LIBRARY DISCARD

Adventure Westward

Eric Acland

Drawings by Merle Smith

THOMAS NELSON & SONS

**Public Library Commission
North Central Branch
Prince George, B. C.**

To Lo

who gave encouragement and wise counsel when very sorely needed,

and

For Charles and Bruce

in certain hope that their generation will recapture the spirit of adventure and service that made their country.

© 1967 by Eric Acland

All rights reserved under International and Pan-American Conventions. Published in Camden, N.J., by Thomas Nelson & Sons and simultaneously in Toronto, Canada, by Thomas Nelson & Sons (Canada) Limited.

Library of Congress Catalog Card Number: 67-13919

Printed in the United States of America

1

I suppose, boy and man, we always have the urge to take the devil by the nose and, if we are not wanting in courage, do so.

Leastwise I can conjure up no better reason for changing my mind that bright spring day in Montreal—and my life, as it so happened—letting the brigantine *Duke of Richmond* sail for Bristol without me, forsaking a comfortable berth in my grandfather's Geneva bank for that great and awesome wilderness to the westward.

But then, old comrades of the Royal Americans did lend a hand to the changing of my mind; and, though I knew it not then, I suppose in over three years the challenge and fire of this vast continent had got into my blood and I had become a part of it.

But my thoughts are all agallop and I must set this down by introducing myself. My name is Vere Bayard and I was born seventeen years ago in the Canton of Vaud, on the north shore of Lake Geneva.

A long way, say you, from the shores of the great St. Lawrence. And right you are; but then, a soldier's life goes ill with the home hearth and apron strings. In a way, I suppose, General Braddock and his unfortunate troops were responsible for my being here. Leastwise it was that three-hour slaughter of Braddock and his soldiers on the banks of the Monongahela by scalp-hungry Ottawas and Ojibways that forced the British to the conclusion that a tough kind of soldier with a special kind of training was needed to fight the French and, more particularly, his Indian allies in this vast and rugged country. And so was born the 60th Foot, Royal American Regiment, a lusty force of four fighting battalions, its soldiers recruited in the backwoods settlements of the colonies and its officers mostly from the Protestant cantons of Switzerland with a few doughty Germans and hardy Scots to give flavor to our comradeship. And so, even though since childhood I had been destined for service in the Swiss Guard of the Prince of Orange it was not to be and instead I entered the service of King George of England.

I am not short in stature, nor tall for that matter, and sound in wind if not quite in limb. In truth, I get this limp only in wet or cold weather, for our regimental surgeon, John Graham, made as good a job of removing the musket ball from my right leg as he did trimming and molding again my left hand. There is no better surgeon on any field than John Graham and saving my thumb and little finger was surely a feat of knife and needle. Proud of his handiwork too. How he would rail at me for hiding it from the sight of others, particularly the female sex, in cloak or pocket. "Blast ye, lad," he'd grumble, "do you expect to go through life sitting on your hand after the fine job I did on it? ... You get busy now. An hour in the morning and an hour at night opening and closing it around a musket barrel." And I did, so that now I can grip and hold a rifle barrel as well as any man.

A little over three and a half years ago that was ... and it seems as yesterday. I was as green as the grass on the southern slope of an Alpine valley when I reported to our 1st

Battalion at Philadelphia and I had scarce lost my sea legs before I was on the march, choking with the heat of summer dust and chilled to the spine when I first heard the forest echo with the war cry of unseen warriors. The day we started that march to the relief of Fort Pitt was in fact my birthday—my fourteenth—in the year 1763.

That Shawnee at Bushy Run all but stopped me ever reaching my fifteenth. He jumped me, screaming his scalp cry as I vainly tried to hold a fear-crazed pack horse, and bore me down to the ground as I protected my throat from his slashing knife with my left arm. It was a Royal Highlander who saved me, wheeling about and driving his bayonet twixt the warrior's ribs. I can remember getting to my feet, clutching the wrist of my left hand, and kicking around in the dust for my signet ring. It had gone with my three fingers at the end of a downward sweep of the knife. I valued it much for it was my father's gift the day I left the valley to join the Royal Americans. But I never did find it for it was then that the musket ball struck my thigh and brought me down.

Strange how events set the course for one's life. Truly, if Braddock's defeat caused the Royal Americans to be and so brought me to the Americas, then the victory of Bushy Run resulted in the ultimate reduction of my regiment and my proposed journey home. For there was crushed the fighting strength of the Confederacy of the Three Fires and so ended the Beaver War, and Pontiac's dream of restoring the north and west to the French was whisped away like so much smoke from a bivouac fire. We took our vengeance for Braddock that night and long day when Colonel Henri Bouquet, God rest his soul, forced victory at the very hour when overwhelming defeat seemed certain —and this with a mere handful of Royal Americans and Black Watch.

And there, too, we won peace, an uneasy peace to be

sure. But the black belts of war had scarce left the council fires of the Western Tribes before the penny pinchers at Whitehall had reduced the Royal Americans to two battalions and put the most of the rest of us on half pay. After serving at Fort Pitt, my battalion had been dispatched to Montreal. As junior ensign of the regiment my future was about as bright as fresh lead from a bullet mold.

In truth, I had little stomach for a future in a counting-house nor, in equal truth, did I wish to leave Montreal or my comrades. But circumstances and the fortunes of war are not always attune to one's heart; and so I needs must board the *Duke of Richmond* on the morrow, set sail down the majestic St. Lawrence, highroad to the seas, and leave all this behind. So it was that I left my lodgings, striding in the warming spring sunshine toward the high ground of Battery Royal for a last look at the town I had come to love in this past year.

Not big as towns in the Old World go, for it was home to less than eight thousand souls, but this Montreal was a beautiful town, full of color and excitement and friendly, happy people whose language I had the good fortune, being a Swiss Protestant, to call my own. Scarce a mile long within its moat and walls and less than a musket ball would carry back from the river the town itself was interlaced with the houses and gardens of religious orders—Jesuits, Sisters of the Congregation, the Seminary of St. Sulpice, the garden of the Recollet Friars, and, as if to reach out arms of mercy to wilderness folk, the Hospital of the Gray Nuns outside the walls. The dwellings seemed strong and neat, giving purpose to it all with scampering children that this day seemed anxious to escape from frame and masonry homes to run in the sunshine that had driven the snow back into the shadows. Montreal was awaking from the long winter sleep and everywhere there ran a new urgency, a growing vigor.

I turned through a narrow lane toward the Battery and met head-on four of five canoemen, gay with sash and ribbons, walking arm in arm singing lustily, voices no doubt fortified by the wine of homes visited. Grinning, I crowded toward a house front to give them room.

"Bonjour M'sieur!" they shouted. The one nearest to me, realizing I gave ground to them, managed a little bow. "Pardon, M'sieur, pardonnez-moi."

These were rough fellows, strong and carried away by the revelry of the hour, yet always that Gallic courtesy and friendliness that was the unforgettable mark of the Cana-

dian. I turned for a moment and watched them as they weaved in good voice toward the river. Aye, there was much about this amazing new land I would not want to forget. As I came out of the lane I was hailed at a distance.

"Bayard! . . . Vere Bayard! . . . Wait up!" Striding down toward me was Ensign Christopher Pauli, his cloak thrust open by the quick and urgent movement of his long legs. We shook hands as he spoke: "Madam Soulière told me you had left for the Battery, but I didn't count on your taking short-cuts. Mind if I join you?"

So we walked on together. I thought I knew why he came seeking me, for I had promised to take with me a number of letters to his friends and relatives at Montreux. He was one of the original Swiss officers of the regiment, and letters to and from home were still of prime importance.

"I hadn't forgotten the letters," I assured him. "I intended to pick them up at your quarters this evening."

Pauli gave me a quick look, and a peculiar one by reason of the fact that Potawatomi torture to his nose and left ear gave a sort of permanent quirk to the near side of his broad, honest face. "Letters?" he asked, then quickly answered himself, "Ah, yes, yes, of course. Non . . . no. . . . I didn't chase you with the letters but with an invitation. Dan Clause is coming in from Caughnawaga today and we thought we might all dine at Madam Benoit's."

I nodded my head in approval. "Sounds splendid . . . a farewell party for the homeward-bound infant."

A twisted grin from Pauli, "Well, perhaps, my boy, perhaps. Whatever way you want to look at it." He quickly changed the subject. "Slow down, lad. Whatever happened to that gimpy leg of yours? . . . I expect it's my age again."

I shortened my stride and smiled inside me. There were two subjects that Christopher Pauli could be counted on to introduce. First, his graying hair to give reason to mention he had been the senior ensign in the regiment for five years; and secondly, the matter of his unpaid allowances. I beat him to the second one.

"Ah, yes, graybeard," I said with mock conviction. "But think what comfort your allowances are in your old age!"

"The devil take you, boy," roared Pauli, giving me a hearty belt on the back. "After that you can stroll by yourself. I'm off for Madam Benoit's, and I'll see you get salt pork for dinner." He left me but then paused and called back. "Full regimentals, Ensign Bayard, and well turned out. . . . We don't want to run foul of Captain Clause, you know what a stickler he is about dress."

I laughed. Poor Dan Clause, now Indian Agent to the Mohawks at Caughnawaga was a notoriously unregimental officer. "By the way," added Pauli in an unconcerned tone, "John Nordbergh will dine with us; he particularly wants to meet you."

"But why Lieutenant Nordbergh? I never spoke to him in my life. Besides, I thought he was in New York, trying to wangle command of a company."

"No, he's here, arrived this morning as a matter of fact." Pauli spoke slowly as if trying to be offhand about something important. "Probably Brigadier Haldimand asked him to keep an eye on you. Eight o'clock then at Madam Benoit's." With that Pauli hurried away before I had a chance to question him further.

As I plodded up the slope of Battery Hill John Nordbergh took hold of my thoughts. Why? I asked myself a dozen times, why should he of all people wish to see me on this day? Had he been Swiss he might well have wished to use me as courier but he would hardly expect me to carry tidings to Sweden. Of all the engineer officers of the Royal Americans I suppose John Nordbergh was by far the most mysterious.

Some said he was of Russian birth; others that his father had been Consul of the Empress. It was common gossip in the mess that he came to the regiment under the sponsorship of both Lord Halifax and Lord Granville who had promised him a company in reward for services of a secret nature in both Sweden and Russia. But the mystery man was still a Lieutenant, God be praised, for there was a gallant company ahead of him in seniority.

Then I thought of Frederick Haldimand, dedicated first Governor of Trois-Rivières, and how he had chosen Lieutenant Nordbergh for the work closest to his heart, providing a better life for the good Canadians. The iron mines and the St. Maurice Forges were his projects and I suppose in their way as important a victory as Bushy Run. I recalled that they provided work for close to a thousand Canadians and no one would gainsay that the Swede was responsible. Thus, I put my troubled mind to rest. It was as Christopher Pauli suggested, only interest in my welfare on the part of Brigadier Haldimand, now in command in Florida. "Uncle" Frederick, as I knew him, was a close friend of my grandfather and had spent his boyhood in the Canton of Vaud and had sponsored me for a commission in the regiment.

By now the spring sunshine was slanting away rapidly and quick, cold dusk was not far behind. The peaked towers of the seminary and the spires of the churches were already dark fingers against the sky and here and there toward Lower Town warm lights started to wink from house windows. I started slowly toward my quarters, turning up my cloak collar against the chill night air and dismissing Lieutenant Nordbergh entirely from my mind. After all, this was my farewell to the New World. At least so I thought.

2

It was fifteen minutes of eight before I left my lodgings and hastened with long strides through the dark alleys of Lower Town toward my rendezvous. By now a chill wind swept off the river and gusted through the laneways.

I walked close to the walls and houses for protection, perilously close as it transpired. Without warning, the door of the house I was passing was thrust open, catching me full broadside and half spinning me about. I had forgotten the ever-present danger of walking close to these Canadian houses whose doors swing wide on the thoroughfare itself.

The warm light from the open door shone full on my uniform and the open-mouthed soldier, whose strong arm had swung it, stammered in a confused Irish accent, "Sure am sorry, Y'r honor . . . I . . . I."

I replaced my silver-laced tricorn hat with as much dignity as I could muster and was on the point of reprimanding the unfortunate fellow when my eyes focused on his charming companion. She was a sprite of a girl with an infectious smile about the corners of her mouth. I know if I could see her eyes more clearly they would be dancing with mirth.

She curtsied prettily. "Bon soir, M'sieur le Capitaine,"

she said. There was music in her voice and wisdom, too, beyond her years, for why else would she up-rank me?

"Bon soir, Mam'selle," said I, with a bow fitting to the occasion. Then I strode on my way forgetting my ruffled dignity and the fellow who was the cause of it.

Thinking of the girl, my good humor returned quickly as I walked. So charmingly Canadian. Friendly, courteous, yet full of the joy of living and quick humor. I would miss these good Canadians. Madam Benoit, for instance, a good soul if there ever was one. For almost seven years now her establishment had provided good meat and wine for officers of the Royal Americans, and a great deal more; for us Swiss it was in very truth a home across the seas. Of all our four battalions there would be scarce an officer, from those present at the taking of Montreal until this day, who would not gladly draw his sword in defense of her honor. She always kept the long table before the fire for us and the mural covering the opposite wall was unquestionably her proudest possession, and ours too, for that matter. Lieutenant Jamette had worked on it, on and off, for close to six months. His Swiss village with its neat brown houses and flagstone roofs and red geraniums might have been any one of a hundred dear to our hearts; but there was no mistaking the snowy, sun-struck peak of the Matterhorn that dominated the work. Poor Jamette did not live long to enjoy his work of art. He was slain and scalped by Pontiac's warriors in the treacherous attack on Michilimackinac four years ago next month. Someone had written under his signature on the mural, "Mort sur le champ d'honneur."

I ran down the stone steps two at a time, lifting my sword scabbard as I did so, and as I burst in the door Christopher Pauli was there to greet me. As we shook hands he put his mouth close to my ear. "Some of our Bostonian friends have commandeered our table . . . make light of it to Madam."

And not a moment too soon had he warned me for Madam Benoit, in her snowy starched apron, descended like a ship in full sail, wringing her hands: "M'sieur," she cried, "I am so unhappy." And indeed she was; and for a moment I thought she was going to give way to tears. "Those Bostonians have taken your table. I begged them not to, but it was no use and I couldn't afford trouble. You know how it is these days."

I tried to calm her by patting her shoulders. "Now, now, Madam, what matters where we sit?" I pulled a serious face. "Providing, of course, we eat well."

Her face lit up. "Ah, oui, M'sieur, your favorite . . . partridge pie."

"With cabbage?"

"Oui, M'sieur . . . and tourtière." She was all smiles now.

"Good, good!" I exclaimed with enthusiasm. "With partridge pie who cares about the table." Thus reassured Madam Benoit flounced off to her kitchen, with a toss of her head at the long table as she sailed by.

As I hung my cloak and sword-belt on the wooden wall peg Christopher Pauli fetched a tall, lean officer from the fire nook. "I don't think you two have met," he said. "Lieutenant Nordbergh . . . Ensign Bayard." He had a firm enough handshake, but I had a feeling his eyes were looking into me. They were the palest blue eyes I had ever seen in any man, the color of clear river ice.

"I am delighted this meeting could be arranged," he said with a slow smile. "I have heard much of you from Brigadier Haldimand."

We seated ourselves at one of the two smaller tables for, as Pauli said, there was no use waiting for Daniel Clause, he could be counted on to be late. Henri, the establishment's wine-steward, boot-boy, and general factotum, lit the tapers and poured the wine.

"I understand you propose to sail tomorrow," said Nordbergh. I nodded.

"Pleased to be leaving America?"

"Not exactly," I admitted. "But then, beggars cannot be choosers. I'm so far down on the seniority list there is little hope of a posting to either battalion."

"Pity," said Nordbergh, and let it rest at that.

The late arrival of Captain Clause seemed to touch off a bedlam of noise between greetings all around, the scraping of chairs on the flagstones as they were pushed back and his much too loud and long explanation for his tardiness, claiming a lengthy meeting with the Mohawk chiefs had outrun the clock. Above it all, it seemed to me, the strident loud talk from the long table seemed to be fanned up to a new pitch. We could not help but know that their sallies were directed at us, but like most soldiers of the Montreal garrison we studiously ignored it. Scarce a day passed now without merchants and soldiers being dragged before the magistrates charged with insulting behavior the one to the other. Too often, to our thinking, the result was a flogging for the soldier and an apology and a small fine for the merchant.

So we addressed ourselves to the good fare, enjoying the partridge and tourtière to the obvious pleasure of Madam Benoit, who hovered about like a mother hen with chicks. Now and again we would pause as one of the other produced a morsel of regimental or army news or gossip.

"Tell me," I asked Pauli. "What is the last word from Whitehall on your claims?"

Pauli snorted like a startled horse. For three years now he had been trying to collect and 'twas said that General Gage in New York had to employ an extra secretary to handle the correspondence on the matter, between briefs and memorials and affidavits.

"You wouldn't believe it," he started.

"Oh, yes, I would. I heard about it in Quebec," broke in John Nordbergh.

"My Lords of the Treasury," announced Pauli in mock solemnity, "have come to the decision that it would be a dangerous precedent to make such payments to Ensign Pauli unless he produces the necessary vouchers. If the said vouchers have been inadvertently destroyed, then Ensign Pauli should produce not less than two witnesses prepared to swear to the details and fact of such destruction."

A roar of laughter followed his little speech. We all knew the facts and the jest was as humorous as it was grim. Pauli had spent six months' pay out of his own pocket buying winter food for his little garrison at Fort Sandusky, and food and blankets for hungry Indians to boot. Then in the spring, Ottawa and Wyandot warriors took Sandusky by stealth, put the garrison to death, save Pauli whom they reserved for the amusement of their women, and put the torch to the blockhouse. Pauli was lucky to escape and make his way to Detroit, but his scars he bears as evidence.

"Well, now," spoke up Lieutenant Nordbergh, "seems to me we have the answer at this table. All you have to do is produce the Ottawa braves who set fire to your office and get affidavits from them. What better man to do that than Captain Clause; he knows every Indian in the West and his powers of persuasion are equally well known. Might even get his father-in-law's assistance; that would do it."

Neither Clause, who resented any inference that he had obtained his posting as Indian Agent for the north and west through the good offices of Sir William Johnson, Superintendent General of Indian Affairs, whose daughter he had married, nor poor Pauli, who really needed his back pay, found much humor in this sally. It was time to change the subject.

"Oh, by the way," spoke up Clause, "does our young

friend sail on the morrow or is he going adventuring in the West?"

There was a silence then. No doubt amused at the bewildered expression on my face, Nordbergh answered him, "I don't know, haven't asked him yet."

"What's this all about? About the West, I mean," I asked.

"It's a long story, Vere, but the nub of it is I leave for 'Mackinac shortly. How would you like to come along? It would be to work for Alexander Henry on Lake Superior."

There was a long silence in which I am sure they all enjoyed the astonishment that must have showed on my face.

"You mean Alexander Henry the fur trader?" I blurted out.

"Yes," said Nordbergh. "He does have license to trade on Superior. But fur trading is not what we have in mind."

He pulled a rough piece of metal from his pocket and placed it on the table. It held our eyes; it was dull and hard and in a manner of speaking, beautiful.

"This is what he has in mind . . . copper!" After a time he went on. "Mr. Henry has asked me to look at the deposits and assess their value, and as the General also wants a plan for improving the fortifications at 'Mackinac, I can kill two birds with one stone."

Of course, I thought, what better man than John Nordbergh. I recalled the wonders he had performed at the St. Maurice mines and forges at Trois-Rivières. I had heard he had built it up until thousands of pounds of iron were produced monthly, not to mention stoves and kettles and the like sorely needed by the good habitants.

But they were waiting for me to say something. "I don't know. . . . I don't think I should care to work for a Bostonian," I muttered.

Lieutenant Nordbergh stopped Madam Benoit as she

bustled past his chair, intent on providing for the needs of two officers of the 10th who, along with three Canadian ladies, had by now taken possession of the only remaining table. "One moment, Madam," he said. "Tell me, is M. Alexander Henry known to you?"

The good woman's face rippled into a sea of smiles. "Ah, oui, M'sieur, but everyone knows le Bel Anglais, a good man, and a friend to all. Is he coming back from the West?"

"I'm afraid not, Madam, not for a time at least."

"Ah, that is a great pity. There are not many here now like le Bel Anglais. . . ." Disappointed, apparently, she went on about her business.

"Well, Bayard," spoke up Nordbergh, "does that answer your fears?"

I still was not satisfied. "It's not clear to me. This le Bel Anglais, the Handsome Englishman, Alexander Henry, sounds like a Scot to me."

Captain Clause put down his wine glass and shook a long finger under my nose. "The trouble with you, m'boy, is you don't yet understand these Canadians, they have everything simplified."

"How so?" I asked.

"Well, if you are French speaking and put on airs, you're a Frenchman. If you are English speaking, drive a hard bargain, naggle with your canoemen about wages, horse-trade with the Indians, and shout off your mouth about the danger of Papists and foreigners, you're a Bostonian—the rest of the newcomers are English. Got nothing to do with where you were born or where you hail from. Simple, eh!"

I grinned. "Hm," said I, "and now would someone please tell me what the Handsome Englishman is?"

Lieutenant Pauli leered at me with the misshapen side of his face.

"You are dull-witted. Clause made it quite clear, I thought. He is New Jersey born and bred . . . came up here as a provisioner with Amherst's army and liked it, so he stayed."

Dan Clause thought it fitting to add more. "He is about the only one of our traders who has the interest of the Indians at heart, as well as his own. Gets along well with the Canadians too. That is why General Gage gave him license for the whole of Lake Superior. We could trust him."

Nordbergh ceased tracing a design on the cloth with his fork and looked at me seriously. "Well, now, Vere, we seemed to have disposed to your doubts regarding Alexander Henry . . . what think you now of adventuring in the West?"

I stared hard at the piece of rugged metal, then picked it up and felt its cold and chipped surface as if weighing it against my future. As I turned it the candlelight seemed to burnish it. "It seems so far away. Is it known to exist in great quantity and how would we get it out?"

Lieutenant Nordbergh nodded slowly as if half in agreement with my questions. "These things have yet to be worked out. But it's fine, pure metal, as fine as any I've ever seen. In Quebec I spent some time with Abbé Grandpré and he produced Jesuit missionary records that state quite positively there are rich deposits on . . ."

Christopher Pauli interrupted him by clearing his throat loudly.

Then he filled in the silence by lowering his voice and speaking in French. "Our friends at the long table seem more than a little interested in the subject. Perhaps we talk too much, no?"

Nordbergh exploded. "Gad, yes. I am a fool!" He reached out and pocketed the nugget of native copper. As he did so I half turned in my chair to look at the merchants and my eyes met those of the man at the head of the table. He was a big man, loose-mouthed, and he sprawled more than he sat.

"You see," he growled to his friends, "look at them . . . wearing the King's uniform and talking the enemy's language. And what are they talking about? Jesuits and Papist orders. I tell you when we got rid of those Canadian-loving generals, Murray and Haldimand, we didn't go far enough."

I half rose in my chair. "Sit down, Bayard!" snapped Captain Clause. I sat as Clause added more quietly. "They are only looking for trouble, don't accommodate them."

Christopher Pauli loudly called for more wine and the tension eased. I felt the hot blood of my anger cool slowly and the merchants seemed to transfer their unwanted attention to the two officers of the 10th and their ladies.

"Of all people, don't clash with Zeke Hutt," advised Daniel Clause in a lowered voice.

"The big man at the table end?"

Clause nodded. "He was one of the ringleaders of the group that forced London to recall Governor Murray. He is as dangerous as a wolverine and about as trustworthy."

I managed a half-hearted smile and an attempt at humor. "A Bostonian, I presume."

"So say the Canadians . . . but our friend is really from the Ohio country."

Zeke Hutt. I pondered over the name. It seemed to have some association with the past. Then I remembered.

"Wasn't he the man who had trouble with Ensign Nott a few years ago?" I asked.

Dan Clause nodded. "Aye . . . and he has never got over it. He and two other merchants, Grant and Chown, were fined £30 apiece and made to apologize for insulting behavior before the whole garrison. He's had a jaundiced eye for the Royal Americans ever since."

I suppose he read my thoughts, for he added quickly,

"Don't get any fancy notions, Bayard; that was in the days of the military government and now that these civil administrators have taken over, Hutt and his gang are riding high, even in the courts."

By now the two officers of the 10th had had enough of the crude remarks from the long table and escorted their ladies out, white-faced and tight-lipped. As one passed our table he caught my eye and shook his head in a gesture of silent disgust. Their departure served only to add fuel to the flames.

Zeke Hutt shouted raucously for the landlord and when Madam Benoit appeared from the kitchen, wiping her hands nervously on her apron, he roared at her as if to frighten her back.

"You want business, woman, eh?" he shouted.

"Ah . . . oui, M'sieur. Oui."

"Then, by God, you'll speak English, none of that foreign jabber."

Madam Benoit shifted feet and looked to us as if for help.

"Come on then!" shouted Hutt, as his cronies laughed at the woman's discomfort. "Say yes, yes, Y'r Honor."

In stammering tones Madam Benoit did her best to oblige and Zeke Hutt seemed to look about him for more means to bait her and entertain his friends. His eyes came to rest on the mural of the Alpine village.

"And look you," he ordered with a long glance in our direction. "You'll get rid of that foreign claptrap from your wall. Understand?"

The woman only stared back at him, her face completely vacant.

"This . . . see!" he shouted. With that he hurled the wine from his mug. It splashed against the mural and ran in dark blotches down over Lieutenant Jamette's signature at the bottom. "We'll have no work of foreign . . ."

I was on him before he could finish or caution could take command. The weight of my rush and his wine-softened legs more than made up for the difference in our size. He crashed down to the flagstones with me on top.

He seized my silver gorget and twisted it until the pendent chain bit into my neck. I tried to get my right hand about his bull neck and he lurched over as I felt myself forceably raised to my feet. Captain Clause had me by one arm and Ensign Pauli the other. They held me back as Zeke Hutt, grasping the oak table, pulled himself to his feet, his face blotched with rage.

"So . . . ," he snarled, voice shaking, "the foreign cockerel shows his true colors. You'll get satisfaction for this, I swear it." He half turned toward his friends. "You all witnessed this attack. I'll see him rot in jail for this."

My breathing was easing, although both Clause and Pauli still held me fast. " 'Tis satisfaction I want," I managed to reply, although still consumed with anger. "Satisfaction for the honor of a brave man whose work you smeared. . . . Satisfaction with pistols at dawn!"

There was a long silence. The other merchants seemed to have their eyes on Zeke Hutt who, for a moment, looked surprisingly like a trapped animal.

Lieutenant Nordbergh broke the spell. "I would be pleased to act for Ensign Bayard," he said, his voice calm and reassuring. "I suggest we meet at the mill outside the Recollets' Gate . . . at five o'clock." There was a pause. "Are you in agreement, gentlemen?"

I nodded, but Hutt gave no sign or word in reply, although his friends seemed awake with expectation. Then he favored me with a round oath and a look of hatred I had not before encountered the equal of, as he turned and reached for his greatcoat. The others followed suit and, leaving us standing, went ill-tempered into the night.

3

It seemed hours to me, although I suppose it was but a few moments, before anyone spoke. I had an increasing sense of having acted rashly. It was Pauli who broke the silence. "Jove! That's done it," he said with feeling. "Now I suppose they are trooping off to a magistrate to swear out a warrant."

Lieutenant Nordbergh poked at the fire for a time. "No, I don't think so," he said finally. "Zeke Hutt cannot afford to lose face in front of his friends, but I'm wondering just what trick he will try."

Dan Clause had resumed his seat at the table and sat tapping the top of his snuffbox. "Tell me, Bayard," he asked, "how good are you with the pistol?"

"Fair," I said, with some modesty.

"Good," said Clause. "And certainly you have a bigger target than he. Looks to me, m'boy, that come dawn you will render the King a good service."

I seated myself, wondering at the meaning of the remark. "I don't understand..."

Clause glanced at Nordbergh, who stood rocking on his heels, back to the fire. "Should we tell him? It would give zest to his affair."

The Swede smiled. "I see no harm. No one could question our loyalty, or our ability to keep information back of our teeth."

Clause snapped the lid of his snuffbox shut. "Did you ever hear of a Marylander named Captain Joseph Hopkins?" he asked.

I shook my head. "I think I recall hearing of Hopkins' Rangers."

"That's him."

"Wasn't he in trouble at Detroit," butted in Pauli. "Selling beer to his men at a profit, or something like that."

Clause nodded. "And the commanding officer, Detroit, got into a peck of trouble for not arresting him for court-martial."

"But what's that got to do with Hutt?" I asked, not in the humor for service gossip.

"Patience, my boy," suggested Clause with a wry smile. "If you people would stop interrupting. . . . The fact of the matter is, Hopkins went over to the French."

Interesting, I thought, but of no great import. After all, we had been at peace with the French for almost four years now, and I said as much.

Captain Clause snorted. "H'mm," said he expressively, "but it's what he is doing for the French, or maybe trying to get the French to do. You see, he's in New Orleans trying to persuade . . ." he glanced sidelong at me, "our late enemies that they could get this country back if he got the Western Nations to take the warpath for them."

Christopher Pauli laughed. "Look," said he, "Pontiac was crushed once and for all at Bushy Run, and you yourself say the Ottawas and Ojibways are now our friends. It sounds like a wild scheme to me."

Captain Clause made a face. "Perhaps, perhaps. But if a force of four or five battalions were to march nor'east from

Louisiana, how long would it be before the black belt would be at their council fires? . . . Remember this, Pauli, our traders have been robbing them right and left, and they still remember the French traders as their friends."

There was a silence. We all knew that Captain Clause was more than Agent to the Mohawks at Caughnawaga, he was also responsible for intelligence respecting the Western Indians and more than likely knew more than we did.

"But what has this to do with Hutt?" I asked finally.

Clause went on as if I hadn't spoken. "Four letters from Hopkins came into New York and were . . . were, shall we say, intercepted by General Gage. One of them was for Zeke Hutt; the contents were most interesting. It was delivered to him today, sealed of course."

Dan Clause favored Nordbergh with a knowing smile and I assumed that Nordbergh, just in from New York, had been the courier.

"But why," I asked, "don't you have him arrested?"

"Because, my young friend, we have bigger fish to fry." He shrugged his shoulders. "After all, we would be glad to give Hutt to the French, if they would have him, but there are far more dangerous men involved."

"The other three letters, who were they for?" I asked.

Captain Clause looked at me hard for a moment. "That, Ensign Bayard, is not your concern . . . leastwise not for the present."

Pauli rubbed his twisted face with his thumb. "One thing I will say, the Western posts are in good hands. With Robert Rogers in command at 'Mackinac, God help any Indian renegade with a bloody hatchet. Rogers could lick them with a quarter the men."

Clause studiously examined the top of his snuffbox and Nordbergh picked up the poker and directed his attention to the fire.

"Well . . . couldn't he?" pressed Pauli, irritated at the lack of agreement.

Dan Clause pursed his lips. "Maybe," he said laconically. "Maybe."

Lieutenant Nordbergh dropped the poker on the hearth with a clatter to bring the conversation to an end.

"Look," said he, "it's a quarter of midnight and our young friend needs sleep for his nerves tonight."

They agreed and we were soon buckling on our belts and slipping into our cloaks. "You had best bed with me tonight, Vere," suggested Nordbergh.

"I would stay clear of your lodgings, can't tell what Hutt and company might try to pull off there—besides I have a fine brace of Swedish pistols; would like to see how they fit your hand."

I agreed thankfully, for I had little stomach to pace the night out alone. Christopher Pauli and Dan Clause shook my hand warmly and wished me well on the morrow. "Don't get rattled, and take your time," advised Christopher.

"But not too damned long," added Captain Clause.

As we parted company at the corner of the next lane Dan Clause left with a special request. "No winging shot, mind. A good clean mortal wound in the chest. Won't settle for anything else."

I started to feel a little sick and shaky for it was my first affair and I think Lieutenant Nordbergh sensed it. He linked his arm in mine as we walked together. "Not to worry," said he. "Remember, God is on the side of the just; keep that in mind—and the Manual of Arms—and you'll be all right."

I slept but fitfully that night, twisting and turning on my cot and trying to keep my mind off the duel, but rising now and then to feel the butt of the Swedish pistol and to taut the nerves and muscles of my right arm. It had been a strange night this, one that had been designed innocently enough to launch me back to a quiet life of pen-pushing in a Geneva bank. My mind jumped about like a jack rabbit in sage brush from the dream of copper mines in the wilderness to the scheming of vile men and the Western Nations being prodded to war again. There were two things I had no answer for and they troubled me. Why should Zeke Hutt, a successful merchant, who was in the van of every effort to discredit the Canadians, be interested in the French cause? It didn't make sense. And why that strange tension when Major Robert Rogers' name was mentioned —the finest Indian fighter and bravest man we ever served with. That, too, didn't make sense and it troubled me. I tossed about until John Nordbergh spoke in the dark.

"No sleep yet, Bayard?"

"No."

"Don't worry about the outcome. You're steady and with quick reaction. Have no fears."

"It's not that, it's everything that happened tonight. Some things I don't understand."

"Such as?"

"Well, for one thing, why would Zeke Hutt be interested in the French cause. You know how he works to keep the Canadians down, their language, their religion, holding meetings, sending memorials to London. Well . . . you know."

There was a chuckle from the darkness. "Vere, I am afraid you have not learned to measure men," he said.

"How so?"

Some time went by as if Nordbergh was searching in the dark for the right words. "I suppose it's what a man believes in that counts. Now Hutt and a whole lot that followed the army in after we licked the French came here for one purpose only—to make their fortune as quickly and as easily as possible. They have one loyalty and that is to their purse. So the greater control they keep in their hands the better for what they believe in. You know, Bayard, men like Governor Murray, Brigadier Haldimand, yes, and even General Gage, believed in something else. They believed it was high time the Canadians were given half a chance. The French never gave them that much, and if this were done, together we could make something of this country."

"But what could Hutt gain from an attack from the West?" I asked.

"Perhaps more territory, fur concessions, anything or nothing. If it didn't look good he could just stay where he was. You see when a man is entirely concerned with his purse there are no rules other than that."

A silence; then I asked. "And Robert Rogers—where does he fit in? Surely there is no braver nor more loyal officer than he? You remember what happened the day the battalion marched out of New York for here? There wasn't a man of the regiment who didn't take part in storming the debtor's prison to release Rogers."

For some time I thought Nordbergh was never going to answer, but then he did. "That is something I would rather not talk about," he said, "but keep this in mind—it is possible with the years for any man to change. Sometimes it's rum, sometimes debt, sometimes greed. In fairness, though, one should hold hard to the memory of a man's good years."

And that had to serve to settle my curiosity, and thus pondering I dozed off. When I awoke Lieutenant Nordbergh was loading the pistols carefully in the light of a candle.

As we walked through the Recollets' Gate the first rose-fingers of dawn were pointing in the sky and the gray outline of the old mill looked cold and forbidding.

"Looks as if we're the first here," said Nordbergh, "I

hope he doesn't keep us waiting too long, not before breakfast."

The wind was coming in strong, directly off the river, and we sheltered in the lee of the mill wall. "Keep moving about," he advised. "Keep your blood circulating well, so you don't stiffen up."

It was a good quarter hour before we heard them. First a sort of murmuring, like a flock of geese away off; then we saw them coming through the Gate.

"Good heavens!" exclaimed Nordbergh. "He is bringing a gallery with him. Now what the devil does that mean?"

The group of men, there must have been eight or ten, turned off the road and up the path toward where we stood. It was easy to recognize Zeke Hutt, he was half a horse length in the lead and striding along.

"I don't like the look of this—he's up to something," muttered Nordbergh.

I recognized some of the men as those with Hutt at Madam Benoit's; others I had never before laid eyes on. Lieutenant Nordbergh moved forward to meet them and I saw him open his pistol case, obviously offering Hutt his choice. Hutt shook his head and the man closest to him produced a horse pistol. Even at that distance it looked like a small cannon. The group of men broke away from Hutt and clustered close to the wall of the mill. They seemed to be handing over the proceedings to Lieutenant Nordbergh.

"Gad, I'd like to know what this is about," he muttered to me as he opened the case for me to take a pistol. "Be on your guard, boy!"

Now Hutt and I were back to back; I carried my pistol high and close to my upper chest.

"Ten full paces, gentlemen . . . and in accord with my count!" Lieutenant Nordbergh's instructions were crisp and clear. "On the completion of the tenth pace you will turn and fire."

I looked at the men against the wall. They looked like a row of crows watching, watching.

"Ready, gentlemen? March! Un . . . deux . . . trois . . . quatre . . ." With each count I marshalled my thoughts. "Long strides, relax, lock the right arm, take your time, steady, . . . cinq . . ."

Instead of the count of eight I heard a shout. "Vere . . . en garde!"

I wheeled to my right automatically and as I did something bore across my chest, tearing away cloth and the second button on my coat. Then I heard the pistol shot.

I turned full about, spread-legged. Hutt had a look of

utter disbelief and wonderment on his face. From his empty pistol a whisp of smoke rose skyward.

I extended my arm, aiming my pistol at his chest. "No! No! No!" he screamed. "It was a mistake; I slipped." He wet his lips with his tongue, face ashen gray as the color left it. There was a terrible, long silence, and looking at the fear in his face I began to feel sick. I knew what I must do. I raised my pistol and fired into the air.

The men against the mill wall had their eyes fixed on Zeke Hutt like as many rabbits held rigid by a garter snake. He stopped trembling and the color slowly came back to his face. Suddenly, he found use in his legs and half-staggered, half-strode toward Lieutenant Nordbergh, and as he did so rage took the place of fear.

"I was tricked!" he roared. "Foreign swine counting in another language." He grasped the horse pistol by the barrel and swung wildly at Nordbergh who stood firm, his face showing only utter contempt. Two or three of the men came forward and pinioned Hutt's flaying arms. They eased him away, mouthing curses, and down the path toward the Recollets' Gate.

We watched them go for a time in silence. "Gad—I'm a sheep-head," said Nordbergh at last. "It wasn't until I started the count that I realized what he was up to."

"How could you know until it happened?" I asked.

He took my pistol and put it back in the case. "It should have been obvious—the reason for the gallery. He brought those men as witnesses and after he had murdered you it would have been their word against mine. They would have sworn it was a fair duel and that would be that."

He put the case under his arm and then looked hard at me. "You made a bad mistake. You should have shown him no mercy; you should have shot him down. Now you have made an enemy for life, and a dangerous one."

I laughed at his fears. "How so? Surely to spare a man's life doesn't make him an enemy."

Nordbergh shook his head. "Hutt will never forgive you. So long as you live you will be walking testimony of his murderous treachery."

By now the sun was up and the warmth of a new day was spreading across Montreal. Blue smoke from a hundred chimneys gave evidence of stirring life. It was good to be alive on such a day. John Nordbergh must have read my thoughts for when we came to the Recollets' Gate he suggested we walk the ramparts back to our quarters.

"The morning sun will brace us," he said. "Besides it's good for the soul."

From the top of the wall the river seemed to spread out in quiet and lazy strength, here and there patches of rotten ice floes moved listlessly, gray dirt against the blue water of spring. A small ship already under half-sail moved slowly through them (under the command of a Canadian pilot) like a toy sailboat through lily pads.

I stopped and pointed. "Look! For heaven's sake, there goes the *Duke of Richmond*, and with all my boxes and gear on board."

Nordbergh chuckled. " 'Tis she all right. But not with your boxes."

"How so?" I asked, already wondering how I would get them back.

"Beeause they are safe stowed at the King's Wharf. Pauli and a detail fetched them ashore. I am surprised at you, underestimating your comrades like that."

"But when—or how—not in the dark . . . ," I stammered.

He laughed. "Oh, no; yesterday high noon."

"But then—but then I didn't know about the copper or the western venture. Nor had I changed my sailing."

Nordbergh grinned and slapped me hard on the back.

"And that, my young friend," said he, "is the second time you've underestimated the Royal Americans in as many minutes."

"The devil take you!" swore I, with my first laugh this day. "Let's stride out; I'm beginning to feel the need of breakfast."

He put his arm on my shoulder. "You may not make your fortune out of copper, Vere Bayard—but then you may. One thing I swear to, your life will not be dull."

Deep in me I knew he was right, and suddenly the world about me sprang alive and my very blood seemed charged with it. I looked far to the west and wondered without fear what lay ahead in that great wilderness that seemed to stretch to the end of the world.

4

River ice held fast that year until almost mid-May and while men of the canoe brigades spent their advance pay in merrymaking and gay nights, the adventurers in the fur trade and the "bourgeois," as the proprietors were called, bit their quill pens to their thumbs staring at the red side of their fat ledgers, for each day of delay meant money lost.

But for me it was time well gained, for it gave me a week in which to shop around for warm, plain clothing, blankets, gun with rifled barrel and fowling piece, powder and shot, and all the odds and ends needed to sustain one in the wilderness. At that it cost a pretty penny, for while there were still such bargains in the marketplace as fancy silver, snuffboxes, brocaded waistcoats, and the like, left by departing French officers, one had to drive a hard bargain at this season for things needed in the nor'west.

Lieutenant Nordbergh and I took our baggage and belongings to a stone warehouse inside the walls near St. Mary's Gate. Here there was an atmosphere of urgency and seemingly ordered confusion. Clerks bustled about with marking pens and papers; and here and there experienced voyageurs, guides, and winterers looked over the bundles with a wary eye for those not sufficiently securely tied for the journey, pausing to complain, now and then, with a vigorously pointed pipestem.

Sections of merchandise being sorted and packed were ranked under the names of the guarantors—Frobisher, McGill, Forrest Oakes—and at last we found the Alexander Henry consignment where a much harrassed but obliging clerk made the best of our late arrival.

"It's this late shipment from New York," he explained with a sweep of his hand. "If we hadn't been a week behind, thanks to the ice, it would have been too late, and that would have been a nice kettle of fish."

"You mean this is only part of the freight?" I asked.

"Good heavens, yes," he replied. "This is only the tail end; we've been packing English goods all winter, came down by bateau from Quebec. That is all at La Chine, ready for loading."

By this time our odd assortment of baggage had been wheeled in from the cart and deposited at the clerk's feet. He was too polite to grumble but rubbed his chin in a gesture of concern, no doubt wondering how his men could get that lot in neat ninety-pound packages, or pièces, as they must.

"You haven't met your guide yet?" he asked.

"No," said Nordbergh.

"André Perrot! André Perrot!" the clerk shouted, and from a corner where carrot tobacco was being wrapped in linen came a short man in voyageur dress.

"André, these are your two passengers for Michilimackinac—Lieutenant Nordbergh and Ensign Bayard."

As we shook hands the voyageur's weatherbeaten face broke into an almost toothless grin. "Dat is good," he said. "When I 'ear two passengers, I say this not good luck journey. But soldiers; ah très bon!"

John Nordbergh laughed. "Some passengers are difficult, yes?" he asked in French.

André Perrot shrugged his wide shoulders. "They do not mean to be, but it is a long journey, nearly a thousand miles—and when you're in a canoe for forty days, tempers sometimes..."

"When do you think the brigade will leave?"

"Maybe tomorrow, maybe next day," the guide said with a shrug. "Today we will have all the freight at La Chine and my canoes leave today. Maybe with luck we could make it tomorrow."

I looked at the goods still to be packed in the ninety-pound pièces, carefully wrapped to protect the contents from water and weather and each pièce containing, as far as possible, assorted merchandise rather than goods of one kind, with each ending with two ears at the top for easier handling. And I wondered how he could hope to leave in less than a week. He must have read my thoughts.

"The carts are waiting, M'sieur," said André. "And I go now to send my canoes up. They will be at La Chine by nightfall."

"And the engagés—will they be ready for departure?" asked Nordbergh with a knowing smile, for the difficulties of guides in rounding up missing and revelling canoemen at the time of departure was a standing joke.

André grinned. "Ah yes," said he. "No trouble this time, instead of three or four days to spend their pay they have had two weeks." He shook his head woefully. "It wouldn't last that long at wine and cards." I knew these tough voyageurs got half their pay before they left and wondered what it amounted to.

"Depends," said André. "Steersmen, about 300 livres; middlemen, 150."

With the livre worth less than a shilling it seemed little enough for the value of the cargo entrusted to their care (for each canoe was said to carry £500 worth of cargo) or for the dangers of storm and wind and white water.

"I go to the canoe yard now," the guide said, adding an invitation to join him. Lieutenant Nordbergh, who had some final matters to attend to at headquarters, declined, but I gladly accepted the offer out of honest curiosity and to take time off my hands.

We walked out the gate and eastward along the shoreline, André keeping up with a short and quick pace that was almost a dogtrot, the red tassel of his wool cap bobbing from side to side, and greeting each voyageur we met with "Bonjour." We had not gone as far as a musket ball would carry before we came to the canoe yard, acres of color and feverish activity surrounded by the hum of voices, good-humored banter, and snatches of gay songs, as seasoned northmen put final touches to the care of their fragile craft. I suppose there must have been two hundred canoes, great and small, and four hundred men at work. We passed through a row of giants, up-ended and being caulked. "Canots du maître," explained André. "Used on the big lakes."

"They also call it the Montreal canoe?"

"Oui, M'sieur."

They seemed about forty feet long, and André explained that a crew of fourteen men was needed to handle one. "No good on the long portage," he added, as if in defense of his own craft.

We had not gone another hundred yards, weaving our way past birchbark canoes being caulked with pine pitch by gaily dressed canoemen, before we came to the eight for our brigade.

André looked at them with ill-concealed pride. "All new," he explained, "from Trois-Rivières."

They were "canots du nord," about twenty-five feet long and made to carry a crew of eight and three thousand pounds of freight. The men had already decorated them with stripes of green and red and some had gaudy works of art, such as Indian heads or horses painted on their bows. Beside each was equipment that André now checked carefully: two oilcloths for covering cargo or to be used as a sail; a short mast to fit the block in the middle of the canoe; a giant sponge for bailing; two lengths of stout rope, neatly coiled; and the paddles. The paddles were painted in almost every color of the rainbow—red and black, and green and blue. Most of them seemed to be little more than two feet long, and, judging by their number, I could only assume they were used by the middlemen. A longer paddle, I take it, was used by the steersman.

I did note that each canoe had one paddle or pole of prodigious size and length and my curiosity got the better of me. "Avant-de-canot, the bowsman," explained the nearest man, taking his short pipe out of his mouth to do so. "For the white water in the rapids."

André became more engrossed in his duties for he had to move these crafts nine miles upstream around the Falls of St. Louis to La Chine, and I could see I served only as a hinderance. I took my leave of André Perrot and his crews and walked back through the sally port below the fort and through Lower Town to headquarters. Every now and then I met up with a group of dancing, singing, and revelling voyageurs, young and old, sometimes with arms about the waist of a laughing girl, sometimes singing lusty canoe songs in which nearby residents joined in the chorus as they leaned out unshuttered windows. These men were leaving for months (in the case of the "hivernants," the "winterers," perhaps for years), and they made certain their last hours in Montreal were happy ones. I was filled with wonderment, and some apprehension, at this new world I was committed to.

John Nordbergh arrived at my lodgings soon after

breakfast the next morning with a military driver and a kind of hooded gig to carry us the nine dusty miles to La Chine. It was a beautiful day of glittering sun that pointed up the faint green-bud haze of the trees. As we trotted through the Recollets' Gate and passed the old stone mill I recalled my last visit there and it seemed an age ago.

"It looks better this morning," said Nordbergh, reading my mind.

"Yes," said I. "I wonder if I shall ever see Zeke Hutt again? I hope not."

"I wouldn't count on it," he laughed. "Bad pennies do have a habit of turning up." Little did we know how right he was or how soon it would be!

Despite the hour we did not have the road to ourselves and many times on the journey our driver had to turn out and pass heavily laden carts moving ponderously with freight destined for the far West and North. And now and then little groups of people—men, women, and children—singing and laughing, and some sad, each bearing along in their midst a swaggering and brightly dressed voyageur.

Jouncing along after passing such a group with waving children I grew reflective. "I'm sorry for these Canadians," I said, more to myself than anyone else. "Not much of the fur-trade money is going to them. But what else have they got? Nothing."

John Nordbergh struck my knee with his fist. "I'm glad to hear you say that, lad. Many times I've heard Brigadier Haldimand say the same thing when he was pouring his own money, without even a thank you, into the St. Maurice Forges. 'These Canadians are good people,' he used to say, 'but they must have work and industry. We cannot build a country on beaver pelts that go out of it.'"

"Maybe," said I, "but look what happened to Uncle

Frederick and Governor Murray. They were removed because they thought like that."

Nordbergh laughed. "So . . . does that change anything? The greed and selfishness and smallness of men will always be with us. But so will the truth and facts." He reached in his pocket and produced his nugget of copper. "See this, boy?" he said. "This may be one of the answers—and there will be others. Here, take it. It will remind you, besides it may bring you good luck."

I looked at it. It was hard and many-sided, but strong and full of color. I put it carefully, almost reverently, in my tunic pocket and wondered what would come of it all.

As we approached La Chine it was like driving into a fair or fête. Despite the shouts of the driver the tired horse could make but little headway through the throngs of people who cared but little for their own safety or the comfort of others. Eventually we gave up and Lieutenant Nordbergh dismissed the driver and we walked through the people to the water's edge. It took us some time before we found our brigade. It was not easy even then to find our guide for André Perrot was in the midst of his family, consisting of Madam Perrot and fifteen children, from a sixteen-year-old daughter with dark flashing eyes down to little Hypolite, still in arms but bellowing lustily. André introduced us to them with much pride and swagger of his "ceinture flèchée," a gaudy sash from which hung an equally colorful sac-à-feu, or beaded bag, in which voyageurs kept their most treasured possessions. As we made the rounds of the Perrots, great and small, a platoon of the 10th Foot went by at the double.

"Wonder what they are up to?" mused John Nordbergh, looking after them as their scarlet coats and flashing bayonets disappeared around the first bend.

But soon we were caught up in the laughter and good nature of our voyageurs' relatives and friends, for one had produced a fiddle from somewhere and the whole crowd was soon swinging into "la ronde." A young voyageur, his hat gay and jaunty with bright feathers, led all in the exciting words of a canoeman's song.

"Look!" said John Nordbergh, seizing my arm. "There goes Dan Clause—as if the devil was after him." I looked in time to see a horseman disappear behind a grove of willows. "It's him all right, and that's the way the troops went. Come on, lad, let's see what's up, these people are here for a time yet."

We slipped away and walked quickly to the willow trees and just beyond, but not far. Before us unfolded a strange scene, four big canots du maître being unloaded pièce by pièce by their crews while on the bank a lieutenant of the 10th and Captain Clause directed the soldiers in slashing open the carefully tied or sewn pièces. Clustered about, watching in silence, stood the families and friends of the voyageurs.

Captain Clause's greeting as we walked up was short and terse. "Damn his eyes," he swore. "He all but got away with this. Just look at it! There is a smuggled keg of rum hidden in almost every pièce. And look at that, close to a hundred gun barrels, all rifled, and kegs of swan shot, to boot. Every item banned for Indian trade."

An old voyageur, obviously the guide, worked with them, pointing out those packages thought to hold contraband. There was a commotion behind the crowd of silent onlookers and the noise of restless horses being pulled up short. The crowd parted making way for an urgent man.

"Le bourgeois!" said the old voyageur, and the fear in his face was noticeable.

"Gad," said Nordbergh. "Your bad penny has turned up already!"

It was Zeke Hutt, breathless and livid with rage. He bore down on the two officers punctuating his oaths with swings of his heavy stick.

"What are you doing with my goods?" he shouted. "I'll have you stripped for this!"

"You mean they *were* your goods," replied Captain Clause coldly. "Including over 100 gallons of rum in pièces marked otherwise, rifled gun barrels, and swan shot. These are now seized in the name of the King."

"Trying to ruin me, that's what you are doing," Hutt shouted. "This brigade was to be at Toronto this month and we'll lose all the spring pelts there. I'll speak to Governor Carlton about this. He knows how you military are interfering with trade."

You could almost see Hutt's mind toting up his losses pound by pound as the troops methodically continued to rip open pièce after pièce. Then his desperate, shifting eyes fell on me.

He came forward with stick raised high. "So it's you that's responsible!" Two soldiers dropped their muskets and seized his arms, scuffling in the dust to hold him back.

The old voyageur stepped toward him. "No, M'sieur," he said almost apologetically, "I was the one; I reported the freight to the soldiers."

For a long moment Hutt looked at the Canadian in disbelief. "You? You? You foreign swine, after I paid you good money. How much did they pay you, eh?"

"They pay me nothing, M'sieur." He paused for a minute. "I see what is 'appening at the ware'ouse and it troubles me. So I go back to Terrebonne and tell my curé. The good father he say, 'Jean, dis is bad, very bad—you report it to the soldiers or I never again endorse your permit.' So, M'sieur, I 'ave to do dis. I 'ave a big family and I 'ave to work on de canot."

The poor man's explanation seemed only to add fuel to Hutt's temper until Captain Clause stepped forward and confronted him with facts.

"Look you, Hutt," he said with authority. "This brigade will not leave for Toronto; I have picked up your license. I am sending the goods back to Montreal. You can either go back quietly and wait until the hearing or you can go back under escort and in irons."

John Nordbergh nudged me. "Come on, Bayard," he said in my ear, "or we will miss our brigade."

We slipped away through the curious people, our stride quickening and lengthening as we went. "You see," said John Nordbergh. "I knew he would turn up again, that bad penny of yours. And mark my words, lad, you haven't seen the last of him yet."

When our point of embarkation came into view as we passed through the willow slash we could see we had no time to lose for the most of the crews seem to have already taken their places in the northern canoes.

"We are ready to leave," André called out as we approached. The earlier gaiety seemed to have gone entirely. Several women were crying openly or holding their hands to their faces to cover their sadness. The children were either rushing about in childish ignorance or, as children the world over, waving farewells too far in advance.

"You will travel in my canoe," the guide informed Lieutenant Nordbergh as we reached the water's edge, adding to me, "and you in the second."

As I was helped into the craft by canoemen solicitous of brittle gum and frail bark to assume my cramped seat amidships, younger voyageurs were catcalling to their girls on the bank, voices full of banter and bravado but not quite hiding the sadness in their hearts.

With a salvo of orders and shouts between the guides

and the bowsmen we moved quietly out and the eight deep-laden canoes moved forward upstream. For a moment the paddles stopped as if controlled by a single mind and heart, and a shout of farewell and encouragement, punctuated by the waving of red caps, went up from the crews. But it was only for a moment and even before the current had caught us we were gliding ahead with each powerful stroke of the paddles.

Nearly a thousand miles lay before us and as many untold adventures. I looked at the Canadian canoemen. Their faces were set in determination, with the look of strong men with confidence in themselves and their life.

5

If I thought we were clear of Canada and heading deep into the unknown with each strong thrust of the paddles, then I had reckoned without the good Sainte Anne, patron Lady of all voyageurs.

We had gone scarcely fifteen miles, the length of Lake St. Louis, and my legs already cramped, before my feet were on firm ground again and the canoemen were easing our craft, sometimes almost waist deep in icy water, through the rapids of Ste. Anne.

Having considered carefully the height and swiftness of the water, André Perrot had made the decision to work half-loaded canoes with cordelles, or lines, up the rapids. Four of each crew, the "mangeurs de lard" or pork-eaters as they dubbed the less experienced men, portaged the goods over the carrying place while the others with infinite care worked the canoe through the rapids with skill and patience.

"Do we load again when we get through?" I asked a husky fellow as he picked up two ninety-pound pièces without so much as a grunt.

"Non, M'sieur, non," he replied, scarce keeping the disgust at my ignorance out of his voice. "This is the night for Our Lady Sainte Anne." And so it was indeed.

While some of the voyageurs secured the canoes and saw to it that the freight was well stacked and covered, others built eight fires and over each fire was hung the huge tin kettle or pot that each canoe carried. The pots were more than half filled with water and the fires well stoked to hasten its boiling, then eight quarts of dried peas and a couple of pounds of pork, cut in thin strips, were added to each.

And thus, having set in motion the means of feeding over sixty hungry men, the Canadians quietly prepared to partake of spiritual strength. Bright and colorful "ceintures flèchées" were retied and each beaded pouch examined to be sure that it hung to look well. Even the thongs that held high the deerskin leggings were tightened up and breech cloths adjusted so that strong thighs were less bare. Then, each satisfied with the appearance of his dress, the voyageurs in small, silent groups made their way to the Chapel of Sainte Anne.

I recalled as a boy reading in the chronicles of Froissart how men-at-arms had knelt at Mass before battle; and it came to me, watching these hard men, kneeling in their little Church of Sainte Anne that this was, in a way, the same thing. Certainly some here present would never return, for there is no more dangerous an adversary than the fury of the elements or the cruelty of angry waters. For most if would be months before they again knelt at Mass and for the "winterers" it might be as many years, if ever.

Having confessed their sins to Almighty God and prayed for the intercession of their Lady, the voyageurs quickly gathered about the steaming kettles and gave voice to rousing songs, for now must be enacted the second tradition of the encampment at Sainte Anne. André Perrot, accompanied by bowsmen from the canoes, went to the landed freight and uncovered one section.

The voyageurs left their fires, cheering and shouting, they horseplayed their way to the uncovered goods and here each man was issued with a gallon keg of rum which must do him the whole long journey to 'Mackinac. And need it he will if he is to survive the numbing cold of icy water or the drenching of rain from which there is no drying out save from his own body heat. Even so, judging by the increasing volume of songs around the fires, I fear that many a keg was broached that night and some would go short when more was needed before the nearly a thousand miles were ended.

Fortunately, perhaps, it was not long before the evening meal was ready and I had my first experience with the dining habits of the Canadian voyageur. First the kettles, now filled to the brim with a steaming, mush-like substance, were removed from the flames. Then eight canoemen squatted in a circle around each pot and began to spoon into their hungry mouths, with amazing rapidity, the hot concoction of peas, fat and pork, not stopping or even pausing until each had had his fill.

Being passengers, Lieutenant Nordbergh and myself were provided with a makeshift tent consisting of oilcloth and a few poles deftly erected by canoemen. To this sanctuary were brought two brimming plates of the voyageurs' fare, to which I addressed myself with some misgivings. But I need not have for I was hungrier than I had thought, and indeed ate it even with some relish and so expressed myself to my companion as I spooned up the last of it.

Nordbergh grinned and shifted himself on the hard rock. "I agreed—but I fear forty days of it, twice a day, will not add to its taste."

"Good heavens!" said I. "Do you mean this is all we get, every day?"

"Yes, my friend; every day a quart of peas and four ounces of pork for every man-jack of us."

I made a wry face. "Come, come," said Nordbergh with

a laugh. "It will make a man of you. Look at our Canadian friends. On this they do twelve hours' paddling a day and carry two or three hundred pounds at a time over long portages. It must be the peas!"

In Canada there is but little twilight at this time of the year, and it was not long before we could see the voyageurs only as obscure shadows against the light of their fires, although their songs, laughter, and chatter carried strongly in the cool night air.

"I don't know about you," said John Nordbergh, "but I'm turning in. I hear we move early."

After undressing, I tried to make myself as comfortable as possible on the hard ground, but despite many folds of blankets I gave up. "There is one thing about it, John," said I. "If we were too comfortable at night we couldn't face twelve hours of that cramping canoe on the morrow." The voyageurs were singing a chanson of their own devising and I tried to fill in the words carried away by the wind off the water.

I awoke with a start and, raising myself to my elbows, peered out of the flapless tent. It seemed quite dark but there was a feeling of movement about.

"Alerte! Alerte!" The shout outside caused me to throw aside my blanket in sudden alarm.

"Lève, lève, nos gens! Get up, get up, men!"

I lay back then, more asleep than awake, but as the commotion outside increased so did my sense of guilt. I was pulling on my breeches when the oilcloth above was snatched away revealing a grayish sky and dim stars. "Pardon, M'sieur, pardon," said a shadow of a voice. "We 'ave to 'ave the poles for de canot!"

We finally stumbled down to the water's edge, finding our places in the canoes with the help of our voyageurs' guiding hands. The darkness was changing fast now and as the canoes moved out on the black waters a wedge of ducks winged low over us so close one could hear the swift, rhythmic beat of their wings. Over behind the chapel a crowing cock heralded a new day.

Lead by the bowsman the crew broke into a canoe song; it seemed to concern the arrival of spring and new loves and old loves. Fair enough, thought I, but songs before breakfast on an empty stomach with a cold wind whistling down on us did not fill me with enthusiasm. Even so, the rise and fall and thrust of the paddles in steady time with the chanson did fascinate me. I pulled my great-coat higher up around my neck, and hoped for the best.

Thus we travelled without check or missing a stroke for about an hour when there came a sudden cry from the lead canoe, echoed in turn by the bowsmen of the others.

"Allumez! Allumez! Allumez!"

The forward thrust of the canoe ended immediately and dripping paddles were rested on thwarts. The canoemen settled back off their knees and rested against convenient freight as they opened their sacs-à-feu and filled clay pipes. This was the voyageurs' ten-minute halt for a pipe of his beloved tabac, which to him marked both time and space. "Une pipe" represented one hour of paddling and four miles of progress.

The canoeman closest to me was a grizzled veteran of the North. Pierre Dupuis, of the Parish of Ste. Geneviève, had not only a tongue for tall stories but a remarkable face to go with it. From the near side he seemed to have little face at all below the hairline and an eyelid that was permanently closed, but on the off side his jaw and face seemed to be perpetually reaching out for his right shoulder. This was the result, he informed me, of being slapped by the fore paw of a standing bear when he was wintering as a young man beyond Le Grand Portage. This grotesque appearance was added to by his shuffling, lopsided gait, caused by the same bear chewing his left leg after he had been knocked down by the blow to the head. He had been saved by his Indian woman, who drove the bear off by striking it over the snout with an axe.

"Ah, M'sieur," he said with some feeling. "She was a good woman, that one." Which at the time and under the circumstance I thought to be somewhat of an understatement.

It was to old Pierre that I now turned with my gnawing, increasing problem of hunger. "When do we have breakfast, Pierre?" I asked.

He probably grinned on the off side of his face but I saw only the near-side mask. "Trois pipes, M'sieur—always it is so!"

Good heavens, I thought, three pipes—that is three hours and twelve miles after we start.

"Your belly flapping against your backbone?" the old northman laughed. "Ah, that is bad. Not enough peas and pork last night, eh? Maybe tonight you eat your fill, eh?"

He puffed away on his short clay pipe in silence for a moment before going on with more enthusiasm.

"Ah yes, M'sieur, tonight is one big night."

"How so?" I asked, encouraging the old one's desire to talk.

"The second night out," he said, as if that should explain everything; but recalling my greenness he went on, "This is the time for 'La Ronde'—and me? I am the "Old One." You'll see, M'sieur, and there isn't a brigade that wouldn't want me for the Old One."

This statement brought teasing protestation from other members of the crew countered by outbursts of good-natured profanity from Pierre Dupuis. But not another word about "La Ronde" would he say, obviously desirous that I should come to this traditional event unspoiled by any preconceived expectations. The more so in that apparently he had a lead part to play.

With the bowsmen breaking into song we were again on our way up the still waters of the Lake of Two Mountains. About two hours later, when I was all but weak from hunger, the eight canoes changed course and headed for the north shore. Our guide must have had this spot in mind, for there were no rocks and it was possible to bring the heavy-laden canoes in to within ten feet of the shore without danger of damage. Even so, the water was two or three feet deep and Lieutenant Nordbergh and myself, not a little embarrassed, were carried to dry land on the broad shoulders of two voyageurs. I salved my conscience by telling myself that after all the deerskin leggings and bare thighs of the canoemen was a better garb for this than my white breeches and black regimental gaiters.

No sooner were we ashore than eight fires were built and blazing and as many canoe-kettles strung over them to warm the "soupe" left over from the feast of yesternight. In due course, the thick concoction of peas and pork having been warmed through, the Canadians again squatted around the pots, spooning in the mixture with even greater speed and enthusiasm. Indeed, so did I, for hunger gives a free hand to the chef.

As Lieutenant Nordbergh and I sat in the sun emptying our plates for the second time our guide came to inquire as to our well-being.

"Breakfast taste good?" André asked with a smile.

"Indeed, yes," replied Nordbergh. "It must be sustaining, considering how your men work."

Half in hope I said, "You have no change in the diet?"

"But yes," replied the guide with a wise grin. "Coming down from 'Mackinac we have dried Indian corn instead of peas and sometimes fat instead of pork."

But he had one word of encouragement. He suggested to keep our guns, powder, and shot handy. "There will be chances for a deer, or a bear. Even a brace of ducks would be welcome, and next week there might be a few wild strawberries and partridge eggs for the finding."

He raised his head, looked at the sky and breathed deeply as if smelling the air. "It looks like good weather all day. By encampment we should make the foot of the Long Sault."

Within the hour the empty kettles, and the passengers, in that order of importance, were reloaded and we moved forward again, the chanson sung with greater vigor and the dipping paddles once more back to their steady, rhythmic thrust.

For the next "pipe" we lay to opposite a settlement on the north shore. Actually, it was the Indian Mission of the Seminary of St. Sulpice, and I could see the smoke of two distinct villages, separated by a church located on a point of land in the shadow of the two mountains that gave this lake its name. The quiet grandeur of the scene for a moment sent my thoughts back to Switzerland and other villages nestling in the shadow of mountains on the water's edge.

I wondered why two villages instead of one. Pierre Dupuis had the answer. "Algonquins to the east, and Iroquois to the west," he explained. "The Brothers brought them away from Montreal—too much strong drink."

"And how do they get along?" I asked, recalling the bitter enmity between these two Indian races.

"Très bien, très bien," replied Pierre." Until you...," he checked himself, "until the Bostonian traders got in there with rum. I hear there has been the devil to pay."

It was not long after that we entered a sort of strait, which was in fact the mouth of the mighty Ottawa River. Suddenly the gay voyageur song they were singing ended in the middle and paddles came inboard, red caps were snatched from the head and the northmen bowed in prayer. As they raised their heads they made the sign of the Cross. This, I discovered, was the traditional personal prayer rendered unto God by Canadian voyageurs whenever they entered a new water course venturing into the unknown.

André Perrot's forecast of our progress that day was, if anything, conservatively estimated. We arrived at the foot of the Long Sault before the sun had scarce started to drop. The canoes were brought up to within thirty feet of the shoreline and passengers and freight were again carried to ground on the strong backs of the Canadians.

The encampment was made under a stand of giant hardwood trees and the firewood gathered with such speed and urgency that it was no time at all before the water was heated in the kettles and the inevitable eight quarts of peas and two pounds of pork added. While it was cooking, and the cooks stirred the mixture and fed the fires, the voyageurs decked themselves in all their proud finery. Men with seniority of service, steersmen, bowsmen, and winterers affixed waving red plumes to their caps. I noticed old Pierre Dupuis, off by himself beside a maple tree, carefully adjusting his feathers to an appropriately rakish angle on his cap, then trying it on, turning his misshapen face this way and that. Of all the middlemen, it seemed he was the only one not a "pork-eater," and eligible to wear these badges of honor.

It seemed to me that the "soupe" was consumed with extraordinary speed that night and John Nordbergh and I had hardly started our second plateful before the guide came striding into the midst of the fires, with the confidence and swagger that comes with command.

"La Ronde—La Ronde—La Ronde!" he announced, and the signal set the whole company in action, as if by sixty-four individually pulled strings.

Two filled sacks appeared as if they had been conjured up from behind some towering oak. These were stood on end about five paces apart, and the old voyageur, Pierre Dupuis, strode out, wearing his blue capote and tall, gay plumes nodding from his cap. He held an empty kettle under one arm and seated himself on one of the sacks with no less dignity than a monarch on his throne. To the other sack went the youngest "pork-eater" of the brigade, with a neck like a young bull and hands the width of an axe-head. He, too, held a kettle and although he lacked the confidence of the Old One he swaggered just the same. It was his young, strong voice that started the traditional dance.

> Ce sont les voyageurs
> Qui sont sur leur départ;
> Voyez-vous les bonnes gens
> Venir sur les remparts?
>
> Sur l'air du tra, lal-dera
> Sur l'air du tra, lal-dera
> Sur l'air du tra, lal-dera
> Lal-dera!

After the young man's song had told of the voyageurs' departure it was Pierre Dupuis' turn to sing advice. With a wisely wagging and gnarled forefinger, he recommended patience for the long hours at the paddle and the tiring portage.

> Mets d'la racine de patience
> Dans ton gousset;
> Car tu verras venir ton carps
> Joliment sec,
> A force de nager toujours
> Et de porter;

>   Car on n'a pas souvent l'crédit
>   D'se sentir reposé!

Then came the chorus! All the voyageurs joined hands, as the Old One and his young confrère beat out the time on their kettles, and danced in a great circle, their gay sashes swinging in unison. As they gave strong voice to the lilting words of the chorus the whole forest seemed to reverberate and the tall timbers nod in approval.

>   Lève ton pied, ma jolie bergère!
>   Lève ton pied, légère!
>   Lève ton pied, ma jolie bergère!
>   Lève ton pied, légèrement!

And so it went, the young engagé starting with a new stanza, "Au revoir père et mère," and, in reply, Pierre Dupuis commencing, "Embarque-moi dans ton canot," and the dancing chorus again. There seemed no end to it and as they warmed to the dance the Canadians became more vigorous and vocal. Certainly, Pierre Dupuis had a répertoire that would have gone on until dawn, and whenever the young man faltered there were plenty of prompters.

It was a night of a million stars, this second night, and from our tent we watched the dancing forms of the voyageurs, enlarged by the shadows cast by the firelight, and when sleep came to us the canoemen were still in good voice with endless songs of love and of their hazardous calling. Little they cared, this night, that the Long Sault faced them at the break of day.

6

The break of day brought with it a steady drizzle of rain sufficient to dampen down a man's good spirits, but to our Canadians it only served to add zest to their labors as, stripped to the waist, they faced the first portage of the long journey.

The Long Sault, three miles in all, caused our canoes to be unloaded thrice and the freight carried over rocky paths made the more hazardous by rain.

I had been told that before we reached Michilimackinac there would be forty such portages, some longer, some more dangerous, all testing the sinews of the strongest man, but I had not expected such witness of skill, endurance, and speed as I saw that morning.

As a gray dawn came, the voyageurs were already adjusting their "portage collars," a type of harness to aid them in carrying their loads. So far as I could tell it consisted of a strap, about three inches wide, doubled back in such a manner as to provide for a number of smaller straps or thongs. One pièce was securely tied top and bottom with two sets of the small straps and then swung onto the back of the "pork-eater" so that it rested on the small of his back. The collar, or the double end of the wide strap, was then over and on the head, at which time the voyageur seemed to lean slightly forward; at the same time the bearer would heave up another pièce, ninety pounds, mark you, and place it on top of the one already secured. Some of the men were adding a third when stopped by the guide. The footing was too treacherous this morning and a broken leg or even a sprained ankle would mean only delay.

Then off at a steady dogtrot to the first "pose." This, I discovered, was about a third of a mile, and I learned that distance over a portage was measured by the number of "poses," just as distance on water was measured by the "pipe." There the load was dropped and the Canadian trotted back for his second. Not until all the freight was brought to the first "pose" was a start made to move it to the second. No man slacked; indeed, each seemed to strive to move faster and carry more than his fellow, as dictated by the extraordinary pride of the voyageur.

Each canoe was carried by the bowsman and steersman and by the time the first "pork-eater" and his load arrived at the end of the portage the canoes were in the water, some twenty feet from the rocky shore and ready for loading. Without hesitation the voyageurs waded out, sometimes almost up to their waists and placed each pièce carefully in its alloted place, for nothing must be done either by rock or rough handling to damage the frail bark.

Lieutenant Nordbergh and I carried our guns and hopefully made two or three sweeps back of the portage path, but nary a bird or animal did we see. Obviously it was no day for the hunt and wild life had gone well to cover, seeking protection against the rain. So it was back to warm "soupe" for breakfast at the end of the first portage, and good it tasted, too, even to us, let alone the Canadians who had moved twelve tons of freight and still held fast to their good humor.

Once the brigade left the Long Sault, the last of the seigniories had been passed and not even an isolated farm appeared on either side of the wide, slow-moving Ottawa—nothing but the endless giants of primitive forest. Thirty miles or so on we passed an old French trading post and fort surrounded by a stockade; it looked deserted and lonely. And again, at the mouth of Rivière du Lièvre, we passed another trading post at which a dozen or so Indian canoes, loaded with fur, had just arrived from the wintering grounds. Both banks of the river seemed high and dry, and here and there, where a break in the forest formed natural meadowland, the grass was already green with promises of lushness. I wondered how long it would be before man found this rich and wonderous countryside and made it his home.

Indeed, beauty and grandeur seemed to unfold with startling surprise. It was high noon on the following day that we drifted in the slow current for "une pipe" opposite a breathtaking waterfall on the left bank. It was created by a river that must have been close to four hundred yards wide, its waters dropping, I judged, fifty feet over sheer rock into the Ottawa. The noonday sun striking the spray produced a myriad of colors in rainbow-like hues. What a magnificent curtain, thought I.

Pierre Dupuis, sucking on his pipe, gazed at it for a time in silent admiration, although he must have seen it fifty times or more.

"Rivière du Rideau," he said at last. Ah, I thought, how appropriate—the River of the Curtain.

We moved up the mighty Ottawa, now moving as if the ages had set its course by the opening of the rocks to let it pass, thundering toward the sea. Strangely, after the last pipe the voyageurs did not break into their usual chanson, but dipped their paddles in mute silence like men about to enter some great cathedral. After a short time I heard a distinct and increasing rumble as if some giant stirred the vitals of the earth.

"La Grande Chaudière!" said old Pierre gruffly, as if this should be sufficient explanation. "The Great Kettle." Well, I think, what sort of a wonder of nature can that be? My own eyes soon answered my question.

La Grande Chaudière, The Great Kettle! How well the French explorers had named this great caldron of furious white water, ironbound by rock. Here the turbulent river, rock marked and savage, seemed to divide its troubled waters, half of it dropping down some thirty feet into a devil's hole of a chasm, cascading spray and foam high in the air to be caught up by the sun and crowned by a rainbow. No man knows for sure whence go these angry waters save that some secret channel deep down must pass the rushing waters onward.

The steep rock banks made this portage as dangerous as it was awe inspiring. It took twelve voyageurs to lift each canoe up the rock face to higher ground, and as the Canadians carried the freight over smooth, flat rock they were drenched by the spray from the falls. Three miles or so upriver we encountered the Second Chaudière Portage, and five miles further again the Portage des Chênes, no doubt named in honor of the ancient oaks that stand sentry along the portage path. Here, where the water moves swiftly to its appointment with the Great Kettle, the empty canoes were cordelled up through channels studded with black rocks.

We encamped that night under the oaks, wearied from exertion and strain endured in overcoming the obstacles of rock and wild water. Ahead, the great river widened out into Lac des Chaudières and seemed to promise twenty-five miles of placid, calm, and serenely moving water. It was a welcome thought after this day.

As we waited for the kettles on the fires to heat, John

Nordbergh and I climbed a small knoll, the better to view the great beauty that unfolded ahead. We judged the lake to be almost two miles wide even close to where it narrowed to enter the turbulent rapids we had just passed and where clusters of rock formed tiny islands, many sporting greening trees, to split the waters rushing downward. To the west, as far as our eyes could see, the river looked like placid glass, all rose tinted by a glorious sunset that filled the sky over the horizon.

André Perrot, having completed his check of the overturned canoes, joined us.

"It looks like better going tomorrow," said Nordbergh to the guide by way of greeting.

André shrugged his massive shoulders. "Perhaps, M'sieur, perhaps. I hope we can use our sails going up Lac des Chaudières, but you never can tell."

"That sunset," said I, "It seems to promise fair weather."

André laughed. "You know, always sunsets are like that on Lac des Chaudières, yet always different. But blow! I've seen bad ones on this lake; they come up fast, as if they bounce off the mountains."

By now the sun seemed to be drawing off all the reds and blues and greens from the sky and taking them to himself. It became a great orange-red ball and dropped with startling suddenness behind the mountains to the west.

When dawn came there was a great stillness in the air and scarce a ripple on the lake. However, after one "pipe" it seemed to freshen, and sails were hoisted in the hope of extra speed.

The canoemen exhorted "la Vieille," the Old Woman of the Wind, to produce favoring breezes. Some of them cast a pinch of tabac on the water as they sang "Souffle, souffle, la Vieille"; and by the time we made shore for breakfast a slight breeze came up in limpid gusts, rippling the surface of the lake water in odd dark patches.

André Perrot paced about more restless than I had yet seen him. Indeed, he ordered the men to get on with breakfast when the "soupe" was not yet lukewarm in the kettles. His apologies he reserved for his passengers.

"I don't like the look of it—too still," he explained, raising his head and breathing the air in deeply. "We may have to make an early encampment."

I looked up at the sky; it was clear and blue, except for an occasional cotton-wool-like cloud moving majestically with the air currents. Seldom had I seen a more peaceful sky, but I kept my thoughts to myself.

We hadn't been back on the river long before a fish-tail breeze from the south and southeast sprang up and the sails were raised to take advantage of it. An island appeared dead ahead, almost in midstream, and the brigade changed course so as to pass between it and the north shore. It was a rocky island with a cluster of wind-deformed pines clinging bravely to it. As we drew abreast, we saw a number of laden canoes close by the rock face; and the breeze carried toward us the sound of a gutteral, dirgelike song, and moments later we heard the wailing of women.

"Indians burying their dead," said old Pierre, pausing in his stroke long enough to make the sign of the Cross. "That is a bad omen."

The canoes seemed well laden with fur and I presume their dead had been brought down from the winter hunting grounds.

After "une pipe" the wind veered around until it seemed to be coming straight down on us and the sails had to be stowed. By now the water had become choppy so that, with only two or three inches freeboard in the heavy-laden canoes, the bailing sponges had to be brought into use. We had travelled perhaps another four miles, but there was no thought of the beloved pipe now. I could see André Perrot standing in the bow of the lead canoe anxiously scanning the shoreline, which for some time now presented only sheer rock rising twenty or thirty feet out of the water.

Up ahead the sky had turned pitch black and where the light ahead of it struck the lake there seemed an eerie shape that looked almost like a funnel moving down on us. Lightning forked its way over the mountains set back from the river.

A sudden shout from the lead canoe was carried down to us on the wind. The guide who had been easing in toward the shore for some time now gave directions to the brigade by pointing over the starboard quarter. Through the spray and over the pitching of our canoe I could vaguely see a sandbank that appeared to have formed across the river side of a marsh; and for this refuge the canoes now turned.

The waves were breaking over the bow and as we turned to starboard and dropped down in a trough, for a moment I thought we had foundered. The bowsman and steersman used their long paddles like giant levers and the middlemen thrust powerfully, their paddles forcing the craft ahead against wind and water. We took water heavily over the port bow, but there was no time now for bailing; it was a race against the full fury of the mountain-born storm to be defeated only by brawn and skill.

As each canoe was beached a half of the crew strained to hold the craft steady with the rise and fall of the waves so that it would not be pounded or crushed against the shore, while the others moved swiftly to unload the cargo. Just as the driving rain struck a shout went up. The last canoe of the brigade was in trouble! It was about fifty yards offshore, the crew already overside, up to their necks in water, trying to push the craft in. Men rushed out to help, and once or twice it looked as if all had been completely engulfed by the storm-driven waves; but gradually, battling every inch of the way, they brought her in. She had struck a submerged tree trunk, ripping open the birch bark like so much matchwood.

While the voyageurs struggled in the face of the driving rain to cover the freight with oilcloth, John Nordbergh and I ran up the beach toward a stand of hardwood that stood to the west of the marsh, in the hope of finding shelter. We threw our oiled cloth over a low willow bough and sat there, holding it up for protection and wondering if we were not really wetter than the weather outside.

"Well," said I, "I have one suggestion to make."

"Good," said John, moving uncomfortably in his wet breeches, "and what might that be?"

"The next time you try to interest someone in a mining adventure, see to it that it's a little closer to civilization," I said with some feeling. For a moment John grinned, then his expression changed. The water running down the willow trunk against which he was leaning had changed course to the inside of his tunic collar.

Fortunately at sundown the storm abated almost as quickly as it had come, and by some miracle of experience the voyageurs had found enough dry wood to get the kettles boiling. For the first time I really appreciated hot peas and pork. Sleeping wet is bad enough, but on an empty belly to boot, it would be asking too much.

As we spent this most uncomfortable night a distance from the overturned canoes, under which the voyageurs slept, it was full daylight before we awoke. Lieutenant Nordbergh was first on the shoreline and he called back in a voice of surprise that sent me hurrying to join him.

"Look, Vere!" he called, "I think we are in business!"

By now I could see down the shore to the canoes, and the sight that met my eyes made me pull up short. Every bush, willow tree, and stump lining the beach had blossomed forth in a gay, many-colored garb of stroud—the coarse trading blankets—blue and scarlet cloths, serges and flannel, not to mention shirts and undershirts that for color outdid Joseph's coat. On the sand in front was an array of other objects set out in the morning sun. Indian fusils (flintlock muskets), painters' colors, brass and tin kettles by the dozens, twine, nets, and carrot tobacco.

"We must be," I said when the surprise wore off and I found my tongue. "At first I thought we had opened a laundry."

As we walked toward the array of goods, two voyageurs clowned along the shore in mincing steps, with shawls of the brightest colors I ever laid eyes on draped about their stalwart shoulders. A roar from a bowsman ended their caper and they proceeded to hang the shawls on a branch of cut-leaf maple. Other Canadians were still opening watersoaked packages and sorting out material to dry in the sun. Beads, snuff, silver earbobs, bracelets, and awls were sorted out from gay handkerchiefs, gartering, and fettering.

Fires had already been lighted under the kettles of "soupe"; so it was clear our departure would be delayed for some time.

We walked down to the canoes, where fifteen or twenty of the more experienced northmen were at work repairing the damages. There was not one but there were two rents in the underside of the craft that had run afoul of the sunken tree trunk; obviously, it had protruding branches that had done the damage. The voyageurs had cut away a whole section of the bark and were replacing it with sheets carried in the bow of each canoe against such an emergency. One man was already sewing together a strip using "wattape," the fine root of the red spruce, as thread. Later the joints would be gummed as pine-tree gum was applied with the aid of a torch. Voyageurs were in fact now recaulking the other canoes for fear the storm or portage handling had loosened the brittle gum; and men moved back and forth from the fires with lighted brands.

Even though the sun had now come out in summer warmth and the lake had long since lost its anger, it was conceded that the day would be spent before the goods were dry and repacked in appropriate pièces.

"Strikes me," said John as we stretched our legs on the sand after breakfast, "strikes me, that game should be on the move this morning after holing up for the storm."

I agreed that such was likely; and so we got our guns, and with hopeful good wishes from our Canadian comrades we started back in the bush, skirting the edge of the swamp for dryness' sake. Although heavily wooded with tall hardwood timber, the terrain proved to be cross-cut by almost perpendicular shale banks rising twenty feet or so and running parallel to the river with a plateau of trees and the occasional meadowland patch, a hundred yards or so in depth, before the next rise.

We worked our way some distance along the first plateau without seeing anything, although we did hear two partridge get up ahead of us in a clump of spruce. We agreed to split up. I was to work the higher level with John taking the woods below.

I scrambled up the shale bank, making as little noise as possible and, once at the top, walked a hundred yards or so without seeing so much as a chipmunk. A strong patch of pure sunlight ahead indicated meadowland and I walked toward it. On the edge of this clearing I was amazed to see a granite boulder some ten feet high. It was as if some giant had walked away and forgotten it after some prehistoric game of bowls. Fascinated, I walked around it and on the far side found clefts in the granite from which grass and wild-raspberries sprouted. Using these for a foothold, I climbed to the top of the rock.

From this vantage point I could look down on the whole of the clearing, a lush green carpet fringed with forest giants. The rock was warm from the sun; so I sat down and then lay back, stretching out my legs, with the occasional swat at an inquisitive wasp. After a time there was complete stillness. Then I heard a twig snap and raised my head cautiously. I all but fell off the rock. There, not twenty-five yards away and browsing in the clearing, was the biggest buck deer I ever laid eyes on. I rolled over and raised my gun from the rock, taking care that the butt did not strike. He must have heard the click when I pulled back the hammer, for he raised his head and snorted in alarm. But I got my shot away and dropped him, and a second was not needed.

The sound of my shot echoing through the woods below brought Lieutenant Nordbergh on the run. I went to the edge of the shale bank and called him up.

"Jove!" he exclaimed, still out of breath, looking down at the buck, "Couldn't you have picked a smaller one. It's a long way back to camp."

But we solved that problem by walking a half mile to a rocky point that looked down and over the marsh and the sandbar. We fired a shot to attract the attention of the men below and signalled for help. It wasn't long in arriving, for the Canadians had already guessed that we had had luck.

And that night we feasted on venison. There was plenty for even voyageur appetites and a ham besides, smoked by one of the cooks and carefully wrapped for the benefit of the passengers' future use.

Nor was my venison the only change in diet that day, for three or four Canadians had walked a hundred yards or so along the shore to the mouth of a small creek where they netted three bags full of fish. And another had found a clutch of duck eggs in the wild rice on the edge of the swamp.

That night under the stars and before the winking embers of eight fires the Canadians made merry with song and dance. And now without good reason, for they had dined well and the freight was all repacked awaiting the break of a new day and the launching of canoes made sound by the craft of good canoemen.

7

As far as I could judge, taking into account the twists and turns of the great river, the brigade's course up the Ottawa was west-northwest and as each day passed both portage and recharge became more difficult and hazardous. Precipitous rock and angry white water constantly tested the skill and the strength of the voyageurs. At many a portage, in fact, we hardly came to a rapid without seeing pathetic, lonely clusters of tall wooden crosses. Here Canadians had lost their battle against cruel waters.

At the head of Lac des Chaudières we faced the Portage des Chats and a carrying place along a ridge of high, uneven rock. The rock stretched out across the river in a parade of pinnacles between which the high water roared with the power of a million horses. Above, for six long miles, Lac des Chats was studded with small rock islands between which the river swept with such strength that the half-loaded canoes had to be cordelled up, with a swift, dangerous return for the remainder of the cargo.

The Portage du Grand Calumet came two days later and this, it transpired, was the longest portage on the Ottawa. Close to two miles by my reckoning and over a small mountain through desolate, rocky, spruce-pocked country.

At the end of this portage a day was taken up in examining and recaulking all the canoes lest damage and wear sustained in rough water or by rock should endanger our progress.

While the Canadians plied gum and torch or mended and strengthened with "wattape," Lieutenant Nordbergh and I took our fowling pieces and went out after wild pigeons. I would not call it sport, for all that was required was to fire into a mass of birds when they took flight before us, rising above the spruce trees like clouds of gnats on a warm summer evening. But then we were not out for sport but rather for sustenance, or at least a needed change of diet. So we filled two sacks as the result of the slaughter, sufficient to provide an evening meal for all the voyageurs as well as for ourselves.

That night around the fires voyageurs whittled down to convenient size pieces of limestone-like rock they had picked up on the portage. "Pierre à calumet" they called it, and I was told by our guide that both Canadians and Indians prized it highly for use as pipe bowls, so much so that the portage was named in its honor.

By noon the next day we passed Fort Coulonge, a trading post that seemed to be getting a fair share of fur, judging by the number of Indian canoes pulled up before its stockade. Fifteen miles or so above Portage des Deux Joachims, at the mouth of Rivière Dumoine, there was another post equally busy but not so preoccupied with trade that the Canadian trader and his Algonquin wife did not insist that Lieutenant Nordbergh and I partake of typical Canadian hospitality, including the provision of wine, which he proudly informed us was made from the flower of the wild elderbush.

For some time now we were destined to sleep on hard rock. Gone were the lush meadowlands of the lower Ottawa and we seemed weighted down by the hardness and vastness of a land composed of mountains and rock, stunted spruce, and wind-deformed pines. Even the tall hardwood trees had fled before its harshness.

It was in this rough and awe-inspiring country that we approached the Portage du Roche-Capitaine with the rocks rain-swept and dangerous to stand on and the river water high and mad from the late spring thaw. In a way, it was our farewell to the Ottawa and I would that this day's events could have been otherwise.

The angry waters roared through a narrow channel created by a large island, and in their midst, withstanding the crashing foam, a giant rock standing high and named Le Capitaine. André Perrot considered at length the difficulties of the rocky portage that snaked its way through stunted spruce and mountainous terrain. He decided, at last, to cordelle half-laden canoes through the channel made deep by the run-off and covering rocks otherwise dangerous at low water.

Laboriously and carefully the half-loaded crafts were eased up the channel by ropes, with the voyageurs more often than not up to their knees in water or clinging perilously to the rocks, keeping the canoes clear of the destructive rock face.

The return for the remainder of the freight was breathtaking. Time and time again, as the rushing water thrust a canoe this way or that, disaster seemed inevitable; but the furious paddling of the voyageurs as they kept the bow head-on, combined with the agile work of the bowsman's pole in warding off the canoe from a jagged rock, seemed always to achieve the impossible.

John Nordbergh and I stood on a high point watching in silent admiration the skill of the northmen. Seven canoes went by to their rendezvous with the freight that had been left behind, and the eighth came plunging through the white water for all the world like a runaway horse that every so often the rider manages to check before it crashes madly away again. Again and again steersman and bowsman, standing high, set the craft away from rocks.

Then, so swiftly that it seemed our eyes deceived us, it happened. The bowsman thrust powerfully to keep the fast-moving and pitching bow away from a jagged rock. His pole broke... he went overside headlong, and seemed for a moment to rise from the white water and throw his weight between the craft and the rock. The steersman shouted an order as the canoe hung for a second on the verge of a fatal swing across current. A middleman near the bow dropped his paddle and picked up a pole from the bottom of the canoe, poling furiously in place of the lost man. At last the canoe was brought back on safer course.

In seconds the craft was out of reach of the man overboard and there could be no turning back. For a moment his head appeared above the churning water, then he raised an arm; whether it was a gesture for help or one of farewell no man will ever know. Once I thought I caught sight of his body in the whirling rapids farther down, but I could not swear to it.

That evening there was no chanson about the fires and the voyageurs sat like lonely men, drawing on their pipes, wrapped in thoughts known only to themselves. A group had gone into the woods seeking a tall straight poplar; this, with a broad-axe, they fashioned into a cross standing ten feet high. It was planted with twenty-seven others, many now leaning with the weather, and each telling all who voyage past this place that here a Canadian gave up his life in cruel waters.

André Perrot, of all, seemed the most lonely this night. His decision it had been to décharge rather than to portage, and his alone. It had cost the life of a comrade. In such matters the burden of command weights heavy on a man.

We engaged him in conversation hoping to ease his mind, but I don't think we succeeded to any degree. "This place must have a bad reputation," said John Nordbergh. "I see there have been many losses," he added, with a toss of his blond head in the direction of the pathetic cluster of crosses.

André nodded. "Yes," he agreed. "Three years ago my brigade coming down lost a canoe and three men here." He paused for a time and then went on as if talking to himself. "I was a bowsman then, like Jean Brunnet. God rest his soul. It is strange, three years ago I promised Madam next year no more voyaging; I will stay and work the farm." He shrugged his strong shoulders. "And last year Jean had thought the same, but now it is too late."

"You knew him a long time?" I asked.

"But yes . . . many, many years we voyaged together. We started as pork-eaters together. He was a good bowsman, Jean, none better. A good man from the Parish of St. Sulpice."

"Did he have a family?" asked Lieutenant Nordbergh.

The guide shook his head sorrowfully. "Ah, yes . . . poor Madam Brunnet. They have nine children, all girls except the first-born . . . Jean-Marie, a fine strong boy. This is his first year as an engagé, with a brigade that was to leave the week after we did. Jean told me Madam was against the boy voyaging; she'll like it the less, after this."

André left us then, wandering down to the canoes and running his hand over the caulking as if by habit rather than with a purpose.

Three days later the brigade left the great and powerful Ottawa, after having journeyed four hundred miles over its placid places and though its roaring defiles, and at the Lazy Portage entered La Petite Rivière, a small river as the name implies, that seemed in actual fact a mere necklace of rapids and cataracts. At last, after crossing innumerable ponds and small lakes we arrived at a lake called Nipissing, and here sails were hoisted to take full advantage of a good breeze. But by noon the breeze had stiffened and the brigade just had time to make a small island composed of rock and storm-dwarfed spruce before the full fury of the blow hit us. Even so the Canadians had to work like beavers, waist deep in water, to unload the freight and bring the canoes to the sure safety of the rock.

A shelter was made for John Nordbergh and myself in the lee of a rock outgrowth that stood some eight feet high, and we made a small fire from such wood as we could find on the windswept island. Whether it was the sudden squall, or the wetting, or the interminable and inevitable peas and pork, or the ache in my leg, or all put together, I know not; but I was not in good heart and I must have worn it on my face.

"Travel weary, Vere?" asked Nordbergh, squinting at me through fire smoke.

I nodded. "Perhaps."

"Cheer up, lad. Less than a day's journey and we will enter the French River. They tell me it is less than sixty miles down the French to Lake Huron and that will end the portages."

I eased my left hip, trying to find a more comfortable position on the rock, while Nordbergh lit his pipe from a fire brand. He watched me out of the corner of his eye.

"The trouble with you is . . ." he said between puffs, "you haven't yet caught copper fever."

I grinned in spite of myself. "Never heard of the disease," I replied. "Or, for that matter, much about this confounded copper."

He threw a couple of sticks on the fire, settled back against the rock and, for a time, looked like a schoolmaster considering how much his pupils might be expected to absorb.

"Well," he said at last, "to do the subject justice I can only begin at the known beginning, which, so far as we Europeans are concerned, was probably the Island of Cyprus."

"The Greek island in the Mediterranean?"

"The same," said he. "As a matter of fact there is where we get the name copper—*cuprum*, according to the Romans."

For a good while, pausing only long enough to relight his pipe or to feed the fire, the Swedish engineer recounted the ancient wonder story of this reddish metal. How, for thousands of years, the Greek and Roman empires had drawn on the cuprum isle for the sinews of war and peace until at last the ore itself ran out and the Romans ran drifts or cuts below water level to collect ground water, charged with copper sulphate, in jars which slaves carried to the surface, where the sun evaporated the water and the copper sulphate crystallized.

And how three thousand years ago Phoenician traders had founded the Rio Tinto mines in Spain and with tin from Cornwall had made bronze. On this resource had flourished their empire. But the deepness of the mines and their flooding by water had, in the end, defeated even the conquering Romans. True enough, miners had found the first Cornish copper in the reign of Good Queen Bess but not until our century had Cornish miners gone deep down for the rich lodes needed by the civilized world.

"I know of no metal," said Lieutenant Nordbergh, as he poked the dying embers of our fire, "nor, for that matter of any other material thing that has had more to do with the progress of man than copper."

I thought for some time before I dared venture my doubts, and tried to make my point with an old French proverb. "Point d'argent, point de suite. No money, no future. I mean, with Cornwall able to supply the most of the world's copper, how can we hope to compete, even if we find it, by carrying it a thousand miles through this wilderness?"

John Nordbergh smiled and shook his head. "This, my friend, is an adventure in discovery not a job in a counting house. But then, I suppose a straight question warrants a straight answer. Perhaps we won't compete, perhaps we will; but I know this much, if we find copper of good quality in quantity, some day the world will be grateful."

He eased over on his side as the rock-bed grew harder under his lank, prone body. "You see, the copper in Cornwall is deep down, far below the tin, and water is the problem. Men strain their hearts out day and night at the pumps, but always the water seems to win."

"Then you think that Cornish copper will be flooded out, or disappear, like that of Cyprus and Rio Tinto?"

"Of course . . . some day. It is just a question of when. Now they are trying to invent engines to pump out the mines; even if they succeed it will be costly mining."

The Swiss in me set me after hard facts. "And what would copper be worth if we found it?" I asked directly.

The engineer snorted. "Jove! I'm not at all sure you wouldn't best be at your Geneva bank. Oh, it's worth about eighty pounds sterling a ton, but the price is rising and they say it may reach one hundred. And, before you ask, it costs thirty pounds a ton by voyageur canoe from Superior to Montreal."

After that sally Nordbergh proceeded to wrap himself in his blanket and deserted me to my thoughts. I sat for a long time staring past the fireflies that were the embers of the voyageur fires. The moon came up, giving black outline to the overturned canoes under which the travel-weary Canadians slept.

The magic and almost madness of it all took tight hold of me. Was this, indeed, a fool's errand I was on or was it an adventure with a prize so rich no man could measure. I thought of the man into whose service I had elected to go—le Bel Anglais! Although I had not yet set eyes on him, his character portrait had been painted for me by soldiers and traders and voyageurs, and even Dan Clause had vouched for the fact that the Indians had faith in him. Certainly the facts spoke for his determination and courage. Twice had young Alexander Henry seen his fortunes destroyed in the path of violence. The first time in 1760 when he lost three boatloads of merchandise on the Rapides des Cèdres, his entire worldly possessions; and the second when Pontiac's blood-crazed warriors brought pillage and slaughter to Fort 'Mackinac three years later. Indeed, le Bel

Anglais' life had been saved because of Indian and Canadian friends. But still he had begun again with little to build on save strong hands and a fair mind. Hardly, though I, a man to set out on a fool's errand.

Two loons, out on the dark waters, laughed one to the other, filling the night air with weird derision that seemed to shock the very stars. John Nordbergh stirred in his blankets, mumbling.

"Not abed yet?" he asked, my blanket-wrapped and seated form visible to him against the white moon.

"No . . . I have been thinking."

The engineer chuckled. "Aha! So the copper fever is taking hold so soon."

"Perhaps," I agreed, "perhaps."

He turned on his back and cradled his head on his hands. "Well, Bayard, it is a venture that may lead anywhere. You can build your dreams as high as those stars and still be short of where it may lead." There was a long silence before he spoke again, as if choosing his words.

"And it's not only copper, methinks," he said at last. "The time I spent with the good Jesuit fathers at Quebec searching for reference to copper in the writings of their missionaries was more productive than I bargained for. Not only were copper deposits indicated but also mention was made of silver."

"You mean they found silver?" I asked.

"No, they did not, but obviously the Indians had and in the Lake Superior region. Medals and bracelets made of silver, and twice mention was made of a crucifix carved by Indian laymen out of silver. I was shown one; so far as I could tell it was virgin silver."

"But surely," said I, "surely, if there was silver there and Christian Indians knew of it the missionaries would know where it could be found."

John Nordbergh snorted. "My young friend, despite the fact you lost fingers to one, there is still a lot you don't know about Indians. Copper, and apparently silver, is a sacred trust so far as the Ojibways are concerned, and they are not prepared to share it with any man. Can't say I blame them."

"How far will they go to protect these sacred mines?" I asked.

"That, my friend," replied Nordbergh drily, "remains to be seen."

He rolled over and rewrapped himself in his blanket. "Now you had best get some sleep," he advised. "Tomorrow we enter the French River, another sixty miles or so of rapids and portage before we reach the big lakes."

But it was a long time that night before sleep met up with me and it was not the hardness of the rock, nor the mad laughter of the loons, nor even the howling of wolves, that kept me awake. I wondered, down the ages, how many men had in fact walked in my moccasins, filled with doubts, yet dreams, with foreseen difficulties and hardships, yet stirred with a strange excitement that would brook no defeat. The Greeks, the Romans, the Phoenicians, all these and more had turned the rich storehouse of the earth into man's slave and companion. Was I, too, to join this unnamed company of adventurers? And then sleep found me and remained with me until the cry "Alerte! . . . Lève, lève, nos gens" sent me wandering, half asleep, to the water's edge in the first gray light of a new day.

8

To enter the French River, which was to carry us close to sixty miles in a southwest direction, the portage of the Chaudière des François had to be traversed—a rocky, treacherous carrying place of more than five hundred paces. I sensed that our Canadians had become unusually tense, and jovial good humor and chanson had given way to a kind of serious and close comradeship that men attain before facing a common danger.

In a way, I thought, they are not unlike troops on the eve of battle. And when the canoes were afloat and loaded, poised for the long drop toward the lake of the Hurons, it seemed to me that their customary prayers over paddles at the rest were longer and even more devout.

We had not gone many miles before I realized why, for the tortuous course of the island studded French River was little more than a tilting-ground to test all the skill and nerve of the voyageur, with death riding the bow of each canoe of the brigade through a roaring frenzy of cruel water and rocks.

Even the scene seemed to be set for it. During the whole course of the wild river I don't think I saw a foot of good earth. Rising high, back as far as the eye could see, were rocks and rock faces with, here and there, deformed and dwarfed pines clinging desperately to life drawn from barren rock. Islands studded the water, but, in fact, they might more accurately be called rocks of giant proportion with little or no vegetation to break the grim monotony of their hardness.

Between such barricades the divided waters rushed headlong with power and force toward the inland sea. In many places these dangerous channels were no wider than twice the width of the canoe and bowsmen and steersmen, standing high and tensed for action, time and time again parried off disaster with split second thrusts and turns of magnificent timing and strength.

So, in God's mercy and thanks to the courage and skill of our Canadians, we in due course arrived on the north shore of Lake Huron. Here the brigade rested a day while each canoe was carefully checked and each seam recaulked with pine pitch; now portaging was over and only the wind-swept waters of the great lake lay ahead. Forty-two portages lay behind us from Montreal and the voyageurs' songs seemed more gay and carefree than since we left Ste. Anne.

Our course for the next few days was in a westerly direction, coasting the north shore; and the second day brought us to a necklace of islands strung across our path, turning and extending westward as far as the eye could see. We made camp at an isle the voyageurs called La Cloche—the Bell—and after our repast of never-ending peas and pork our guide took us to a stretch of level ground where stood a rock on end.

André picked up a stone and struck the rock. It rang like a deep-toned steeple bell echoing and ringing in waves. "Voilà! La Cloche!" he exclaimed, grinning at our surprise. It wasn't long before the canoemen joined us, each in turn trying his hand at La Cloche until the island rang, with the northmen adding their voices in chorus at appropriate times.

It was Perrot who caught sight of the canoe in the distance before it disappeared behind a neighboring island, to reappear again in a minute or two. "An express from Montreal," he told us. "And he's making good time even against the wind. Headed for 'Mackinac."

John Nordbergh had brought his telescope along, the better to scan the distant islands, and he trained it on the canoe when it reappeared. There appeared to be a crew of six and the rhythmic movement of their paddles never faltered as the canoe rode the white-capped waves like a sea bird.

Nordbergh with his glass trained on the express swore under his breath and handed the glass to me. "Have a look at the passenger!"

I picked out the hunched-up figure amidships and brought the telescope to bear on his face. There was no mistaking it, even in profile. "Zeke Hutt!" I exclaimed, in amazement. "What on earth is he doing here? I thought he was trading out of Toronto."

"Whatever he's doing, I'll swear bodes no good for somebody," replied John, adding softly, "Let us hope it's not copper."

"Do you know Master Hutt?" I asked André Perrot.

The guide nodded slowly, then shrugged his shoulders in Gallic expression that spoke stronger than a tongue. He turned and walked back to the encampment. "Well," said Nordbergh, "I gather our Canadian friends think no more of Zeke Hutt than we do. I'd give my eye teeth to know what he is up to." Then he stopped suddenly and added, as if talking to himself, "Of course! . . . The Hopkins letters that were intercepted in New York." He put a halter on his tongue and I realized from the firmness of his mouth that questioning would be to no avail, so I let the matter drop.

We travelled some ninety miles westward on Lake Huron, our course taking us closer to the chain of islands than to the north shoreline. Then, where the lake narrowed at its western extremity, the brigade changed course and headed in a southerly direction. As we lay to for "une pipe" betwixt two islands, the canoes riding up and down on the lake-swell like so many gulls, old Pierre nodded at me and pointed westward to where the lake seemed to funnel down into a long bay, between a large island and the north shore.

"The road to Superior, my friend," he said. "The Falls of Saint Marys are about thirty miles in." He puffed away on his pipe in silence for a time as if his memories were too sacred to share.

"You know Superior, eh?" he asked at last. I shook my head. "Ah, but you will, my friend, you will."

I grinned at the Old One, trying to make light of his seriousness. "Is that a promise . . . or a threat?" I asked.

He scratched his chin stubble with his thumb and looked at me, dead serious. "Both, my friend, both."

After a time he gabbled on. "Ah oui. . . . The Lake of the Ojibways. I've seen storms on that lake with waves running higher than a full-grown pine . . . and deep, some say in places it has no bottom, save hell itself." At this he made the sign of the Cross.

"The Indians claim 'tis the home of the Great Manitou who will bring evil to any not his children who build lodges there."

I laughed out loud. "Come now, Pierre. If it is the home of the Great Manitou it must be heaven itself. Surely that is welcome enough."

My light heart was not in tune with the Old One's

thoughts. "Tiens!" he growled, "One learns not to laugh at such things."

I was rather glad that our steersman at this point chose to end the rest and our Canadian canoemen were away again giving full-throated voice to a voyageur song.

It seemed to me that the voyageur songs grew stronger and more gay as we passed through the narrow channel known affectionately and almost reverently as "Le Grand Détour." This, indeed, was the water road taken by strong men who ventured into the unknown North and West.

On our right was Pointe du Détour, the cape that served as a hinge between Lakes Michigan and Huron, and on our left l'Ile du Détour. But most important to the Canadians, and to their two passengers, was the fact that now just forty miles of open water across the Straits of 'Mackinac was the end of our journey.

We encamped that night on Ile aux Outards, being driven in by a sudden squall; but it took more than driving rain to dampen the spirits of the men. They sang and danced about the fires long after darkness fell, teasing the young engagé with wild tales of the revelry and sport to be found at Fort Michilimackinac on the morrow.

Nor was there any tardiness in leaving their blankets in the morning. Indeed, we were afloat and on our way before the sky to the east had scarce been touched by the rising sun.

The brigade travelled about nine miles into a choppy swell before I made out the gray outline of an island. At first sight it seemed a hump-backed object, like a giant whale breaking water.

Old Pierre grunted. "L'Ile de Michilimackinac . . . the Great Turtle."

As our canoe pushed closer under the rhythmic thrust of the paddles the resemblance became more obvious.

"It does look like a giant sea turtle, at that," I agreed.

"Michilimackinac means Giant Turtle in the Ojibway tongue," the old voyageur explained. "It's very strong medicine to the Ojibway . . . always en garde protecting Ke-che-gum-me—the Great Water, the Lake of the Ojibway."

"This is Superior," I suggested. Old Pierre nodded vigorously as if pleased with the pupil's progress.

We put in at the island for our first meal of the day although in truth there did not seem much time devoted to it, for the Canadian canoemen scarce took time to bolt down a few spoonsful of the inevitable "soupe" before decorating themselves in their traditional finery in preparation for their arrival at Fort Michilimackinac now just six miles across the water. Gay sashes and brightly beaded pouches to swing bravely from them were brought out of each man's sack and modeled jauntily by the wearers, feathers too reappeared in the caps of those who had been "hivernants," true men of the north, and none wore them with more pride than old Pierre even though he now used a porkeater's paddle. As we watched the voyageurs plume themselves André Perrot joined us.

"Only six miles to go . . . and the weather looks to hold fair," he said with a broad smile. "What do you think of the Great Turtle?"

We cast our eyes over the sloping round rock behind us. "Well, from the water at a distance there is a resemblance," said John Nordbergh, without too much enthusiasm.

"Old Pierre tells me the Indians consider this some sort of a holy place," I filled in.

André nodded seriously. "But yes, the Ojibway consider it to be a place favored by Ke-che-mum-e-do, their god. Indeed, there is a legend that the first white men landed here naked and hungry and met a crane and a bear who took them to their lodges, fed them and warmed them. The

Crane and the Bear are the two great clans of the nation."

The guide adjusted the knot of his sash more to his satisfaction, adding, "And just as well that it was so, for we Canadians have always been welcomed in Ojibway lodges."

"Well," said I, half seriously, "I hope they feel the same about the rest of us."

André thought for a time before he replied. "They are a friendly, honest people. So long as you have traders like Alexander Henry and Jean-Baptiste Cadotte they will . . . but if they are cheated or robbed—" He shrugged his shoulders. "They are great fighters, the Ojibway, once they take up the black belt."

André Perrot strode away in his moccasins to where the canoes were being prepared for the last short leg of the thousand-mile voyage.

"H'm, I wonder—" said Lieutenant Nordbergh, "I wonder where our friend Master Zeke Hutt would fit into that statement."

"Strange," said I, "that is exactly what was on my mind."

It was mid-afternoon and under a hot summer sun when we first sighted Fort Michilimackinac from the straits. As our canoe pitched steadily from a strong easterly swell I strained my eyes, hungry with curiosity, to see the form of this place that was the most westerly outpost, the taking and holding of which had cost so many lives of my regiment. At first it was but a brown burr on the shoreline flanked on the eastern side by white dots that were Canadian farmhouses.

"That's her!" grunted old Pierre with a strange quality of elation and satisfaction in his voice, although he must have been through this a hundred times or more. "Fort 'Mackinac . . . been standing there since Père Marquette came."

But it was not the fleur-de-lis of France that flew over the old fort now; and one of the first things I spotted was the twice-crossed flag of England flying high.

As the canoes of the brigade drew closer, the rhythm of the paddles seemed to grow faster and stronger. Indeed, the canoemen had a host of friends ahead and in time one could see a crowd gathering on the shore west of the fort, as news of the arrival of the brigade had obviously become known. The whole area on both sides of the fort seemed to be taken up by canoe yards, and craft of all sizes and shapes were being loaded or unloaded. I remarked on their numbers.

"But yes," agreed old Pierre. "Fur is moving down now and there must be two hundred Indian canoes in by the looks of things."

At last under the dun-colored wooden walls of the fort I saw the familiar blue facings on scarlet—men of my own regiment—and I felt pride stir in me. I straightened my shoulders despite the heat. The Royal Americans had served well this gateway to the unknown West.

The walls of the fort seemed to enclose a small town, for I could see the roofs of several houses and the spire of a chapel. I would judge the palisades, of unpainted, dingy-looking wood, would enclose two or three acres; but it was hard to judge, for it was irregular, almost hexagon in shape. We seemed to be heading for the Water Gate, which was flanked by canon-bearing bastions, and I was surprised how close the water came to the palisade, for there seemed to be hardly any beach at all.

"Crowded out, that's what they are," Pierre grumbled. "It's best to land to the east o' the fort and take the goods along the road to the warehouses inside the Land Gate. But there can't be room and we'll have to carry through the fort . . . hot as hades it will be."

But I had the feeling there was another reason for his complaint. I suspected his friends, Indian and Canadian, were with the increasing throng by the canoes further down the shore, for it was there his eyes were fixed rather than on the gate dead ahead.

Two officers of the Royal Americans were given the compliments of the guard as they hurried through the gate to join two or three men already at the water's edge. Our first canoe was in now and André Perrot was being welcomed and congratulated by a round of warm handshakes. Lieutenant Nordbergh joined the group and I was hard on his heels, wading ashore to my knees in water while the voyageurs held their laden craft clear of the shoreline.

Lieutenant John Christie seized fast hold of me almost before I was on dry land, embracing me with both his arms in a bear hug. John avoided handshaking even though he always wore gloves. He had much of the flesh burned from both hands pulling burning shakes off the roof at Fort Presqu'île after Pontiac's warriors had set it afire with fire arrows and pitch-balls.

"Let's have a look at you, lad!" thrusting me away the length of his arms. "So . . . the infant has turned man, eh? Well, you've picked a man's world to come to, and that's no word of a lie." John wasn't going to let me forget, bless him, that when we served in the same battalion of the regiment I was the junior ensign and far from dry behind the ears. And, I suppose, he was still senior lieutenant in the regiment, at least from point of service.

Captain-Lieutenant Frederick Spiesmacher joined us with a little formal speech of welcome which, for him, was a veritable flight of oratory. I had served under him. He was one of these conscientious German-Swiss officers who always looked worried and usually was.

"You are in command here, sir?" I said, rather than

asked, trying fatuously to fill in a painful silence.

"Ah no, Bayard, no . . . but command of the troops, ja, ja."

John Nordbergh came to my rescue. "Look, Vere . . . I think it's high time you met Alexander Henry."

There were two gentlemen talking to André Perrot and as we approached them the shorter of the two turned toward us.

"Mr. Henry . . . this is your recruit, Ensign Vere Bayard," said Nordbergh. For a moment I was taken aback, for I had expected a giant in seven-league boots. Surely this little man could not be "le Bel Anglais." But he was.

"We are certainly glad to have you here," he said in a quiet voice that had the quality of truth in it as he shook my hand.

"And, and I'm glad to be here, sir," I stammered. Even at this first meeting he had captured my loyalty and devotion. Perhaps it was the firmness of his handshake, or the frankness of his gray eyes, or the good humor that seemed to hover at the corners of his mouth, or all those things or more. I know not; but I knew he was one of those rare men who were born to command and to be respected and to be loved. I was well pleased.

"Well, now," he went on. "My partner and I have work ahead of us with this freight and I suggest you spend a few hours with your old comrades, and getting familiar with 'Mackinac. John Christie will make both a good guide and a good host. Besides, you will welcome a change from pork and peas." He paused and smiled broadly, tapping André Perrot on the shoulder as he did so. "Now, André, I mean no disrespect of the voyageur fare. How could I? . . . I know the kind of men it builds." The guide grinned with pleasure.

"Off with you then," said Alexander Henry to me. "There is a cot ready for you in my quarters and I'll have your gear left there. I will see you this evening."

As we passed through the Water Gate we caught sight of Captain-Lieutenant Spiesmacher and Lieutenant Nordbergh disappearing in the direction of the Commandant's office. As was to be expected, Spiesmacher was losing no time in voicing his troubles to the engineer officer.

"An unusual man, this Alexander Henry," I said, half aloud, still a bit taken aback at the appearance of "le Bel Anglais."

"Unusual?" John Christie snorted. "He is a just man . . . and, Gad, you don't know how unusual that is around here."

He said it with both feeling and conviction and it disturbed me, for it was not like John Christie to be overly critical of his fellows.

We hadn't gone ten horse-lengths within the walls before the heat struck me. It was like a wood-fired oven with the sun beating down strong enough to parch grass. I supposed that was why there wasn't any grass and not even a solitary tree to break the glare or provide shade. I spoke of it to Lieutenant Christie.

"Hotter than hades, and there is no let-up," he agreed. "You're just lucky you don't have to wear regimentals. The trouble is the palisade turns back any breeze off the water and there is no shade. If it's any comfort to you, it's as cold in winter as it is hot in summer."

Soldiers, stripped to the waist, were carrying water from the well to gardens between the barracks where, obviously, they hoped for fresh vegetables.

We walked past two rows of dun-colored and unpainted barracks, one of which was for officers and traders. John Christie pointed out the door of Alexander Henry's quarters, adding, "But I don't advise you to enter until after sundown, unless you want to fry like an egg."

The little church and the Jesuit missionary-priest's house behind it was made of logs. Next to the church was a long, low building, that served as Officers' Quarters.

"Let's go through to the land side," suggested my guide. "As a civilian you'll be interested in the trade . . . if you don't mind the smell."

Actually it met us before we got there—a strong, acrid smell that seemed to hang on the hot, breathless air like an odious pall. As we approached a row of barnlike buildings near the far palisade it grew worse.

"Raw furs, pelts. Fragrant, eh?" said Christie, screwing up his Celtic stub of a nose. "Fancy you going in the business."

"Not me," said I.

"But you're to be with Alexander Henry?"

"True," said I, "but not the fur trade. Copper."

John Christie looked at me hard for a moment. "Well," he said slowly with a lowered voice, "take a word of advice from me. Don't talk about it . . . leastwise not hereabouts."

He changed the subject quickly. "Have a look in a warehouse. You won't linger, I'll warrant."

I walked just inside a wide-open, double door and was met by a pungent heat-wave that all but knocked me down. Inside, scores of men, voyageurs and clerks, labored all but naked, the sweat glistening on their bodies. Some sorted piles of pelts, others manned giant presses or were sewing up "pièces" of the right shape and weight ready for the canoe brigades returning to Montreal. It was the winter's harvest from the North and West.

I did not tarry and quickly rejoined Lieutenant Christie who had wisely waited on the threshold. "I had no idea so much moved through 'Mackinac."

"That's just one of four warehouses. They say over half

the fur cleared through Montreal passes through here, and each year as beaver becomes scarcer in the East the proportion increases. Let's go out toward the Canadian settlements for a breath of air."

At the Land Gate the sentries, obviously doubled, were having trouble keeping a crowd of curious Indians out of the way as traders' men carried stores and furs in and out. To my surprise there were no children or women, and some of the men were feathered and others wore paint.

"Are there always this many warriors about?" I asked as we worked our way to the dusty, winding road and turned eastward.

"Heavens, no. They are not from the villages. They are in for the Commandant's Grand Council. A thousand of 'em—Potawatomi, Ottawas, Mississauga, even Dakotas from the Mississippi, that we have to keep under escort lest the Ojibways slit their throats."

We had just passed the perimeter of the fort when Christie took to a little path that lead toward the water. We stopped under the welcome shade of a giant maple. John Christie took off his tunic and loosened his stock. "Thank God, there is a breeze here off the water," he said.

I seated myself on the top log of the fence that ran under the tree. A brindle cow on the other side, being busy with flies, did not even raise her head.

"I suppose this Indian Conference accounts for Spiesmacher's worried look—that and his chronic lack of humor."

John Christie shook his head. "No. If any officer in the British army had the right to worry, I'd say it's poor Spiesmacher."

I was surprised both at the statement and the sincerity in Lieutenant Christie's words. I put my surprise into words.

"Great Ceasar! With Robert Rogers as Commandant? . . . I couldn't imagine an easier post than commanding troops for Rogers."

Christie looked at me as one would at a child who just announced that the moon was made of treacle. He opened his mouth to say something, then shut it on second thoughts and shook his head woefully.

"Well, for a start," he said, slipping the halter from his tongue, "now we have a thousand chiefs and headmen from all the Western Nations here for a Grand Council . . . and where is Mr. Indian Agent, the man that Sir William Johnson and General Gage in New York authorized to treat with Indians? In our ruddy guardhouse, arrested for his own protection, as much as anything else."

If it had not been for the seriousness of his expression I would have thought John Christie was the author of a bad joke. Now, particularly since the Pontiac trouble, the word of the Superintendent-General of Indian Affairs, Sir William Johnson, was indeed law when it came to dealing with the Western Tribes. That, at this time, his officer should be locked up in the guardroom was a fact I found hard to believe.

"But when . . . and why?" I asked.

"Yesterday afternoon about this time the Commandant and the Indian Agent, Benjamin Roberts, started brawling in the square in front of the well. Started over nothing. Roberts asked to be provided with a blacksmith's shop for the Indian Department and Major Rogers refused; said he could use the fort forge when it was not in use. One thing led to another until Roberts called the Commandant a traitor—and a lot of other unpleasant things. I thought Rogers was going to kill him! Fortunately, it was close by the guardhouse and I had a file of men over in short order to drag Roberts away."

"And what about the Grand Council? Surely the Indians must know."

"No," replied Lieutenant Christie emphatically. "That

they don't. Major Rogers continues to run the Council meetings . . . that's another problem. He has already handed out almost four thousand pounds' worth of presents and rum, and raised another five hundred pounds from the traders. How on earth he ever expects to pay that amount I don't know. He surely knows Spiesmacher would never sign the vouchers, and certainly General Gage and Sir William would never agree to the expenditure."

He stood up and slipped into his coat, straightening his stock. "One thing for certain . . . Major Rogers has bought the personal loyalty of the Western Tribes, for good or for evil, no matter who pays for it."

We started back toward the fort in silence. I felt anger at first and then bewilderment. Major Robert Rogers had been a hero and idol of fighting men on this continent for too long for loyalties to be other than deep rooted for this iron man of the long march, the valiant leader on a hundred frontier raids, the warrior among warriors. We both remembered the day in New York when the men of our own regiment, on the very day of our departure stormed the jail and released Major Rogers from his debtors' prison, and how the officers of the regiment, we included, knowing what was afoot, dallied over breakfast so that the mission might be accomplished.

"And what sort of a fellow is this Benjamin Roberts?" I asked at last.

"A boot-licking little popinjay!" John spat out in reply. "And now I have Corporal Clossen under charge for planting his boot forcibly on Roberts' rear end in the guardhouse. Oh, he did all right . . . you know the way the troops feel about Rogers, but he'll get the lash for it."

We trudged along with the dust of the road alive in the slanting sun and had almost reached the Land Gate before my friend spoke again.

"I'm sorry, Vere," he said. "I know exactly how you feel. I did too; but when you live with it for a time you come to recognize the truth. I really think Robert Rogers is going slightly mad; that and too much brandy and rum. Sometimes I doubt my own sanity. That's what comes of living on a powder keg with the fuse already lit."

There was an even larger crowd of Indians at the Land Gate now and extra sentries had been added. It struck me then that this was the very gate that treacherous Ottawa warriors had stormed through in pursuit of "a lacrosse ball," a Trojan Horse game that ended with the slaughtering of the garrison. Poor Jamette, he didn't have a decent fighting chance. Then I remembered his mural at Madam Benoit's . . . and Zeke Hutt . . . and the talk of mysterious letters from the French. The third letter . . . could it be? And if Robert Rogers had won the loyalty of the Western Nations.

"No . . . it's not so!" I said aloud.

"What's not so?" asked Lieutenant Christie after returning the salute of the sentry.

"Nothing," I mumbled. But I feel sick at my own thoughts. One does not even think such things of a brave man without feeling something less of a man yourself.

9

On the morrow, long before high noon, I began to wonder if I had not taken leave of my senses. The acrid stench of raw peltry spread out from the warehouses and fouled the air even beyond the stockade; flies swarmed and attacked one's body with persistent monotony so that one's hands could not be still for a moment. All the while dust clouds raised by shuffling moccasins and military boots parched the lips and caked body sweat.

To this shadeless hive of outpost activity had been added the perfidy of ambitious men, perhaps even treachery. This, all this, I had willfully traded for the gentleness, peace, and security of my beloved Switzerland. But the die was cast and, at least for a time, I must honor my agreement, though I resolved to stay not one sun-up longer than my conscience dictated.

So thinking, with brown dust scudding about my gaiters I trudged despondently across the parade in search of my employer. I met him as he emerged from the wide, barnlike door of the second warehouse, mopping sweat from his face and waving aside the flies that had followed him from the oven-hot darkness inside.

"Ah," he exclaimed, "I was just coming after you." His

eyes seemed to sum up my downcast face, and he added quickly, "Come, lad, let us go find a cooling drink ... at least this place has cold well water."

In his stifling quarters, Alexander Henry lost no time in outlining his immediate plans.

"We have no time to lose," he said, fanning himself with papers off his pine table that served as a desk. "For the present I am tied up with the trade, 'twixt the goods that have arrived and furs coming in daily from the northwest—but I must not let that put our mining plans out of step. For that reason, I shall rely on you to keep things moving." A quick smile, then, "I suppose you will take on the task of both secretary and manager to the Adventurers into Superior."

I loosened my stock, the better to breathe. "And where do I start?" I asked listlessly, almost rudely, which is not, I assure you, my usual wont.

Mr. Henry seemed not to hear and began sorting papers on his cluttered desk. "I think we must have a meeting of all of us concerned. Yes, we will do that tomorrow morning." He gave up his paper search long enough to wipe his face with a towel, adding, "Although, in truth, I know not how we can reason in this heat, and the room holds it all night."

I suggested it might be appropriate to meet out beyond the stockade where breezes off the straits, if there were any, would be an advantage.

"Excellent," agreed Mr. Henry. "There will be only five of us." He paused and grinned. "I hope Mr. Secretary can manage to keep notes on his knees."

"Whom do you wish to attend?" I asked.

"Just Henry Bostwick, Jean-Baptiste Cadotte, Lieutenant Nordbergh, and you and me. I'll see Henry and Jean-Baptiste at the warehouse—perhaps you would inform

John Nordbergh, tell him it should not take long . . . not more than an hour or—"

A clerk, stripped to the waist and obviously harried, came panting into the room. "Mr. Henry," he said, desperation in his voice. "There is a brigade of Indian canoes with fur, I think from the north shore . . . and we are having trouble getting that last shipment into the Montreal brigade. André Perrot says you are going to use some of his men here and . . ."

Alexander raised his right hand, which silenced the little man.

"I shall be down in a minute . . . right on your heels." The clerk disappeared more satisfied but still fussing.

"Well, Bayard," said Mr. Henry. "You see what I mean?" He looked ruefully at his desk. "I can never find anything. I hope you can bring some kind of order to those papers. If you can find and sort out those having to do with the copper venture, it would be useful for tomorrow's meeting."

He stopped at the door, turning to face me, "And don't let 'Mackinac weigh your spirits down, lad. I loathe the place, too, perhaps with even more reason than you. I'll guarantee, once we are on the march, we will see as little of it as possible."

I managed what I trusted was a hopeful smile. "Thank you, Sir. I confess I have little liking for it."

"Good lad!" he said. "There would be something wrong with you if you didn't hate it—but at the moment it is a necessary evil."

He went out the door and as he passed the window I called after him. "Mr. Henry . . . what hour is the meeting?"

"Whatever hour you think best, Ensign Bayard," he replied and then was off with that firm, swinging gait I was to come to know so well.

I rubbed my chin with my thumb, planning my attack on the littered desk. "I loathe the place with more reason than you," he had said. Ah, that he had. Looking from the open window across the heat-ridden and dusty parade toward the chapel, it was all too easy to recall the horror of the massacre that Alexander Henry had survived in this place; for here, not so long ago, he had witnessed the deaths of fourscore friends and comrades by scalping knife, tomahawk, and torture.

Pontiac's blood-seeking warriors had then set torch to his stores. For the second time since coming to this northland in search of fortune he had lost all his worldly goods and had stood, all but naked, to begin again believing in his future and in the future of this vast, hard land.

Yet, for all these hardships, here was a man who still held fast to understanding for others, ready with a word of cheer or a firm handshake when the going got rough for others.

I felt ashamed at my own faintheartedness and my yearning for comfort. After all, I told myself, the Ottawa knife that took my fingers at Bushy Run probably ran with blood here on that fearful day and so, in manner of speaking, I was one of the brotherhood with a stake in the future of this place. As my thoughts so ran, my eyes watched Alexander Henry across the square in animated conversation with two voyageurs. I saw him leave his discourse and turn and stoop to comfort a wailing Indian child lost from its mother in this strange white man's world. "Le Bel Anglais!" I said to myself aloud. Aye, indeed, le Bel Anglais!

I smiled, I suppose for the first time since I had set foot in Fort 'Mackinac, and I turned to the paper-strewn desk with a will and desire I had not previously felt in me.

I have often since thought on that first meeting of the

Adventurers into Superior. As a formative meeting, I suppose it lacked much in formality. Even so, it gained more, much more from the determination and character of those who took part. These were men who, once having set their course would finish it, despite the worst that man or devil had to offer.

Alexander Henry, whose habitual good humor neither the flies nor the heat seemed to stifle, wore his coat as befitted the occasion. But he removed it and draped it, folded, over the top log of the fence before seating himself on a convenient pine stump. I made myself as comfortable as possible on the grass close by him, stretching out my gaitered legs and loosening my tunic buttons.

Jean-Baptiste Cadotte, who had walked out from the fort with us with scarce a word to say the whole way, selected a spot where he could lean back against the fence and get some shade from it and at the same time be within touching distance of le Bel Anglais. It was a gesture born of mutual respect and close comradeship. He carefully and methodically began to fill the bowl of a stubby clay pipe. He was a short man but with shoulders as wide as the length of a broadaxe handle and his barrel chest, showing through his open shirt, had the color of well-seasoned oak. It occurred to me that if any white man had the right to name this land his own then Jean-Baptiste had that right by both birth and life.

As I watched his strong fingers gently pressing down precious tabac into the pipe and his good-humored, weathered face, I found it hard to realize that this was the man whose legend ran in seven-league boots through Detroit to Niagara, to Montreal and Quebec, and even to New York and London.

Indeed, were it not for this extraordinary Canadian, and his wife, I doubted that this strange business meeting would ever have been held or, for that matter, that we would have been alive this day to curse the flies and heat, let alone to plan the rich taking of copper from the earth. Certainly Alexander Henry would not have been here this day, for it was Madam Cadotte who had saved le Bel Anglais at the massacre of Michilimackinac, and had stood between him and the torture knives and brands of Pontiac's warriors. Madam Cadotte, God rest her soul, was an Ojibway woman whose wisdom was matched only by her tireless courage for she it was, and she alone, who persuaded the war chiefs of the Ojibway nation not to accept Pontiac's bloody belts at their council fires. That hot, terrible summer when we fought with our backs to the forest it was said that Madam Cadotte's canoe was scarcely ever out of the water and that her moccasins at council fires stood on such distant shores of the North and West that they were unknown to my people.

Her voice and that of Jean-Baptiste were heard at these council fires, and were heeded. Two thousand Ojibway warriors did not take up the war-axe.

The sound of voices and the dust-muffled shuffle of marching feet on the dusty road to the fort ended my thoughts and brought my two companions to their feet and caused me, out of curiosity, to rise from the grass. A large group of Indians, escorted by men of my regiment, were moving from the waterfront in the direction of the Indian encampment. Its smoke hung like a distant cloud in the hot, still air.

For a time both men watched in silence. It was Jean-Baptiste who spoke first.

"Dakotas!" he said. There was apprehension in his voice. He looked at Alexander Henry in the manner of men when they share a common fear.

Mr. Henry slowly shook his head. "I suppose Major Rogers is seeking friends wherever he can find them—no matter how far afield."

The Canadian shrugged his strong shoulders. "Then I hope the soldiers will be on guard. Certainly, Waub-o-jeeg will not sit at the same fire."

Mr. Henry resumed his seat on the pine stump slowly, as if he had suddenly found the hot air more exhausting. "Well, my good friend, at least events transpire in accordance with our fears—though Heaven knows there is little comfort in that."

The two men half-smiled as their eyes met. Suddenly I recalled the gossip and the consternation of Montreal and New York merchants when news came that these two men had formed partnership to trade in the West and North. "Every Indian west of 'Mackinac will trade with them," seemed to be the chief complaint. Hardly sufficient grounds on which to try to have the Governor cancel their license, but I well remember that try they did but to no avail.

I longed to know why the arrival of the Dakota chiefs for the Grand Council troubled these two, or for that matter why Waub-o-jeeg, the White Fisher, famed war chief of the Ojibways should be involved. But I kept tight hold of my tongue. In good time these things would be revealed to me, but now patience must be in the saddle.

This much I did know, that I had cast my lot with two extraordinary men! Le Bel Anglais, son of the colony of New Jersey, a man of proven courage, held in good repute by men of all races, tongues, and color; and Jean-Baptiste Cadotte, the Canadian, born of this vast wilderness, whose father had come before the turn of the century to serve his kind here. I found this thought strengthening my spirit. The company was good and they had my undoubted loyalty from this day forward.

Lieutenant Nordbergh, his long legs all but outstriding his apologies for being late, arrived with Henry Bostwick, who obviously had difficulty keeping up with the lanky engineer. The English trader had no apologies on his tongue but confined its use to grumbling about the heat and the fact that Captain-Lieutenant Spiesmacher had insisted he not unload goods at the Water Gate.

"Blasted soldiers!" he swore. "Who do they think they are?"

At first, I thought to come to the defense of the Royal Americans, but I noted the others were grinning broadly. I had yet to learn that Henry Bostwick was a constant and confirmed grumbler. He even grumbled about his left ear itching, much to the amusement of others, for Mr. Bostwick had lost that member of his anatomy by torture at the fall of Fort 'Mackinac. It was after that that he and his fellow trader, Ezekiel Solomons, were taken to Montreal for ransom.

"Well now, gentlemen," broke in Alexander Henry, putting his hands on his knees and leaning forward on his stump seat. "We all have work to do and the sooner we start this meeting the sooner it will be over." He paused for a moment and looked hard at me. I was trying to balance papers on my drawn-up knees in what I hoped would be considered a business-like manner.

"I have asked Ensign Bayard to keep notes of our meeting," he went on, "at least of our plans and decisions. As you know, outsiders are now concerned in our efforts and we cannot expect people in London to invest money unless they are kept fully informed."

Le Bel Anglais paused for a time and the only sound was the sucking noise from Jean-Baptiste's pipe. "And that," he said at last, "brings me to the important news that came by express a short time ago. Mr. Alexander Baxter has arrived at Quebec and will be here within the month."

"Well now—that is something," Bostwick interrupted in a jubilant voice. "London does mean business or they wouldn't be sending their man out. Any word of a Royal charter or what money he has been able to raise?"

Mr. Henry shook his head. "No, but I would think the report he makes on his return will have a bearing on both."

"Baxter will swing it if anyone can," said Lieutenant Nordbergh. "He has the ear of the right people in London, at least he used to have."

Alexander Henry looked surprised. "You know him, John?"

"Slightly. I knew his father better. His father was Consul

to the Empress of Russia. The younger Baxter has always moved in Court circles. Seems to me he is a close friend of Charles Townshend, which should be useful now that Townshend is in grace again with the Cabinet."

Le Bel Anglais smiled wryly and shook his head. "Well," said he, "we will try not to hold that against him." He added, nodding at me with mock seriousness, "I suggest, Mr. Secretary, that that comment be deleted from the record."

Alexander Henry firmly and clearly outlined immediate plans. "While the copper will wait, gentlemen, Mr. Baxter will not. We must move fast so that he will get the most out of his visit. Our first move will be to treat with the Ojibway, and Jean-Baptiste will leave at sun-up for the Falls of St. Marys where he will endeavor to arrange a council with the White Fisher and as many head chiefs as possible..."

Mr. Bostwick interrupted with a quick outburst. "I see no point in that," he grumbled. "White Fisher and other Ojibway chiefs are here now for Rogers' Grand Council. And they sure have been softened up with presents. Why couldn't it be dealt with here?"

Le Bel Anglais raised his right hand and Bostwick's voice muttered its way into silence.

"No, Henry," he said quietly. "White Fisher was here, and his headmen too, but they left on the arrival of their enemies, the Dakotas, and not as you suggest, softened up by the Commandant's lavish gifts.... Is not that so, Jean?"

The Canadian took his pipe from his mouth and nodded gravely. "Oui.... Waub-o-jeeg will not sit at a council fire with the Dakotas."

Le Bel Anglais stroked his chin with his thumb in the silence that followed. Trouble among the Indians was a matter none took lightly, not even Mr. Bostwick. The difference between peace and war might well mean the difference between life and death and these men knew it from bitter experience, although they were not, in the common parlance, soldiers.

"We must not forget," said Mr. Henry at last, as if talking to himself, "that this copper has a special meaning to the Ojibway, and we must respect their wishes."

Henry Bostwick snorted, "I must say they haven't done much with it."

Le Bel Anglais went on as if he had not heard. "The Lake Superior copper is a matter of religion with them, a sacred thing, not a thing for trade," he explained quietly. "I will only treat with them on their own ground. Where the medicine men have an opportunity of putting before the chiefs the meaning of the copper to the nation and I will have the same opportunity. Only then can White Fisher treat well and in a lasting fashion."

There was a long silence to which again only Jean-Baptiste's sucking his pipe contributed.

Suddenly Mr. Henry came to life. "Well now," said he, stirring himself, "I propose to leave for the Falls of St. Marys in three or four days' time. I shall take Ensign Bayard with me. When Mr. Baxter arrives, I hope Lieutenant Nordbergh will be able to travel with him and join us at the falls."

"I see no reason why not," agreed Lieutenant Nordbergh with some fervor. "Particularly as the Commandant has not yet settled with the owners for the reconstruction of buildings at the fort. As his mind is on other things he'll be glad to be rid of me for a few weeks."

"Good," said Mr. Henry. "Our exploration work will take all of that. By the way, André Perrot will be in charge of the canoes. Lake Superior waters are not to be trusted and they are not new to André, by any means."

This news I found much to my liking. It was as if on the eve of a departure on a dangerous voyage one found that an old friend and trusted mariner was to be master of the barque.

After our meeting time took to wing. Mr. Henry, busy night and day with matters relating to the fur trade, left in my hands the securing, selecting, and packing of provisions and powder and shot sufficient to meet our needs. And, in addition, there was the question of suitable presents for the Ojibway chief and headmen—bright calico, white and blue beads from which belts signifying purity, honesty, and blue sky could be woven, and but little rum, for the White Fisher's concern over its misuse by traders was too well known to be ignored even if one wished.

In these matters I leaned heavily on André Perrot's advice. Even so there was the never-ending bookwork to be done, not to mention provision of some comfort for Mr. Baxter such as bedding, a canvas lean-to, a suitable fowling piece, and even a little wine lest the gentleman from London should think us entirely unschooled in the amenities of the good life.

We were to take two canots du maître, which André acquired with some difficulty, for these craft were needed for safe voyage on the deep and rolling waters of the great inland sea. André himself would be in charge of the second one carrying Mr. Baxter and Lieutenant Nordbergh to rendezvous with us at the Falls of St. Marys. There was a little indecision at first as to who should act as bowsman in the first canoe, and I threw my weight in favor of old Pierre, a choice that caused André to smile knowingly and nod his head in agreement. And it was a good choice. The promotion of the Old One to a position of trust not accorded him for years caused him to shed years as the elm sheds leaves at the first frost. Indeed, the very frame of the veteran northman seemed to straighten and grow with a new-found youth and his swagger grew with it.

These responsibilities and the increasing fever of the quest for copper let me, for a time, sometimes forget the shadeless heat and flies, and the stench of the warehouses. From time to time I was even able to bring more cheer to the downcast faces of my brother officers of the Royal Americans. The truth of the matter was that, caught up in the adventure and comradeship of my new service, I ignored the intrigue and evil that was spreading like the smoke from the Indian fires across the parade of Fort Michilimackinac.

But the second morning, and the day before our departure, I was dragged into it by my forelock.

10

In rare good heart I busied myself with my duties, preparing for our voyage to the West in search of riches beyond the dreams of man. Even so, this devil's caldron was not to leave me be and a scarce twenty-four hours had passed after our meeting before I was hauled, head first, into the brew I wished no part of.

I was in the largest goods warehouse, stripped to the waist, selecting and checking Indian trade goods that would serve best as presents, when a runner arrived from the Commandant's office with an order that I present myself immediately.

The soldier, a veteran of the Royal Americans, fidgeted as I took time to look through some bright and attractive calico, betwixt swatting flies and wiping sweat from my body. Finally his fears got the better of him and let loose his tongue.

"Y'r Honor," said he, bending down to my ear, "the Commandant is in a foul taking—an' he doesn't reckon on being kept waiting." It occurred to me that the old soldier would have liked to have added "by a half-pay ensign" but manners and rank forbade it.

I stood up, grinning, and slapped the fellow on the

shoulder. "Come now, my friend," said I, "you wouldn't like an officer of the Regiment to parade before the Commandant like this, would you? My compliments then to Colonel Rogers and inform him I shall attend as soon as I have dressed."

The poor fellow opened his mouth as if to protest at the delay, then closed it without uttering a sound. He walked away, his boot-heels thumping on the pine floor, shaking his head, and, as he picked his way through scattered bales and dodged laboring, cursing men, I noted the spreading sweat stain on the back of his scarlet serge looked uncommonly like the outline of Lake Superior according to a crude map I had been studying. I hoped it was a good omen.

André Perrot, anxious to keep freight for the second canoe to a minimum and knowing by experience the amount of impediments usually associated with a gentleman travelling from overseas, joined me with a word of warning as to the weight of the cloth I had chosen. I retreated before experience though holding fast to some of the brighter pieces which I felt would have particular appeal to the Ojibway. These were set aside for sewing up into water-proofed pièces of required weight and size.

"I have to leave now, André," I explained, as I shrugged flies off my shoulder. "I've been summoned by the Commandant, who, I am told, doesn't like to be kept waiting."

André frowned and shook his head. "That is not good—even this furnace is better for one's health. Watch that one, my friend."

Color, and not from the heat, rose to my face. I had an almost overwhelming desire to come to the defense of the famous Ranger. But I held my tongue, for I knew that André Perrot meant well by his warning. Besides, I reflected as I slipped on my shirt, there was no reason to expect a civilian to know the true metal of a man who had bravely and skillfully led a hundred or more missions across forest and stream seeking out, and often destroying, an enemy that outnumbered him five to one or more, until his very name had become legend wherever fighting men met.

But before I even reached my quarters I began to debate in my own mind the reason for this summons and to recall talk of treason in a Montreal tavern and Lieutenant John Christie's honest Scottish face so troubled by the tortuous courses and plottings of man made greedy by the promise of riches in the West. But as I rubbed myself down I also scrubbed evil thoughts from my mind and with great care checked the buttons and lace of my uniform. Was I not for the first time to meet, in person, Robert Rogers of the Rangers, a giant of a warrior, as loved by those who took the field with him as he was feared and dreaded by his enemies. So thinking, with head erect, I marched off for the Commandant's quarters, hoping that at least I would acquit myself as a soldier.

Lieutenant Christie was on me before I scarce had a gaitered right leg over the Commandant's doorsill. "And where the devil have you been?" he exploded, getting up from behind his table. "The old man will have your hide for keeping him waiting—and mine t' boot."

I grinned at his fuming, thinking much of it is jesting. "Surely," said I, "A gentleman is entitled to the time needed to make himself presentable."

John snorted. "Presentable! Presentable, say you, wait until you see . . ." But he cut himself short as he hurriedly buttoned his coat. "I expect he will place you under arrest —not that I give a tinker's damn except the guardroom is already full and I cannot accommodate another prisoner."

"And," I shot back, "arrange for me to go back on full pay—can't keep an officer locked up on half-pay."

Lieutenant Christie only glowered in reply as he knocked and opened the Commandant's door.

"Ensign Bayard, sir!" he announced. As I stood there trying to focus my sun-struck eyes in the murky room I heard the door shut softly behind me and the click of the latch dropping. John Christie had left me to my fate.

After a time, the shape of a long table, cluttered with charts, took focus, and behind it a glimmer of light from a window. Then the form of a man, back toward me, that seemed to all but fill the window frame.

The silence seemed long and unbearable until at last came the deep rumble of a voice. "It took you long enough to get here."

"I was working in the warehouse," I replied by way of explanation rather than apology. "I delayed only long enough to change."

He turned from the window and faced me. A giant of a man, hands on his waist. I was struck by the width of his shoulders that stretched his rough shirt taut across a barrel chest. Like the voyageur, his life as a young canoeman, had built the top of his giant frame to such strength that neither age or idleness could dissipate it.

The suggestion of a smile came to the corners of his wide, loose mouth and, staring at his roughhewn face, I realized that it had been many hours since it had seen the edge of a razor. His unkempt appearance embarrassed me strangely and a sort of pity took hold of me.

"I regret that I am late, sir," I blurted out by way of making amends.

He ignored my apology. "Sit down," he ordered gruffly making his own way toward the chair behind the table. He seemed unsteady, as if the underpinning was too weak to carry so great a frame.

Indeed, my own head was none too clear and I was glad to be seated facing him. 'Twixt the heat and the close atmosphere charged heavily with the sickly pungent smell of rum I could only pray that this meeting would be short, and I yearned for the sunlight and fresh air.

But Colonel Rogers seemed not to share my desire. He fumbled about among the papers before him until he found a rum mug, which he proceeded to replenish from a flagon. Having satisfied his own needs, at least temporarily, he thrust the flagon and an empty mug in my direction. I declined with as much grace as possible.

As time dragged by I felt more and more like a mouse being watched by a half-amused, half-hungry tomcat ready to purr or pounce on a moment's whim.

"I hear you were at Bushy Run," he said at last, wiping his mouth with the back of his huge hand. I nodded.

He grunted in displeasure. "And me—me," he tapped his chest in indignation, "bottled up at Detroit by Pontiac's warriors like a blasted woodchuck held in his hole by a farm boy's barrel staves. Oh, I'll not gainsay Bouquet did not know how to beat the red devils—he proved he did. But it sits uneasy with me that a foreigner the likes of him knew my trade so well."

So back-handed a compliment to Colonel Bouquet must have brought displeasure to my face for it caused Robert Rogers to grin at me as he added, "No offense meant, m'lad I—have no quarrel with the Swiss—it's other popinjays I lay no store by. Besides Bouquet and Haldimand made the 60th the honest fighting regiment it is—certainly the only line regiment I would serve with."

There was an embarrassed silence, for I knew how hard and long the old Ranger had tried for a battalion or even a company of the Royal Americans but got no farther than a half-promise from Whitehall, and that from politicians in London.

"Besides, boy," he went on, after another draught from

the rum pot, "You are Swiss yourself, and I hear nothing but good repute of your service. Now tell me, now you're on half-pay, like the best of them, do you figure on making a fortune out of copper?"

Suddenly, as if the very mention of the wonder metal had cast a spell his whole manner seemed to change, banter and good humor seemed to melt away like a handful of snow dropped on a hot stove lid. His mouth tightened and his black eyes grew hard and piercing.

"Well, not exactly," I countered, seeking the right words and instinctively on my guard. "I am in the service of Mr. Henry and as much of his time is taken up with the trade I imagine I will be helping out on his copper venture."

The Commandant grunted. "So I hear," he said. "I also hear that there has been a meeting of those interested in what you call the copper venture."

I nodded. Robert Rogers leaned forward on the table as indicating a degree of mutual confidence.

"Tell me, Bayard, has the London agent shown interest —I mean, to the point of interesting adventurers there?"

It was a straight enough question that called for a straight answer or none. I was at loss as to how best to parry it. The Commandant attempted to drive away my fears and end my silence.

He started with a half-laugh, leaning back on his chair. "Ah, come now, lad. I am not one to put off or to fence with. I know a great deal more about the copper on Lake Superior than you probably ever will. When I was in London, His Excellency Charles Townshend was particularly interested in my plans for mining there—only a part, you understand of my proposals for the northwest."

He paused and looked hard at me, no doubt wondering if I had been duly impressed. Apparently he thought I had been. "Now I have heard," he went on, "that Alexander

Baxter is on his way out and that his interest is this copper. He is a confidant of the Honorable Charles Townshend and it is important to me that I know of his plans. Besides, don't forget, I can make or break any such adventure. Surely you must know by now that every Indian nation west of Detroit is my ally."

Another long silence in which I came to the conclusion that whatever the consequences I could be nought but forthright. "Sir," said I, "I have no stomach to fence with you, now or ever. So, in truth, I must say I cannot answer these questions. These are questions that should be directed to Mr. Henry, not me, sir. I have no authority to answer them."

He gave me so black a look that I thought for a moment he would vault the table and crush my ribs in a bear hug or, at the very least, roar for guard and have me placed under arrest for insubordination.

He did neither. After a time the blackness left his face and he became more relaxed. He just stared at me and slowly shook his head.

"What a pity," he said softly, "what a pity, that wars have to end and honest, loyal soldiers are spewed out into a world that has little to offer for either quality."

He got up then and unsteadily made his way to the window. His back to me and no word being spoken, I wondered for a time if, in fact, I had been dismissed.

Then his deep rumbling voice, words slurred, took over. "I'm plagued by little men, will ye understand that," he growled. "Gage and his pen-pushing staff in New York, afraid of his own shadow, watching every penny like an old woman hanging on to her Maundy money. An' that old devil Will Johnson, living like a lord on the banks of the Mohawk, busy convincing Whitehall he has the Indians eating out of his hand. In truth 'tis only the Mohawks, and that because of his woman. But the old fox hates my guts, an' so does that old woman Gage."

I began to wish more than ever that I was elsewhere. He turned, oathing and growling back to the table and, unhappily, to the rum. I could see it had already become master of his tongue and senses. I suppose I still wanted to find excuses for the old warrior of the forest but how could one attempt to justify an officer in his position vilifying his seniors to an ensign—General Gage, the Commander-in-Chief no less, and Sir William Johnson, His Majesty's Superintendent-General of Indian Affairs in the Americas. But I was a captive audience and 'twixt hatred and the tongue-loosing rum, the Commandant had the bit in his teeth now. Black anger took hold of him entirely and he pounded the table with his big fists until the mugs jumped about like marionettes.

"By your face, boy, ye don't like the truth, eh?" he roared. "Well, I'll tell ye the way 'tis, m'lad and ye can judge for yourself. Three months ago, three months ago, mark ye, I asked Gage at New York for a surgeon to be posted here to tend the sick of your own regiment. An' what happened? Today, today, mark ye—when some of the sick have been dead and buried for weeks—I get a letter back that says . . . ," and here his voice pitched high in prim mimicry, "referring to your request for a surgeon, I would again bring to your attention that such matters must be referred to the Commandant, Detroit, the officer in the field to whom you are responsible." Robert Rogers leered at me and added, "As you are a Royal American I thought that little minuet might interest you . . . ," he paused only long enough to refill his rum mug, "an' that old fox Johnson sends up that snivelling runt Benjamin Roberts as Commissary for Indian Affairs to report all matters directly to him—and me already Agent for the Western Indians on the word of the Honorable Charles Townshend and Whitehall. It turns my stomach to think on it. Mr. Commissary Roberts arrives in the midst of my Grand Council with the Western Nations. . . . and what does Mr. Indian Expert Roberts do? Why he spends a week, the little apple-polisher, going around matching otter skins, which he sends to the General hoping that Mrs. Gage will like them."

For a time I thought the old Ranger was going to spit on the floor, but he restrained himself. In fact he fell to silence, then stood and paced the floor which, by his roll, must have felt to him like the quarter-deck of a frigate.

He returned to the window and by the time he spoke again his anger seemed to have gone. "These men have no vision, I guess that is their trouble . . . and they hate a man who has. They see this place only as a miserable hole of a fort, stinking with the smell o' pelts and flies all summer and an icy grave all winter. But not me. This, my lad, is the gateway to a new empire and, by heavens, it will be the capital of it before I am through—an empire so rich from fur and minerals as to make man's imagination poor. Besides, it will stand astride the Nor'west Passage which, heaven help me, I shall find before long."

He wheeled about and looked at me with a degree of steadiness I would have sworn he was not capable of. "And that, my young friend, is where your copper venture becomes involved with my plans," he said, his voice serious and steady.

"It will require time, sir," I suggested for want of anything more useful to say.

He laughed. "Time and money, lad—two things we are always damnably short of—but more than that, my young friend. Leadership and government by a man of vision. And here, not in London or New York, or Montreal; here, on the ground."

The door opened suddenly without knock or warning

and a thickset man crab-walked toward the Commandant's table. I stood automatically and half turned toward him. It was Zeke Hutt.

He saw me and recognized me at the moment I did him, stopping in half stride and staring open-mouthed.

It was Colonel Rogers who broke the ice. "I believe you two have met before. Outside the Recollect Gate, wasn't it?"

I think I nodded, but said nothing. Hutt, having recovered from his surprise, just stared at me with a look so charged with hatred it would have been dangerous to have struck a flint.

Lieutenant John Christie slid into the room through the half-open door and halted behind Zeke Hutt, his face a mask of half-apprehension, half-disgust.

"Ah, Christie!" exploded Robert Rogers, "how the devil did this man get past the guard? I have told . . ."

Hutt butted in with snarling anger, "You told me you would have the information by now."

Rogers moved quickly and silently around the far end of the table toward Hutt; for a moment I thought he was going to strike the man but with an effort he held himself back and his powerful right arm dropped by his side. "When I want to see you, Hutt, I will send for you—until then you stay out of here. Do you understand?"

Hutt's expression changed from fear to a kind of leer. "Whatever you say, Colonel, whatever you say. But I can't keep those two Dakota runners cooling their heels. I'll send them off without your precious infor—"

"Get out!" roared the Commandant, "Get out!"

John Christie took a quick, long stride toward Hutt, seized him by the arm, and half-pushed, half-pulled him out of the door. We could hear Hutt's whining voice expostulating until it was silenced entirely by the open air.

"You made a great mistake, Ensign Bayard," said the

Commandant. "I have the details of that duel. You should have killed him. You may live to regret it."

"That is the second time, sir, that I have been so told."

Robert Rogers' big face relaxed with a smile, "You must learn to treat a rattlesnake as you would a rattlesnake." He shrugged those giant shoulders. "In this country one has to survive—and even if you have to use a rattlesnake for your own ends, keep your powder dry."

He was in complete command of himself now and the rocklike qualities of the courageous Ranger leader began to show through. It was a glimpse of a man that once was and my heart warmed to it.

"Well, now, Bayard, I have kept you long enough— though in truth I know not why you should be subjected to my dreams, and hopes." He reached out for my hand and shook it strongly. "My compliments to Mr. Henry, and will you please inform him that Mistress Rogers and myself expect him to dine with us this night."

As I opened the door to leave he called after me, "Ensign Bayard!"

"Sir," said I, turning.

"I like the cut of your jib, lad, and I wish you luck, and a war, that will take you back to your regiment—you will find the air more to your liking, and comrades t' boot."

"Thank you, sir," said I, and as I bowed I had etched on my mind a picture of a giant of a man, with a straight honest smile and a brightness in his hard, black eyes. It was a picture of Robert Rogers of the Rangers I shall always prize and hold fast.

Alexander Henry took the news of his dinner invitation with as much grace as he could muster and a slow shaking of his head.

"I don't look forward to it, heaven knows," he said. "I've been here before, it's very tragic and very disturbing and the longer the evening, the worse it gets."

This I could understand. "Perhaps you could plead pressure of work," I suggested. "I know you are hard pressed."

He smiled. "I am afraid not—this is a command performance. Particularly as he will want from me information he didn't get from you."

Mr. Henry put his hand on my shoulder. "I want to thank you, Vere, for your loyalty and good judgment in not giving out information on our plans."

"I . . . I . . . did not know what else to do," I stammered. "Things being the way they are I did not know how much Colonel Rogers should be told."

He nodded. "I shall tell him what he wants to know—he'll find out sooner or later. But then, that is my responsibility."

I was behind with paperwork in the office and busied myself there that evening. Work was a good antidote for the emotions that filled my heart and mind; besides there was an accumulation of ledger entries and reports that must be attended to before we left his place.

Mr. Henry must have seen the lantern burning for he came in when he returned, although the moon was long since high.

"You're working late, Vere," he said from the doorway.

I looked up and grinned at him, "Yes . . . I would rather get things in order before we leave."

"And that better be right soon," he said in an ominous tone. He took his coat off and folded it carefully before seating himself on the edge of my cot.

"The dinner did not go well?" I asked, my mind still half on the papers I was putting in folders.

"No—it never does."

"It's a terrible thing—this preoccupation with strong drink—the more so when it's a man like Robert Rogers. I feel sorry for him."

"Yes," agreed Mr. Henry, "I do too, but on that score I feel sorrier for Mistress Rogers, poor woman."

I continued in silence with my work. "Look here, Vere ... for heaven's sake leave those papers be. The fuse is lighted to the powder keg, don't you realize that?"

It was the first and, for that matter, the only time I heard Alexander Henry sound irritable. I found a chair and sat looking at his crestfallen face.

"I'm sorry," he said. "As a matter of fact, Captain-Lieutenant Spiesmacher took me aside after dinner, seeking my advice. The poor man is beside himself with worry."

"Well," said I, "It's quite a compliment."

Mr. Henry ignored my light-hearted comment, and went on in low voice. "Nat Potter has had a falling out with Rogers and has gone to Spiesmacher with a story that Rogers has offered the Northwest to the French in Louisiana. Says he can deliver it to them on a platter, including 'Mackinac and Detroit, as he has the support of all the Western Nations."

I could scarce believe my ears. "But Potter!" I exclaimed. "Nathaniel Potter has been Colonel Rogers' secretary for years. Why, 'tis said it was he who wrote Rogers' two books and got them published in London last year."

Alexander Henry held up his hand to stem my outburst. "Yes, I know that—a Princeton graduate, once in Holy Orders, I have no doubt he has been useful to Rogers, but hardly a man I would care to trust."

"But why would he turn on Colonel Rogers now?" I asked.

"It seems Rogers wanted Potter to carry his plan for a separate government for the Northwest to London in the hope that with the help of Townshend, who is now a leader in the Cabinet, the British government would agree. This, of course, proposed that Rogers would head such a government and also carried with it a very thinly veiled threat that if they were not interested, the French would be. Potter refused and there was a devil of a row. Oh, yes, of course this explains why the Commandant was so interested to learn that Alexander Baxter was coming out, and the more so that Baxter is known to Charles Townshend. What better man to put the plan forward, now that Potter is fear-ridden?"

Alexander Henry was pacing the floor now, hands grasped behind his back; and as he paced to and fro so went my thoughts until the whole brew of my thinking boiled up into disbelief.

"But surely, sir," I exploded at last, "you can't think for one moment that Colonel Rogers would deliberately give his comrades over to the hatchet and scalping knife?"

He stopped pacing. "Of course, not, Bayard—not deliberately. But a man can start a fire he thinks he can control and, before he knows it, it is out of control."

Mr. Henry seated himself again and, no doubt aware of my confused thoughts, attempted to help by giving voice to his own.

"We must not forget," he said, "that Rogers is a very, very desperate man, quite capable of playing both ends against the middle and perhaps not capable of sound judgment."

"You see, Vere," he went on, "Rogers is so far in debt that he dare not set foot in either London or New York where now only the debtor's prison waits for him."

"But surely his appointment as Commandant here would help?"

Mr. Henry shook his head. "To the contrary, he has now become hopelessly in debt—unless his big gamble works. Take this Grand Council of the Western Nations —he distributed four thousand pounds' worth of rum and presents and I would be very surprised if either Sir William or General Gage will approve the vouchers, not when the final result was the winning of their loyalty to Colonel

Rogers. Then there is the cost of his exploration work and searching for the Northwest Passage. As you know he has had Jonathan Carver and James Tute out exploring and mapping for months and he is paying each of them eight shillings a day, which adds up to almost double his whole pay without considering cost of canoemen and supplies."

I had heard in the regiment that Colonel Rogers had interested Whitehall in searching for the Northwest Passage and reminded Mr. Henry of this. He shook his head. "No, he asked the Lords of Board of Trade for thirty-two thousand pounds but not one pound did he get. All he got was half-promises from Charles Townshend, who is about as reliable, and predictable, as a snowshoe rabbit, although at the moment he seems to have the Cabinet eating out of his hand."

Still with a soldier's mind, my confused thoughts turned not unnaturally to the military problems the turn of events brought into focus. If the Western Nations took the war path the garrisons at 'Mackinac and Detroit, already reduced to a bare minimum, could no more stem the bloody tide than I could hold back Niagara with a pike pole. The more so if they were under the leadership of a brave and desperate man.

"What on earth does Spiesmacher propose to do?" I asked at last.

Mr. Henry shook his head slowly. "He really has no choice. He can scarce arrest his Commandant on a charge of treason without evidence other than Potter's story—and Potter is hardly considered a reliable individual. And if he takes precautionary measures, even doubling the guard, the Commandant's suspicions will be aroused and there would be the devil to pay."

"But he must do something."

"Yes, he has sent the information by express to Detroit

—most likely it will have to go to General Gage in New York before an order is issued one way or the other. Captain-Lieutenant Spiesmacher hinted to me that Gage was already concerned over intrigue with the French by a man named Hopkins who has gone over to them."

I thought at once of the veiled words between Captain Dan Clause and Lieutenant Nordbergh in the tavern at Montreal and the mystery as to who the third letter was for. Somehow it seemed no longer a mystery and I had it on my tongue to say so but thought better of it.

"Then the garrison will not be alerted," I said instead.

"He has taken some of his officers into his confidence. It will be up to them to be on the quiet alert, not much sleep for them I expect," said Mr. Henry. He paused for a time. "In a way we have the most important job to do—and because of it Captain-Lieutenant Spiesmacher agreed that you should be made aware of the situation."

"But what on earth can we do?" I asked. "The more so as we are leaving for the Falls of St. Marys. Or are we to stay?"

Alexander Henry smiled. "No, Vere, to the contrary, we will now leave just as soon as André can get the big canoe loaded and in the water. You see, it is at Superior that we will be of most service."

It occurred to me that by so doing we were, in fact, hardly a sizable force on the flank should trouble come, and I suppose my face showed my puzzled thoughts, for he quickly explained.

"You see," he said. "The Ojibway are my friends and I like to think they trust me as indeed they do Jean-Baptiste Cadotte. I know some of the lesser chiefs took presents at Roger's Grand Council but you know that White Fisher left the council because he would not sit at the fire with the Dakotas."

I nodded. "Well, then," Mr. Henry went on, "the Dakotas are more and more under the influence of the French traders down the Mississippi and are pressing harder on Ojibway hunting grounds. We must convince White Fisher of our friendship with his nation and that we are not allies of the Dakotas. If we hold the Ojibway we need not fear any Indian alliance against us in the west."

It occurred to me that as our mission to the head chief of the Ojibway was to seek his permission to invade their sacred copper grounds the two objectives might work against each other and I so said.

"No, Vere," he replied positively, "you underestimate White Fisher. To him, true friendship is not a one-way affair, it's give and take but more than that it's honest dealings and loyalty. That is why he would share nothing with the Dakotas at the council fire, nor would he give friendship to a man who wished at the same time to be a friend of his enemies."

Alexander Henry came quickly to his feet. "Now, lad, when you've finished with your paperwork off with you and find André. Tell him I would appreciate it if we could be ready to leave as soon after sun-up as possible.

I found André Perrot and half his crew asleep in their blankets beside the up-ended canot du maître that was to take us to the inland sea.

Like most men who live close to danger, he was awake the moment I touched his shoulder, his mind clear and alert.

"Oui, M'sieur, we can be loaded by sun-up," he said willingly, meanwhile counting the inert forms of his canoemen. He awoke one and sent him off to the Indian village to warn the seven missing men.

The moon was full and the night clear so that I had no difficulty finding the path that ran close under the walls toward the Water Gate. I had just reached the shadow of the palisade when I heard low voices at the water's edge. I stopped and listened. I could make out three figures, then the flash of a canoe bottom as it was put silently into the water. In equal silence two paddles thrust it swiftly from the shoreline and out into the black waters.

A man walked from the shore toward the gate and I instinctively slipped further into the shadows. The moon caught his face full on and I recognized him. It was Zeke Hutt.

He had just reached the gate and the sentry's challenge rang clear in the night when a hand seized my shoulder and I wheeled about, my right hand cocked to strike.

"Steady, lad!" said a familiar voice. It was Lieutenant John Christie.

"I suppose you are wondering what brings your friend Master Hutt abroad at this hour and what's so important that an Indian express cannot wait for dawn."

"They were Indians then," said I, giving my heart a chance to settle back to normal beat.

"Aye, Dakotas, heading for the Mississippi, I have little doubt. Jove! I'd give ten years' seniority to know what's in that pouch and who it's going to."

"Why didn't you challenge them then?" I asked as we picked our way along the path toward the gate. "You could have stopped the express and seized the pouch, that would have fixed things one way or t'other."

Christie snorted. "And just how do you think our good Commandant would have taken that? He would have had me in irons, I'll warrant, or it would have lit his fuse for him. Then where would we be?"

I had no answer for him.

"I hear you are leaving for Ojibway country tomorrow. I wish you luck, lad. Gad, I wish us all luck, I have a feeling we may need it."

When our ways parted soon after we had passed the

guard he did a most unusual thing for John Christie—he thrust out his gloved and all but fleshless right hand and I took it in both of mine.

"God go with you," he said with deep sincerity.

"And with you," I replied.

As he went striding in the moonlight toward his quarters I suffered a sense of loss and homesickness for the regiment. Then I thought of the morrow already promised by a faint light in the sky to the east and I turned my thoughts westward.

11

The first heat of the morning sun spread a white haze blanket over the waters of 'Mackinac Straits so that we had scarced moved away ten canoe lengths before the dun-colored walls of the fort faded into oblivion. I took it as a good omen, as if nature herself contrived to hide from sight the evil of man.

The fourteen canoemen of our crew bent to their task with light heart and strong arm. The giant Montreal canoe seemed to leap forward like a thoroughbred given full rein. From close by came the sound of a voice and almost at once the rattle of chain as an anchor was dropped. André, riding high in the bow, shouted an order and the canoe veered to starboard just in time. The hull of a schooner was so close to port that I am sure she could have been touched with a paddle.

A naval officer leaning on her rail seemed as surprised to see us as we were to see him. Then he recognized Alexander Henry, who sat amidships. "Ahoy there, Mr. Henry. Run me down would ye? A fine welcome to the West that is."

He got a laugh in reply. "I would have thought Cap'n Sinclair would at least have given us warning on his foghorn."

It was the *Gladwin,* inbound from Detroit, and the two men talked as the canoemen relaxed, their forty-foot craft rising majestically and falling with the swell.

"How long do you expect to be in, Cap'n?"

"If I had my wish, as long as it takes to turn about," was the reply. "But I suppose I'll have to wait on you damned traders."

"I am expecting a load of fur in from St. Marys," said Mr. Henry. "Should be in tomorrow or the day after—just as soon as Jean-Baptiste Cadotte, my partner, can get it here, and it would be a relief if we could clear it on this sailing."

"I expect there is plenty for loading now," said Captain Sinclair.

"Aye, there is—one warehouse is full and part of another."

The seaman swore a good round oath. "I knew it—the weather turns hot as hades, with scarce a breeze, and I have to beat my way up the whole length of Lake Huron with the holds bursting with stinking raw fur—and my God, how it stinks."

Mr. Henry grinned up at him. "Now, now, Cap'n, you wouldn't want the fair ladies of Europe to go without their fine fur would you—just on account of a disagreeable odor?"

For all the banter, the Scottish sailor wished us Godspeed, and we him, as we slipped away after a time. The tall spars of the *Gladwin* could be seen rising clear of the mist, and our Canadians took up a lilting chanson under André's leadership. A hundred miles northwest lay the Falls of St. Marys and the eastern end of the great Ojibway sea.

As we approached Le Grand Détour, the gateway to the Lake Superior water road, a number of canoes, seven in all, appeared dead ahead.

"A fur brigade," said André Perrot, wondering, no

doubt as were our other Canadians, how many old friends they would meet.

"Yes, I expect it's Cadotte's shipment. He expected a good season from the West and he would just have had time to get it moving," said Mr. Henry. As we drew within hailing distance his expectations were confirmed, and he beamed as he noted how low in the water the northern canoes rode. "Jove!" said he, "there's a fortune in fur there."

The lead canoe of the brigade came alongside our craft and a young man greeted us. "Bonjour, M'sieur!"

I was struck by both his youth and handsomeness. He left the smaller canot du nord and we made room for him amidships. Mr. Henry introduced him as Jean-Baptiste Cadotte and, by way of explanation, added, "Knowing his father, Vere, you can see he didn't pick up that handsome face from him."

The young man smiled, revealing even white teeth. It occurred to me that his Ojibway mother must indeed have been a handsome woman.

From his pouch he produced a bundle of bills of lading covering the shipment but Mr. Henry waved them aside. "Give them to the clerk, M. Blondeau, with my wishes that he do all possible to get this shipment on board the *Gladwin* before she sails."

I could see that Jean-Baptiste was having some trouble with the instruction in English so I quickly translated into French.

Mr. Henry laughed. "I am afraid that Jean's English is about as good, or bad, as my French. You won't catch him out on Ojibway though. That is the language they have always spoken at home, French he gets from books, and where on earth he will ever find time for English I wouldn't know."

Jean-Baptiste grinned. "I learn, I tink," he said.

"I'm sure you will, Jean," replied Mr. Henry with confidence. "But don't let your Ojibway or French slip because of it—they are far more useful in this part of the world."

The young man had word from his father of the meeting with Big Feet and the Ojibway headmen. He thought it should take place at Big Feet's lodge, more than a day's journey from the Falls of St. Marys where the medicine men had gathered for the Grand Me-da-we. Moreover as Waub-o-jeeg, the White Fisher, was away, the council should not be held until his return.

Mr. Henry nodded in agreement. "Your father is a very wise man, Jean," he said. "It is important that the medicine men be there to speak of the sacred copper, even though they speak against us. It is also most important that White Fisher be present."

There was a moment's pause. "But where is White Fisher?" asked Mr. Henry, "Strange he is not at the Grand Me-da-we."

The young Canadian replied in French, slowly enough for Mr. Henry to follow. "Two Canadian traders coming in with winter fur have been murdered on the south shore and their fur taken. The White Fisher is out with a scouting party."

"Dakotas?" asked Alexander Henry.

Jean-Baptiste shrugged his shoulders. "Perhaps," he said. "Their raiding parties are not unusual now."

Meanwhile, the seven laden canoes had clustered in close to our big craft and the canoemen shouted back and forth to one another with gossip of the forts and villages at home. I doubt that many questions were answered for they all seemed bent on talking at the same time.

It was Mr. Henry who ended the fest. He called to our bowsman, almost shouting above the din of voices, "Alright, André. We are on our way; these fellows have an appointment with the *Gladwin*."

That night we encamped on one of the numerous islands that marked the entrance to the strait that separated Lake Huron from Lake Superior and, once supper was done and we sat poking the fire-smudge to drive off mosquitoes, I plied my companion for information on the Ojibway, more particularly the full meaning of the Grand Me-da-we and why the Indian called Waub-o-jeeg, the White Fisher, should be of importance to us. I knew I could have no better tutor, less it be M. Cadotte, for Alexander Henry not only owed his life to them after the massacre but had lived with them and under their protection as a friend.

He sucked on his pipe for a time without answering, as if scarce knowing where to begin. "To understand the Grand Me-da-we one must understand their religion," he said at last. "They believe in many spirits, but there is one All Powerful, Gitche Manitou. I suppose we would call him the Supreme Being but I think Kind Spirit is a closer interpretation in our language. They have very firm rules of conduct. Lying and stealing are considered the most serious of sins—these, and being quick to anger. Unlike we Christians, punishment for such things does not wait until after life; a man who indulges in them becomes ostracized by his people."

"And do the medicine men have much influence over the chiefs and headmen?" I asked.

Mr. Henry smiled. "I don't quite like the term 'medicine men,' 'priests' would be more accurate—perhaps 'priest-doctor.' Yes and no—according to the wisdom and strength of the chief, I would say. The Midewi— or society of priests, is certainly powerful as is most priesthoods; in addition, their knowledge of medicine is extraordinary. Indeed, some of them have a knowledge of the use of three or four hundred herbs. They have cured me of fever more than once."

"And what, then," I asked, "is the Grand Me-da-we?"

He poked the fire for a time. "It is difficult to apply to our civilization. It is really an annual conference of the nation's wise men and doctors; add to that its very strong religious meaning and then you can picture the Grand Me-da-we. I suppose in Christian life the nearest example would be the time of Lent, but as you can see, it also has a bearing on the political and social life of the Ojibway."

"And you don't think the priests will be in favor of our going after the copper?"

He shook his head. "I am afraid not—the copper is sacred to them, has been for untold generations."

I had much to learn of this new world in which I found myself and questions posed themselves in my mind before my tongue could give voice to them. Until now I had scarce thought of Indians as anything else than warriors.

"And who is this Waub-o-jeeg?" I asked. "I thought Big Feet was the head chief of the Ojibway."

"And so he is," Mr. Henry explained patiently. "And has been for many, many years. For the whole of his chieftaincy Ma-mong-e-se-da has been a loyal friend and ally of the French; he recruited warriors for Montcalm and was hit by one of our musket balls at the fall of Quebec."

"Then he opposes us," I butted in.

"Not at all. To the contrary, he welcomes us. He seeks peace and friendship for his people. As a matter of fact, after the Pontiac uprising he visited Sir William Johnson on the Mohawk and accepted a belt of white and blue beads as a symbol of lasting peace."

"Then who is the White Fisher—and why is he so important to us?" I asked.

"He is the old chief's son—not much older than you are, Vere—but already he is war chief of the Ojibway and probably the most important Indian west of Detroit. Someday, by the natural course of events, he will succeed his father, but even now his influence is great at any council fire."

Mr. Henry knocked his pipe out carefully. "Now, m'lad, how about sleep? We will be on the move before the ducks in the morning."

But, although I wrapped myself well in my blanket against the chill wind off the water, sleep was long in coming. I remembered John Nordbergh and his stories of the importance of copper, the metal that made civilizations and caused them to crumble for the lack of it. Then I thought of the troubles that lay in our path, a hostile Indian nation, the ambitions of ruthless men pressing northward from Louisiana in search of fortune, the finding of copper—if, indeed, it did exist—the mining of it, and the carrying of it thousands of miles across a cruel wilderness. Surely, I reasoned, the whole thing is a dream born of madness. Close by, even breathing from his blanketed form told me that Alexander Henry was deep in sleep. Le Bel Anglais! I thought and recalled the disasters this little man had quietly and courageously faced and overcome. I felt ashamed at my chicken heart and so found sleep.

Our journey westward started again when dawn was yet only a faint promise over the high bow of the big canoe and the daylight hours unfolded placid scenery so beautiful it looked unreal. Mile after mile of rich meadowlands, lush with tall grass against a stately backdrop of giant hardwood trees on high ground. Thus did the singing paddles push us westward toward the inland sea of fresh water that the Objiway called "Kee-chee-gum-me" which, old Pierre had told me, means, "The Great Water." It seemed to me that the strong-armed Canadians grew gayer with each thrust of the paddle and André Perrot chose songs atune to light hearts.

At last the river seemed to widen out to a lake I judged to be about two miles wide and, as it took us two "pipes" to course it, probably ten miles long. There came into sight, standing high back of the meadowlands, the most magnificent stand of pine I ever cast eyes on. Masts enough for the King's navy and plenty to spare, but it was not so much the timber itself that held one's eye as the way they had grown, as if planned by some master architect. The sight seemed to have an effect even on the canoemen, who must have seen them many times before, for they broke out into a burst of good-will banter, one to the other.

"Six miles from the pines to the Falls of St. Marys," Alexander Henry explained. Even as he spoke the tall pines seemed to recede farther into the background, giving place to tall meadow grass as if setting the stage and making room for the living of man.

Even so, and perhaps because I had conjured in my mind a drab and desolate place in keeping with Fort 'Mackinac, I lost my tongue on sight of our journey's end. By then the meadowlands had widened out so that the cluster of houses seemed set like jewels in the sun in a never-ending emerald carpet.

"There it is, m'lad," said Mr. Henry. "Cadotte's Fort."

And so it was, and the first sight of it took my heart and warmed it. "Look!" said I, forgetting that my companion knew the place of old, "Horses and cows—how the devil would they ever get here?"

Mr. Henry laughed. "And that, Vere, is quite a story in itself. Jean-Baptiste now has a bull and six cows, not to mention a team of horses. And vegetables and strawberries." I gaped in amazement and, soldier or no, clean forgot the fort.

As we pulled in to the rock landing, for it was in fact the beginning of the portage around the Falls of St. Marys, I saw Jean-Baptiste Cadotte standing, hands on hips, waiting to welcome us. But he was not alone; Canadians and traders from the little settlement were there in force and Indian children of all ages scampered about alternately staring at us and gaming about as children the world over are wont to do.

André Perrot, pole in hand at the high bow, had to raise his voice to a shout to hold the attention of our canoemen until we were safe in, as they excitedly gossiped with their fellows ashore.

"Bienvenue, Messieurs," M. Cadotte greeted us, extending a hand to assist Alexander Henry over the high gunwale, his face aglow with smiles. Once we had our feet on firm ground, he introduced me to a young lad who hung back shyly in the little group of boisterous voyageurs, "My second son, Ensign Bayard . . . Michel. He has dreams of becoming a soldier, worse luck, instead of an honest trader, so I imagine he will have a thousand and one questions for you." The boy grinned in embarrassment. He was much more like his father than his elder brother, not as dark nor handsome, but short neither on freckles nor on warm, shy smiles. We became friends from the start.

He tried to keep stride beside me as we followed M. Cadotte and Alexander Henry toward what I could only assume was the fort, though, in truth, in all my service I had not seen anything that looked less dangerous or foreboding. True, there was a palisade all right, I judged about fifty paces on each side; but the whole, like the four houses inside, gleamed white from fresh lime and, looking at the gates as I went through, I wondered if, in fact, they ever had been closed against any man. As if to give authority to its claim as a fort there was redoubt inside made of stout oak and, in keeping with the fitness of things, this alone had not been introduced to the Canadian whitewash brush.

"Oh, good," I heard Mr. Henry exclaim. "I see you got the fourth house finished. I also notice two new ones going up outside."

"Oui," said M. Cadotte, adding with pride, "One for a new family and the other to serve as a warehouse."

Mr. Henry turned toward me. "There was a bad fire here before the Pontiac trouble. Commandant's house burned down and two others. Come to think of it a brother officer of yours, Lieutenant Jamette, was in command with a Corporal's Guard of Royal Americans. So you see, Jean-Baptiste has created it all himself.... Come to think of it, I guess that was the last garrison, eh, Jean?"

Cadotte nodded. "But then my good friend is too modest. He forgot to tell you that it was he who went into the burning house and dragged M. Jamette out the window. And too, with all provisions and powder burned, when we were making a forced march to Fort 'Mackinac, in December at that, and we all came down with snowshoe sickness, it was he that went on alone to get help."

Mr. Henry laughed. "I was hungry. . . . Poor Jamette was not to live long anyway."

My thoughts turned back to my last dinner in Montreal, at Madam Benoit's tavern, and the splash of red wine running down over Jamette's mural. It seemed an age ago already. But as I looked around at this bright and lovely place it somehow made me feel at home that the regiment had had some part in it.

André Perrot joined us for lunch in the Cadotte kitchen, a lunch that turned into a veritable feast, particularly for men who have fared on corn "soupe" for several days. The second Madam Cadotte, a charming Canadian lady named Marie Monet until they were married two years before in the chapel at Fort 'Mackinac by the Vicar General of Louisiana, would have put even the good Madam Benoit to shame with her wild-pigeon pie and cabbage and wild raspberry torte that I returned to for the third time.

The three men soon fell to talk of the bountiful fur harvest and warehousing needed for the year to come. I could foresee a mountain of paper and book work ahead and, between the good food and M. Cadotte's wine made from the flowers of the elderbush, a quill pen somehow lacked attraction.

It was Alexander Henry who saved me. "I think it would be a good idea, Vere, if you had a look around Sault Sainte Marie to sort of get your bearings," adding with a quick glance at young Michel, who had scarce taken his eyes off me since coming to the table, "Perhaps Michel would act as your guide." The boy was on his feet and halfway to the door lest anyone should say nay.

"Wait for Ensign Bayard," broke in his father. "And don't forget to show him our fish factory."

I looked puzzled. "It's true in a way," said Mr. Henry. "Really it's the Indian fishing grounds at the rapids. This fall we are shipping in barrels and salt. We have a contract to supply the garrison at 'Mackinac with whitefish."

"In your spare time, when not fur trading and mining copper," I added in light heart, and not waiting for their retort I took after my young escort.

Despite his short legs, my boots had to move fast to keep up with Michel's moccasins and, once out the shining white palisade, I had to call to him as I paused to admire row after row of the finest strawberry plants I had seen since my boyhood in Switzerland. "Ah, oui, M'sieur," he agreed, although obviously disappointed at the delay. "They came from the Ile d'Orléans on the River St. Lawrence. What a pity you were not here in strawberry time."

"Oh, I expect to be, Michel, I expect to be."

"Bon," said Michel, screwing up his freckles and pug nose in a grin. I turned and looked about me. As far as my eyes would carry in either direction the green carpet of grass spread without a break except that here and there the brown and gold of garden and corn land added a pleasing pattern, pointed up by the occasional house glistening in Canadian whitewash.

"Come, M'sieur," said Michel impatiently, "I will take you to see the fishing ... it is great sport."

And off he went again toward the rapids I could see clearly about half a mile ahead.

"You must have been ... I mean, your father must have been here a long time," I said, increasing my stride.

"Always, M'sieur, always," replied the lad. "You see, my grandfather came here in the service of le Sieur du Lusson, the first commander—that would be in 1671."

"Almost a hundred years ago."

"Oui, M'sieur," the boy added with a quick, shy smile. "But Mama was here much longer—she was an Ojibway lady, a sort of chieftain."

I put my arm on his shoulder. "I know, Michel—your mother was a very famous lady. Why, I heard of her in Philadelphia before I ever heard of Sault Sainte Marie—or Lake Superior, for that matter. You must be very proud of her."

"Ah, oui, M'sieur. I am . . . I am."

By now we had come to the voyageur portage path at the rapids and I followed as best I could Michel's surefooted moccasins so that before long we were close to the churning, frothing water of the falls.

"Look, M'sieur!" shouted Michel. "They catch many even now!"

There must have been a dozen or more small canoes bobbing about in the angry water like so many cockleshells. Each canoe was manned by two men, either Indian or Canadian, both wielding the voyageur poles called "pique de fond" with which they forced their craft upstream and now and then away from some jagged rock. I watched one in particular that seemed farthest in. Suddenly the man in the bow dropped his pole and picked up a net from the bottom of the canoe and threw it into the water. The canoe was allowed to slip downstream, gaining speed all the way as the force of the current caught it. Suddenly the man at the bow heaved in the net, dumping dozens of great leaping fish into the canoe.

"I told you, M'sieur . . . great sport, eh?"

I agreed with Michel; but, watching the crazily bobbing

eggshell craft missing rocks by inches, I told myself it was no sport for me.

"They are big fish, too," I said.

"Oui, M'sieur . . . whitefish, sometimes they go fifteen pounds. But it is not the season now. In the fall a man can easily catch two, three hundred fish an hour."

On the opposite shore a group of Indian women were cleaning the fish and hanging them on racks over smudge fires, for drying and curing. I remarked on it, wondering why they would smoke them when so much fish was available.

"For the winter," he replied. "Sometimes game is scarce or maybe it's for dog food."

We watched for a time, then slowly made our way back to Cadotte's Fort. In sight of it, we saw two Indians leaving their canoe at the landing and go straightway in long, silent steps toward the gate in the palisade. They were young warriors and both wore paint.

"An express," said Michel. "I hope it is not news that takes you away, M'sieur."

But it was. Waub-o-jeeg had returned from his scouting and Ma-mong-e-se-da waited for us at his council fire on the south shore of Superior.

12

Our big forty-foot Montreal canoe was deep laden and at the third "pipe" and about twelve miles out on Lake Superior water, even though we were not yet half across Whitefish Bay, our voyageurs scattered tobacco particles on the waters and exhorted the wind with "Souffle, souffle, la Vieille." And the "Old Woman of the Wind" must have heard, for a breeze from the right quarter gathered strength and the oilcloth sail was rigged amidships.

By now the sun was high, for it had taken André and his Canadians some time to portage the canot du maître, three weeks' provisions, Indian presents, and powder and shot over the narrow rocky portage around the Falls of St. Marys. No wonder she rode low in the water with the addition of fourteen stalwart canoemen and three passengers, Mr. Henry, M. Cadotte, and myself.

Away past the point that horned into the bay on the south shore lay the open water of Ke-che-gum-me—the Great Water of the Ojibway nation. Over three hundred miles long and a hundred in width. The canoe, heavy laden though it was, already lifted and fell in the deep water swell.

It was the most dangerous of waters, according to my

companions who knew it well, where the fury of a sudden storm would drive up the waves to forty feet or more and, if man survived their anger, there still stood the danger of being thrust against the craggy rock bastions of the north shore.

Jean-Baptiste drew my attention to a point on the south shore. "Voila . . . there is Na-do-wa-we-gon-ing—the place of the Iroquois bones. The Ojibways drove back the Iroquois there about a century ago. It was a big war party and the Iroquois never again invaded Ojibway country."

"I didn't know the Iroquois were ever defeated in battle," I said.

"They were there. Not one escaped. To defend one's own country from an invader gives a warrior the strength of ten," said M. Cadotte.

I held my tongue but prayed that he and Mr. Henry could convince the Ojibway that we were not invaders.

We encamped that night on the south shore and it was high noon on the following day when we saw the smoke of many fires on the port quarter. I had never before laid eyes on so large an Indian encampment, summer camp or no, and I would not guess with any degree of accuracy. But counting women and children I would not have been surprised to learn it represented two thousand souls. Maybe five hundred warriors, by a soldier's reckoning. The beached canoes, which across the water looked like a necklace drawn about the half-moon of the point, must have numbered two hundred. The laughter of children and the barking of countless dogs came to meet us.

Before we were in hailing distance it was obvious that our arrival had been anticipated. Fifty of more boys who were playing a noisy game of lacrosse forsook the rough playing field of sand and tufted grass and ran to form groups at the water's edge, leaning on their thonged sticks and watching in silence as a dozen young men moved canoes to make room for our craft and our landing. Our canoemen were overboard now, although almost waist-high in water, easing the big canoe to make doubly sure that no rock or stump would damage her birchbark bottom.

The old chief, Big Feet, was there by the time we had our feet on dry land and, in the manner of the white man, shook hands warmly with Mr. Henry and M. Cadotte. It was obvious even to me that he welcomed them as friends he trusted.

Behind him, in fact overshadowing him, stood the most handsome Indian I ever laid eyes on. He must have been well over six feet even in moccasins and as straight as a young pine. He did not extend his hand as did the old chief, but inclined his head in a manner which could have been either a curt nod or a courtly gesture.

His face, which still carried the markings of red and black warpaint, was inscrutable. It was not friendly yet, on the other hand, it was not hostile. His eyes were alert and piercing as if seeking out some hidden value or evil. It was Waub-o-jeeg, the White Fisher, war chief of the Ojibways, and were it not that I had M. Cadotte's word for it I would never have believed that he was but three and twenty years of age.

What was it Mr. Henry said of him? "The most powerful Indian west of Detroit." Aye, indeed, this young chieftain was a force to be reckoned with.

As we walked through the summer village toward the chief's lodge, half-naked children ran beside us, staring at us curiously, despite the call of their mothers at their summer work of sewing or drying berries to be stored in birchbark boxes. The women turned their dark eyes aside, lest they be guilty of the rudeness of staring, and fixed their attention on their domestic chores. Outside one lodge, a group of old men did not even pause in their game, which seemed to consist of striking a wooden bowl on the blanket-covered ground so that little colored objects would be thrown out to be tallied.

At last we came to a larger lodge where the rush mats of the entrance had been thrown aside and, as we walked by, I stared in. To my amazement, a moosehide tent had been erected inside and draped over this inner sanctum was a startling collection of animal figures, shields, and amulets. I could scarce believe my eyes—they were all of burnished copper!

Perhaps for fear that the rudeness of my curiosity might offend our host or merely to be informative, M. Cadotte explained in a low voice for my ear only. "That is the medicine lodge," he said, "It is in the inner tent that the priest communes with the Spirit of the Great Turtle."

Nearby stood a number of small tepees made from saplings with skin blanket covering, scarce big enough for a man to stand in. In the center of this cluster, women were feeding wood to a fire banked on two sides by stones. As I passed, an old Indian picked up one of the stones and, juggling it on a forked stick, took it into one of the tepees.

"A bathhouse," said M. Cadotte, aware of my curiosity. "Water and herbs are dropped on the hot stone; after sweating it out for a time, a quick dip in the lake, and you're as good as new—well almost."

By now we had reached the chief's lodge, its entrance flap of woven cedar thrown back to welcome his guests. It must have been nearly sixty feet long, with a row of posts down the center. The middle post held high a magnificent carving of Amik, the beaver, obviously the crest of the chief's clan. I had yet to learn that Amik was the totem of a northern clan and that Big Feet had been born a Man-of-the-Thick-Fir-Woods, that he was an Ojibway from the northwest.

Three fires burned low in the lodge as women busied themselves to keep kettles warm so that the strangers to the fires might eat well. And so we did, of venison and fish seasoned with wild ginger and mountain mint and great mounds of Indian corn and wild berries. All the while Big Feet set himself out, by word and action, to the comfort and relaxation of his guests.

White Fisher for a time stood silently in the background until two young warriors, one with a gun in the crook of his arm, came to the doorway of the lodge. The young chief joined them and I could see them talking together in the manner of men who consider serious matters. They were still there when, by reason of having eaten too much for comfort and as my seniors were occupied with matters of their own interest, I decided to stroll in the sunlight of the fresh air.

I wheeled away from White Fisher and the two Indians and, as I did so, almost knocked down a tiny Indian child. At first she was frightened and fear must have quenched her sobs for large tears were still on her face. I reached out and touched the little necklace of colored clamshells she wore and, although she could not understand my words, nor I hers, I made it clear that I thought them very pretty. She managed a quick, shy smile. Then I remembered a small hand-mirror in my tunic pocket. I produced it and showed her how to hold it so that she could see her own face. She giggled.

I looked up quickly, a bit taken aback at the tall form that had arrived in silence. It was White Fisher and our eyes met for an instant across the child. His firm mouth had softened for a moment and at the corners there was the suggestion of a smile. It was the beginning of understanding and of a friendship.

He held out a watch and chain, asking me, in French, to give it to M. Cadotte. "One of my young men took it off a

Dakota; it belonged to one of the traders that was killed."

"They caught up with them, then?"

"Oui, three of my warriors followed them into Dakota territory."

He took the child's hand. "I go now to Red Pine's lodge."

I realized then that the soft, plaintive sounds I heard was the crying of women. He had spoken of three warriors but only two had seemed to have reported.

"Red Pine," I blurted out. "He did not return?"

White Fisher shook his head, and as he answered the hardness of his mouth and eyes was back. "Non, he was shot by a white man who travelled with the Dakotas."

As the war chief and the little child walked away, I wondered how this news might affect our mission. And so thinking and with the silver timepiece in my hand I returned to the chief's lodge.

I could see that the news of the killing of the young warrior by a white man brought concern to my companions, but neither gave voice to their fears.

"The die is cast," said Mr. Henry. "We can do no more than present our case honestly, come what may."

"When is the council to meet?" I asked, wishing it were over.

"Tomorrow morning."

"Tonight the medicine men are seeking the advice of the Great Turtle so it will be known at the council fire," added M. Cadotte for my benefit.

That night in our lodge as we lay back on the rushes, they talked more of our chances on the morrow.

"This killing could not have been worse," said Jean-Baptiste, who had had news from friends in the village. "Red Pine was shot in the back from ambush as he lifted his canoe in the water. There is no doubt now that people from down the Mississippi are encouraging the Sioux, and particularly the Dakota, to make war on the Ojibway."

Mr. Henry was silent for a time. "It's a means of getting possession of this country . . . but a bloody one. I'm not worried about the old chief, Big Feet, he is open to reason and he has taken a blue and white belt from Sir William. It's young White Fisher that worries me. I have a feeling he thinks white men are not good for his people.

I had it on the tip of my tongue to tell of my meeting with White Fisher and the child and the feeling of understanding that it seemed to engender but I somehow lacked the words to describe it and feared my seniors might pin hopes on a mere dream, so I held my tongue. Outside, the shadows had grown longer and deeper and the women came in to feed the fires so we might have more light.

Suddenly the whole lodge seemed to vibrate with the sound of many drums. I sat bolt upright.

"Medicine drums," said M. Cadotte, knocking his short clay pipe out on the nearest fire log. "They are calling members of the Society to attend. Would you like to watch, Vere?"

"It would not be an intrusion?"

"Not at all," said Mr. Henry, as he put on his coat. "In a few minutes there will be a hundred there."

And so there were. By the time we got near the medicine lodge and the tempo of the drums had almost reached a frenzy, a dark, silent throng of Indians formed a thickening circle. We three found a rocky knoll from which to view the better and to hold a respectful distance. A circle of many fires about the sacred lodge was fed furiously by women to provide light and the flames and sparks at times carried so high that they seemed to be meeting the stars. In the red light I spotted our canoemen on the rising ground behind.

As suddenly as they had started the drums stopped, the last beats echoing in the hills behind. In the red reflection of the flames, a man moved into a space left clear before the entrance to the lodge. For a moment he stood motionless, clothed from shoulders to ankle in a cloak made from the winter skin of the weasel, its whiteness given a strange pinkish glow by the firelight. With one motion he dropped the fur from his shoulders and stood naked, save for a breechcloth. Then he began a slow, sonorous incantation, beating time with a circular ceremonial rattle.

"Is he the chief priest?" I asked M. Cadotte in a whisper, for not a sound came from the gathering.

"In a way.... The weasel skin indicates the highest degree of the sacred order of Midewiwin. He is Pale Star, a kusabindugeyu or seer, one who can look into the future. Look, he enters the lodge now and calls on the Spirit of the Great Turtle."

For some time only the voice of the priest could be heard—then a startling, unexplainable thing happened. A terrible noise seemed to come from within the lodge. It was at once a concert of sobs and shrieks, the barking of dogs, and the howling of a wolf pack. Almost at once the lodge itself began to shake so violently that had not the moosehide covering been securely thonged it would have been thrown off. Then silence save for the incantations of the priest. Then another voice, stronger, more powerful, as if it came from ageless time.

"It is the voice of the Great Turtle," whispered M. Cadotte. "He answers Pale Star's questions."

I was gripped and held fast by a mixture of feelings. Of incredulity, of awe, and of fear. I hoped only that the voice of the Great Turtle spoke in our favor. "What does he answer?" I murmured to M. Cadotte.

The Canadian shook his head. "He speaks in a language only the priest can interpret," he replied.

In the morning with the first light I had the gifts carried from the beach, unwrapped, and placed on display in the chief's lodge. The women were busy preparing for the council, rolling the skin blankets and placing them on the outer perimeter, laying fresh cedar and rushes on the floor and building carefully the center council fire. Shy eyes darted now and then toward the bright calico I had chosen to bring, and murmured whisperings seemed to be those of pleasure. At least, I thought, our gifts will be acceptable, Great Turtle or no.

Then the lesser chiefs and headmen began to arrive at the lodge in twos and threes until there were a dozen or more. White Fisher, a lithe, dominating figure in full war paint stood silently with another war chief, Bright Forehead, who had the disconcerting habit of constantly running his thumb over the edge of his ceremonial tomahawk and whose face, distorted by an old knife wound, seemed to wear a mask of cruelty. They wore paint at the conference as a soldier would his uniform.

The head chief, Big Feet, at last took his place at the fire and motioned Mr. Henry and M. Cadotte to sit at his right. I seated myself directly behind them. His war chiefs, White Fisher and Bright Forehead, were on his left and the elders assumed their places in the circle in silence and with great dignity. The ceremonial pipe, at least three feet long, was lighted at the fire.

Big Feet had stretched out before him on the woven cedar mat a belt of white and blue beads, a peace belt conveying purity and clear blue, stormless sky. It was the belt he had accepted from Sir William Johnson at Niagara and signified peace between the English and the Ojibway nation.

Alexander Henry was the first to speak. He spoke slowly and sincerely in English, not trusting his knowledge of the Ojibway tongue on so important an occasion. M. Cadotte translated into the Indian language; once or twice, having difficulty with Mr. Henry's English, asking me to elaborate in French.

"Brothers—our hearts sing that your chief has before him the white and blue belt given him by your great father whose lodge stands to the east on the river of the Mohawks.

"Brothers—we come not bearing such a belt from another council fire but come as brothers returning to our own lodges. We bring presents as does a hunter after many moons' journey.

"Brothers—we do not speak as strangers at your fire. I have lived in your lodges, you clothed me when I was naked, you fed me when I was starving. Twice you saved me from the knives of my enemies. M. Cadotte has lived among you all his life. He took to wife an Ojibway woman who talked as a chief and his sons bear your blood as well as his.

"Brothers—because of these things we come now to your council fire."

Slowly and carefully Mr. Henry told of our plans to seek out and find Misquahbik—the sacred red rock on the shores and islands of the Great Ojibway Water. He told them that their Great White Father's children over the sea needed this rock and would pay well for it, and if this came to be, their hunters and women would be rewarded so that even if the beaver left, hunger would not follow.

Perhaps for the particular benefit of the four priests of the Grand Medicine Society, who sat outside the circle at the other end of the lodge, Alexander Henry gave his word that there would always be enough Misquahbik set aside and left for sacred uses.

After he had finished, the pipe was passed from chief to chief and in silence they considered well the words that had been spoken.

Big Feet then called the chief seer, Pale Star, before the council, to make known the advice of the Spirit of the Great Turtle.

Pale Star, wrapped tight in his weasel-skin cloak despite the oppressive heat of the lodge, spoke without emotion, calmly, slowly, as if choosing every word so that he might not misinterpret the message of the Great Turtle.

"Brothers," he said. "The Spirit of the Great Turtle is much disturbed and unhappy for us his children.

"Brothers—the Great Turtle said the white men would come in such numbers that they would be greater in number than the grain of sands on the shores of Ke-che-gum-me, the Great Water that the white man calls 'Superior.'

"Brothers—the Great Turtle said that all our beaver, and deer, and all other game would be driven from our hunting grounds and our kettles would be empty.

"Brothers—the Great Turtle said the white man would even take our rocks, even our sacred rocks.

"Brothers—the Great Turtle said these would be used by white medicine men.

"Brothers—the Great Turtle said then would come the end of the world."

Pale Star, face emotionless, serious and wrapped in dignity, moved back from the fire.

Then each in turn, first these from the north and west, Men-of-the-Thick-Fur-Woods, the headmen and sub-chiefs spoke: Wagosh of the Beaver Clan, Osinebaw of the Hawks, Cadonia of the Cranes, Ondeh Weas of the Loon Clan, eleven in all and after each the pipe was passed and smoked. Several spoke kindly words of le Bel Anglais and of M. Cadotte, but not one of the elders said "aye" or "nay." I thought, these are confused men and troubled men, waiting, seeking a spark of leadership which might send them this way or that.

Now only the war chiefs were left to speak and Bright Forehead would be first.

M. Cadotte leaned back and spoke in my ear. "There may be trouble here. Red Pine, who was killed when scouting, was his favorite younger brother."

And even before M. Cadotte started his French translation I knew that he was right. Bright Forehead's voice was charged with emotion, and anger seemed to rise in him and hatred with it.

"Brothers—the voice of the Great Turtle has told us what we must already know, that the white man will destroy us.

"Brothers—we fought for the French king and his captains told us we were his children and hunger would never come into our lodges.

"Brothers—the French king took his warriors away and left us to fight without guns.

"Brothers—now men of the French king give guns to our enemies the Dakotas and kill our young men. They take the war path to drive us from our hunting grounds and take our sacred rocks.

"Brothers—the English king sends to us the white and blue belt—but his Captain at Michilimackinac gives many presents to our enemy the Sioux and Dakota and invites them to his council fires.

"Brothers—the Bostonian traders come among us saying they are our brothers, they dull the wits of our hunters so they rob them of their beaver."

As his anger mounted Bright Forehead's speech quickened so that M. Cadotte could not keep pace with his French translation. Not that it was needed, for the war chief's final pronouncement carried the full weight of his anger and mistrust.

"Brothers—all these things are known to us. Are we

women that we should turn our face aside? We must act now. The white and blue belt has no place at our council fire. The red and black belt of blood and death must be sent from fire to fire until treachery is consumed."

The elders stirred visibly. One could sense a stiffening of bearing, a tightening of the lips and two or three seemed to nod their heads as if in hesitant agreement. Gradually, as the pipe was passed, their eyes turned toward the last to speak—the second war chief, Waub-o-jeeg, the White Fisher.

I knew that if he cast his lot with Bright Forehead, the council would follow to a man. My eyes, too, turned toward the young chief and the firm, almost cruel lips and hard black eyes gave little reason for comfort. I felt the sweat run down my back and it was not entirely caused by the heat of the lodge or the thickness of my coat. My entrails felt as if they were gripped and held tight by an iron power.

At last the White Fisher spoke.

"Brothers—Bright Forehead has spoken well. We know that what he says is so—that he has spoken the truth."

He paused. The tension became almost unbearable. I heard M. Cadotte draw in his breath and hold it. At last White Fisher went on.

"Brothers—treachery by those we welcomed into our lodges as friends causes us so great anger that reason goes like snow before the spring sun.

"Brothers—let us not forget that we have also heard true words from the Spirit of the Great Turtle. He has said the white man will come in such numbers as to be like sand on the shore. That he will take our fur and our sacred rocks.

"Brothers—let us not forget that the black and red belt is already being passed—from the Dakotas to all the fires of the Sioux nation. Their war parties are already in our hunting grounds and before many snows have run we will have to defend our villages.

"Brothers—we must not now turn aside those we can trust, now that the treacherous ones arm our enemies.

"Brothers—M. Cadotte and le Bel Anglais have walked beside us many journeys and have dwelt in our lodges many nights. They are our brothers. They are to be trusted. When our enemies have the help of the treacherous ones we will need the help of our brothers."

For the first time there was an almost inaudible yet clear hum of approval from the lesser chiefs and headmen. Heads nodded in the affirmative and exclamations of "Kagat!" "Howh!" ran around the circle like grass fire.

My heart seemed to start again, so noisely that I scarce heard the decision of the old chief as I rubbed my sweaty palms together.

"Brothers," he said, addressing le Bel Anglais and M. Cadotte, "You have heard the words spoken at this fire. We, the chiefs and sub-chiefs present, and the chiefs and sub-chiefs not here present, put our trust in you. Your canoes may travel our waters in peace—and our hunters and young men will lead you to the places where Misquahbik is known to be."

As the presents were given and Henry and Cadotte renewed old friendships with chiefs from distant places the tension gradually eased, although my knees still felt weak when I thought of how close we had been to defeat. And worse, it was more than the success of our copper venture that had hung in the balance. It was men's lives. The thought of the reduced garrisons of my regiment at the frontier posts was not a pleasant one, so I took my cue from my two companions, on whom the strain must have been just as great, and entered into the ceremony with enthusiasm.

André Perrot came to report the readiness of our canoe and he had scarce joined us outside the lodge when we were descended upon by a fearsome apparition. It was a medicine man, clad in the skins of owls and on his head his totem, Ka-Kaik—the Hawk.

He raised a scrawny and trembling right hand. "Ho . . . white men!" he screamed, almost like a falcon after he rises into the blue with his quarry in his claws, "Let not your canoes touch the shore of the Isle of Golden Sands!"

I stared at his face, amazed. The thin nose and the pointed chin seemed almost to meet when he was silent. This and his fierce black eyes made it difficult to distinguish where the hawk-head crest he wore began or left off.

"Ho!" he screamed again. "Any white man whose moccasins tread the Isle of the Golden Sands shall be altogether devoured by the vipers and snakes that rattle. This the spirits tell."

With that he turned and walked, almost hopped, away. I would not have been in the least surprised had he suddenly spread his wings and taken to the air.

"Well," said Mr. Henry, breaking the silence. "He must be the fire and brimstone preacher of the Grand Me-da-we. I suppose every religious organization has one, but his feathers are certainly ruffled."

As we walked through the encampment toward the water I noted several young men painting the palms of their hands and pressing the wet pattern to their faces. A new sound had been added, too—the sound of knives and war axes being whetted. And weapons were being hung on lodge poles, ready to hand. War paint and weapons seemed to be taking over from sugar baskets and berry trays. Even the smoke from the fires no longer hung placidly but fish-tailed about, as if the hated Sioux had cast a spell from the south.

Big Feet and a number of headmen saw us off. White Fisher, standing to one side, motioned me to him.

"M'sieur," he said as I approached. "I bring you this . . . it is yours." He held out the little hand-mirror I had given the child.

"Oh, non," I expostulated. "I gave it to the little girl to stop her crying. It is hers; please give it back to her."

White Fisher looked at me and smiled. "Merci, M'sieur. I shall tell her it is only for smiles, not tears. She was Red Pine's favorite daughter.

Then the tall young chief did an amazing thing—he thrust out his right hand and I seized it in mine, the white man's gesture of brotherhood.

After we were clear of the shore and our Canadians had the big canoe under way, Alexander Henry spoke of it.

"Ensign Bayard," said he, "I have a feeling Captain-Lieutenant Spiesmacher would consider that handshake a duty well done."

I looked at him in surprise for a time. "Good heavens!" I said at last. "I forgot all about the military necessity of winning over White Fisher."

Mr. Henry smiled and nodded wisely. "Of course—that is what made the handshake so important."

13

We were to rendezvous with the second canoe at Batchawana Bay on the north shore of Superior some thirty miles from the Falls of St. Marys and I could not help but wonder how long we might have to lay over, waiting for the great man from London. But my fears were ill founded. They were waiting for us.

When we were still some distance from the mouth of the bay, pitching steadily in a great rolling swell, Mr. Henry passed me his glass. I first picked up the tall, lean figure in regimentals, dear old John Nordbergh, as trim as ever. Then nearby, beyond the cluster of canoemen, a squat figure that swaggered even in the glass—Pierre Dupuis of the Parish of Ste. Geneviève had been given charge of the second canoe and had grown ten feet tall! And the Old One was a good choice, for as André Perrot said, "He can smell weather on Superior when it's just an idea in God's mind."

Ah, there *he* is! I held the glass as steadily as I could on a small figure that paced the beach, hands behind his back, stopping now and then to watch our progress, and then back to his impatience. His frock coat was far too tight and his stock seemed to billow whiteness like scud-clouds in a blue sky.

I gave the glass back. "Well," said Mr. Henry. "And what do you think of *him?*"

I shook my head. "Too much lace."

He put the telescope back in its case. "It need not be of importance," he said. "It's what's above the lace that counts."

I thought how unfair of the fates that the hopes and striving of many men should be put at the mercy of one man, particularly as across a mile of open water that man looked like a popinjay. But I held my tongue for le Bel Anglais was, I was sure, quite aware of the chances of fate.

As it was but high noon our canoe was not beached and Alexander Baxter, Jr., was carried out to it on the strong shoulders of two canoemen. They handled him as carefully as if he were a clutch of partridge eggs and sat him down in my seat. I went overside, after a perfunctory introduction, and waded ashore with the two Indian guides that Big Feet had sent with us, leaving the gentleman from London to entertain Mr. Henry and M. Cadotte—without regrets, I might add. Besides, changing canoes brought with it the companionship of Lieutenant Nordbergh and latest news of my brother officers of the Royal Americans.

We travelled some twelve miles west on the coast and put ashore in a sheltered bay just west of Point Mamainse. I learned that its name was a corruption of the Indian "Marmoaze," meaning "a cluster of rocks." I thought this hardly fair, for while there were rocks, praise be, there was also a deal of rolling acres, rich with giant maples and birch pressing in between craggy mountains.

We camped there that night and John Nordbergh, after getting together his canvas specimen bag and tools for the morning search, attempted to read a geology manual by the light of the fire. I poked at the fire to give him more light.

Down by the water the canoemen made merry, their songs and laughter echoing across the dark water and rising with the sparks of their fire. Not too far away stood the strange, foreign tent that had to be erected each night for the gentleman from London. I poked viciously at an embered log.

"You are making a mistake about Alexander Baxter," said John Nordbergh, looking up from his book.

I felt flustered. "But . . . but I have never said anything about him," I retorted.

Lieutenant Nordbergh closed his book and grinned at me. "You don't have to—I can tell by your face."

I poked again at the log. "Well, I suppose so," I admitted. "He's hardly powder for my flint. But more than that, I don't see why a popinjay like that should have the right to make or break the dreams of men like Alexander Henry or Jean-Baptiste Cadotte. Why should what *he* thinks matter?"

Nordbergh stretched his long legs. "For a very good reason. He knows what he is doing and other men that place their confidence in him know he does. Don't let his mannerisms fool you, Vere. He is a very astute man and if he leaves this country with confidence in our venture, he'll get the money, mark my words. You see, what *he* thinks, is very important."

By the noise from the shore it was obvious that the meeting of the two canoes of northmen was being celebrated as a special occasion. One fellow seemed to be holding the center of the stage and his gyrations brought roars of laughter from the happy Canadians. Amused, we watched and listened more closely. The voyageur turned actor cavorted in mincing steps, hand on one hip, stopping with an elaborate bow, stooping and picking up a small stone off the beach. "Ponmesoul!" he exclaimed. "B'Jove!" There was no mistaking as to who was the butt of the Canadian's mimicry. I automatically looked toward the tent. To my horror, the Englishman was standing in front of it, listening as we were. Worse still, he moved quietly down toward the canoemen, coatless, his white shirt showing clearly in the starlight. I came to my feet, for it seemed only proper that I should intervene. Lieutenant Nordbergh seized my arm and pulled me down. "No," he said. "Don't interfere, just watch!" He was actually chuckling to himself so, dutifully, I sat back all eyes and ears.

The mimic, warming up to the applause of his audience, went through the act again with even greater flourish, his back to the slight figure in the white shirt. But there was no round of applause this time from his fellow voyageurs, merely an embarrassed silence, for they had seen the arrival of the visitor.

"Pardon, M'sieur," broke in the Englishman in impeccable French. "That was very good—but there are one or two things which could be improved upon."

The poor fellow must have been dumbfounded, for he seemed frozen to the spot. "Now watch carefully," said Alexander Baxter, and in mock seriousness and with elaborate gestures, he went through the man's performance.

"And another thing," he said, having finished his final sweeping bow to the stone. "It is not 'ponmeSOUL' and not 'b'JOVE, but 'PON me soul' and 'BY Jove,' accent on the first part, not the second."

The canoeman stood there, still speechless. "Come on, my friend," pleaded Baxter. "Try it again."

But the unfortunate canoeman only shook his head and shuffled his moccasins.

Baxter turned to the others. "Come, my friends—let's give him some encouragement!"

The Canadians entered into the game slowly at first, then wholeheartedly. "Encore, Telesphore!" they shouted, "Encore!" until at last poor Telesphore was prevailed upon to go through his act, which he did with but little enthusiasm.

"Excellent! Splendid!" shouted the Englishman, leading the applause. "Now one thing more—after 'By Jove' and 'Pon m'soul' there must be the snuff."

In a trice, Telesphore was introduced to snuff under Baxter's tutelage and exhorted to draw up strongly. The result was a paroxysm of sneezing that must have all but opened up the seams in the big canoes. The voyageurs were almost overcome with mirth, slapping their thighs, and some actually rolling on the sand.

"Dear me," said Mr. Baxter. "This is serious. I am afraid there is only one cure—good brandy." With that he dispatched a canoeman to his tent for two bottles of his precious brandy. Even so, Telesphore continued to explode noisily even after a fiddle had been found and "la ronde" started with Alexander Baxter an enthusiastic participant in the Canadian dance.

"He is certainly a chip off the old block—young Baxter, I mean," said Lieutenant Nordbergh. "I once saw his father do the same thing with a troop of Cossacks. By morning they would have ridden through the gates of hell with him. I expect that was one reason he was the best Consul the Empress of Russia ever had, at least at the Court of St. James."

Nordbergh bedded himself down in his blankets. I lay awake some time listening to the merriment at the voyageurs' fire and the sound of the fiddle. I fell to wondering what riches were to be found in this wild and vast place and if they were found how we would get them to the outside world. So wrapped in my thoughts, sleep at last found me.

In the next two days fever overtook me, not without reason and with little hope of cure, for, as John Nordbergh put it, "It's chronic and quite incurable." It was mining fever all right; all the symptoms were there.

We worked in two parties and at the end of the day

specimens and notes were compared and Alexander Baxter and John Nordbergh examined closely each find they thought worthy of attention.

I had one disappointment and that was the copper vein that Mr. Henry found and to which we all scrambled. Instead of the hard, half-polished beauty of the copper nugget I still carried as a talisman, it was gray-green and lackluster.

The Indian guide with me spat in disgust. "Kah misquahbik . . . kahwasuh!" And I agreed with him; to me also, it was certainly not copper.

The boyish enthusiasm of the experts, Baxter and Nordbergh, on the other hand, caused my Indian friend and myself to resort to silence though I did manage a feeble "But it doesn't look like copper."

"It's gray copper all right—and loads of it," said Mr. Henry.

Its real name is chalcocite," explained Nordbergh, squatting down and chipping away at it with his small hammer. "Some people call it 'copper glance,' one of the richest of the copper ores and maybe . . . maybe . . ."; but he went no further and devoted himself to his chipping.

The Indian grunted, shook his head and fired one parting shot before he wandered off, "Kahwasuh misquahbik!" Obviously he was a man of firm convictions and thought he knew copper when he saw it.

One of our Canadians it was who made the strike on the second day that brought us up the shoreline more than a mile.

Baxter knelt and picked at the mass of strange, cubical crystals. "Pon my soul!" said he after a time. "It's cerusite, lead ore; this country is a veritable storehouse of minerals."

He got up and carefully dusted off his knees. The canoeman, scratching his chin stubble with his thumb, looked crestfallen at the apparent lack of enthusiasm.

"Probably means there is galena deeper down," John Nordbergh sounded as if he were thinking aloud.

"I expect so," Baxter agreed. "There usually is." He picked up his leather bag and small pick.

Nordbergh had that strange, thoughtful look on his face again that I noticed when we found the gray copper ore. I felt he was holding something back.

"What is galena?" I asked.

"Oh, it's lead ore," he replied, obviously not wishing to discuss the matter further.

It was the last night at Point Mamainse that John Nordbergh dropped his Scandinavian reserve and told me of his own, personal dream. "Mark you, Vere," he warned first.

"I don't want the others to know of it yet. But I am sure there is silver here somewhere, and it's not just what the Irish call a twitching in my thumb. Everything I see seems to confirm it."

"Like a special kind of lead ore—or a copper ore that doesn't look like copper," I suggested.

He laughed. "So you noticed, eh? Anyway, the answer is yes. The lead ore called galena often contains a great deal of silver and copper glance often contains silver—sometimes gold."

"But you had this idea before we found the ore."

"Aye, it was the Jesuit Fathers at Quebec, and their crucifix, that really started me on it. It was carved by an Indian convert and the figure was of pure native silver."

"But didn't they know where the silver came from?" I asked.

Lieutenant Nordbergh shook his head. "No, the missionary priest could not find out, except a calculated guess that it came from the north shore of Superior somewhere."

The engineer-officer raised himself on one elbow. "But not a word to the others. I don't want to set them on a wild goose chase until I have something." He dropped back on his blanket. "But, Vere," he added. "Don't you ever stop looking, boy. It's here somewhere, I'd stake my life on it."

We cruised westward along the coast until our canoes entered the Bay of Michipicoten, a good forty-five miles from our copper and lead finds. It was home country to Alexander Henry, who had once wintered here with the Indians. The bay itself must have been a good ten miles across and was fed by many rivers that poured into it from craggy highlands. Indeed, the mountains seem to rise from the bay itself and tower into the heavens.

The terrain was so rocky and mountainous that there was sufficient time only for geological notes, and searching for minerals on the ground would have to wait. About five hundred yards offshore lay the little island of Nanibojou and, when the waters quieted after a sudden thunder squall, we went across with both canoes, for Mr. Henry had found pieces of virgin copper when wintering there.

While we sheltered in the lee of a rock, M. Cadotte told us the story of Nanibozhu, the Great Hare, whose Being was sacred to the Ojibway and whose body was said to be buried on the island. He was believed to have been the creator of all Indian nations and once lived where the sun goes down but, being warned of the great flood, he built a giant canoe, filled it with animals and travelled east to outrun the terrible waters. Now the spirit of the Great Hare lived on this island, ruling the great Lake of the Ojibway, so that all Indians who travelled on or fished in its waters stopped here to pay tribute to him.

On a rocky island shelf I saw mute evidence of this, for here lay kettles, even broken guns, beads, axes, bows, and mounds of tobacco, rotted by the rains. Our two Indian hunters slipped away from the party for a time and I knew without watching that they too were leaving some object for the personal use of the Great Hare, that the great waters might be kind to us who travelled on them.

The shoreline of Nanibojou gave us copper specimens of the most unusual shapes, and pure copper to boot; none of that gray stuff this, but glass hard, reddish copper burnished by the water and countless ages. Some were only an ounce or two and others as many pounds but all took the form of strange and wondrous creatures, some the shape of animals, others of insects, others like leaves or ferns. Neither Mr. Baxter nor Lieutenant Nordbergh could offer scientific explanation. So not unnaturally I attributed it to Nanibozhu, the Great Hare.

We did not go further on the rock-bastion-rimmed

north shore but, instead, our canoes left the bay on a southeast course.

I knew that the plan was to travel almost the full length of the south coast to the sacred storehouse of the Ojibway, to which our guides were to take us, but a southeast course had me puzzled. Mr. Henry provided the answer with something approaching a sheepish grin. "We are headed for the Isle of the Golden Sands. Leastwise we hope we are. It may take a bit of finding."

"Great Heavens," said I, "after the warning of the Ojibway medicine man!"

He nodded. "Perhaps because of it; the fellow triggered my imagination. Who knows, it may be a floating island of gold!"

We cruised in open water for two days, camping at night on known islands without trace of the mystery isle. Then, when the search was about to be abandoned on the morning of the third day, there suddenly appeared a speck on the horizon that the glass brought up to be an island of about twelve miles around. With every stroke of the paddles our two Indians became more restive and finally we ran alongside the first canoe in the hope that M. Cadotte could reason with them.

But whatever their problem they refused to be placated. "Kahwasuh! "Kahwasuh! they repeated over and over, shaking their heads.

"It's no use," said M. Cadotte, giving up his persuasion, "They say it is the Isle of the Golden Sands and if a white man sets foot on it, the spirits will be offended and violent. They refuse to land."

I looked southward over my shoulder but there was nothing but open water, for the south shore must have been fifty or sixty miles distant.

"What's that just to the left of the island?" asked hawk-eyed André Perrot, standing high in the bow of the first canoe. The glass was put on it.

"It's another island, I do believe," said Mr. Henry.

"Good, tell the Indians we will leave them on it while we visit the Isle of the Golden Sands."

Reluctantly they agreed, but obviously they were still troubled, no doubt wondering if any of us would survive to pick them up.

"We will load with swan-shot," said Mr. Henry before the canoes parted. "Just in case the vipers do materialize."

We made a good landing on the beach, which I noted with some disappointment did not appear to be gold, or even yellow for that matter. With our guns in the crook of the arm, we fanned out and walked inland toward a cluster of rocks.

We had scarce reached them, our eyes on the sand and rocks looking for we knew not what, when Alexander Henry, in the lead shouted a warning. "Look out!"

At that very instant we were attacked by a whirling, diving fury of beaks and talons. They were hawks, dozens of them. My hat was knocked off and my scalp torn at the first attack.

The roar of Mr. Henry's gun brought me out of my surprise shock. I fired into the screaming mass above my head. It was only then that I realized our attackers were literally squadrons of large hawks. We had no chance to reload, but used the butts of our guns to the best advantage possible. Mr. Baxter, unarmed, covered his face and head with his arms and I knocked a hawk off him. It took cloth from his coat sleeve into the air as it rose screaming.

Our canoemen rushed to our aid, bringing their paddles, and for minutes we beat off attack after attack until at last the hawks arose into the blue sky and left us to care for our wounds.

Mr. Baxter sat down on a rock, wiping blood off his face. "By Jove," he said. "I suppose you will tell me your medicine man turned the snakes into hawks for the occasion."

For the first time since the attack started I remembered the warning of the medicine man . . . and his fierce crest, Ka-Kaik, of the Hawk Clan.

Mr. Henry went on with the reloading of his gun and ignored Baxter's comment entirely. André Perrot made the sign of the Cross.

The two men, with the stalwart guard of Canadians armed with paddles, moved off, leaving me attempting to stop the flow of blood from Alexander Baxter's scalp wounds.

"Bless me," said he. "I still haven't learned to keep my mouth shut. I suppose it was a poor jest."

"I'm afraid it was," I replied. "There are some things in this country that can't be explained. So one develops a healthy respect for them."

Nor did we discover what the hawks were guarding. For two days we searched the low-lying Isle of the Golden Sands without discovering a single trace of any mineral. On the second morning I shot a young caribou bull, hoping for fresh meat. But even this was unproductive, for he was little else but hide and bones. Later we stumbled on a veritable caribou bone-yard, whole skeletons frequently with only the antlers showing above the moss. I could assume only that the poor creatures had died from lack of food.

So ended our dream of an island of gold and we left it to the hawks and whatever other powers of nature chose to protect it from intruders.

As we headed across open water for the south shore we had the benefit of a good wind that bellied out our sails and gave an extra thrust to the big canoes. Nonetheless, the white caps increased and I could sense the tension in old Pierre from his place of authority in the bow. He seemed to be forever scanning the skies to the west, now and then raising his head and drawing in a deep breath, for all the world like an old grizzly smelling the wind for scent of danger. The blow increased and the sails were dropped.

The canoemen ceased the rhythmic stroke of the paddles as the wind-lashed waves mounted higher. Now the paddles remained poised when a big wave was met so that the bow would not be driven under the next. Even so, we shipped water and two men wielded the giant sponges, carried for such emergencies, to keep the inboard water down below the danger mark. Twice we changed course, first from southwest to south and then to southeast.

At last, through the blur of driving rain and wind-whipped spray, a finger of land beckoned us, and I doubt not that many a fervent prayer of thankfulness went up from the two canoes. It was Pointe aux Iroquois.

For four days, high winds and rain prevented us from venturing out on the angry waters even with the giant canots du maître but, despite the weather, our party made several sweeping searches among the loose stones for precious minerals.

It was Lieutenant Nordbergh who made the find—a transparent blue stone of eight or ten pounds, charged so much with silver that both John Nordbergh and Mr. Baxter were of the opinion that such ore would run fifty percent to silver. But there was no trace of a vein nor, indeed, were there any other such rocks, so that in the end, we could only guess that the elements or some human agency had carried it there.

"It must have come, somehow, from the north coast," said John wearily, after a day's fruitless searching. "I know, I just know, there is a mass of silver there, somewhere."

But at last the weather broke and we turned westward, in search of the ancient copper to which our Indian guides promised to lead us.

14

Where the great horn of Keeweenaw thrust eighty miles out into Superior from the south coast we found the refugees from war. The smoke of many fires rising from the bay told of an Indian encampment, but it was "trois pipes" before we were close enough to tell that this was no summer camp. There were no lodges, and through our glasses we could see only women and children and old men. There were no young men.

Our two Ojibway hunters knew the meaning of it. They expressed it in one spat-out, hate-filled word: "Nadowe-is-iw!" The Ojibway name for Sioux or Dakota, which originally meant "snake" but which by usage had come to mean "enemy."

Ashore, the old men gave confirmation of war. A strong party of Dakotas—many hundreds the scouts had reported, as many hundreds as there were fingers on one hand—advanced toward their village, which lay southwest of Lake Superior. The women and children had traversed the base of Keweenaw point, some forty miles according to André Perrot, and remained where we found them, awaiting the outcome of battle.

It was a strange camp, quiet, foreboding. Except for the

occasional howling of a tied dog there was scarce a sound as the women went about their daily tasks. Even the laughter had gone from the children. They had journeyed for two weeks, and day by long day they watched and waited for the return of the war canoes.

When we left them we turned northward up the coast of the long peninsula, running close in by the shore and stopping now and then for a close look at unusual rock formations. As we neared the end of the horn, our stops became more frequent and, in proportion, John Nordbergh's enthusiasm rose. The discoloration of mountain streams and quartz veins standing open sufficed to make even the quiet Swede explode with excitement.

"It's almost unbelievable," he kept saying. "Why, this whole great horn of land, nearly eighty miles of it, seems to have a core of minerals, a sort of spine of metal. Lead, iron, copper, you name it and it's there."

"By Jove, yes," agreed Alexander Baxter. "A sort of mineral cornucopia. . . . Pon my soul, there never was a bigger horn of plenty."

We had just rounded the end of the cape and started down the offshore when the two Ojibways in my canoe became agitated, pointing excitedly in the direction of our course. The eyesight of an Indian hunter is something to reckon with but before long even I could see movement dead ahead. It might have been a flock of low-flying ducks for all I could make of it.

It was the war canoes returning, more than fifty of them, and we were ashore making camp by the time they drew abreast. They continued their course without a check for they carried many wounded, and women were needed to care for them. The chief and three warriors turned in at our hail.

The chief, Big Turtle, was no longer young, and obviously physical strain had brought him close to exhaustion. He was given brandy and food, and after he had eaten and drunk he told of their ordeal and victory. M. Cadotte translated for our benefit, the old chief pausing at the end of each statement to give the translator time.

The Dakotas, he said, had come up the Father of Waters, the Indian name for the Mississippi, entering their hunting grounds on a tributary. It was on this water that the Ojibway made their stand and had driven the invaders back. Thirty-five Ojibway warriors had been killed and eight had died from wounds since.

The Dakotas withdrew across the river and the Ojibway, in accordance with custom, dressed and painted their dead for burial, then withdrew fifty arrow flights to allow the Dakotas to return and scalp the dead warriors. The Dakotas did not return.

At this point Big Turtle's voice lost its tiredness and his words seem to hold both anger and disgust.

No Indian, he claimed, not even a Nadowe-is-iw, would so insult a dead warrior by not taking his scalp as a token of the dead man's courage. No, it was the white man that made the Dakotas leave without giving the dead the honors of war. It was the white man who led the Dakotas away.

Mr. Henry broke in with halting questions in Ojibway. Had they seen the white man? What did he look like? Big Turtle shook his head and beckoned to one of his young men. The Indian squatted and made marks in the sand indicating the size and depth of boot-heel tracks. Wah! He is a heavy man, He-Who-Walks-with-His-Feet-Spread. The young man held his arms wide to indicate the man's width of body and so high to indicate that he was of average height. So much they had learned from his tracks and the bruising of tree shoots where he stood or walked in the bush.

After Big Turtle had gone, his young warriors' paddles

flashing in the sun in full pursuit of their comrades, Lieutenant John Nordbergh took me aside from the others. "Well now, my young friend, don't you regret that you didn't dispose of him when you had the chance?" he asked.

"What the devil are you talking about?"

"Not what . . . who. He-Who-Walks-with-His-Feet-Spread!" My blank face revealed my complete ignorance. "Do you mean to say you don't know who he is?" asked Nordbergh with some irritation.

I shook my head.

"Why Zeke Hutt, of course, you ass."

For a moment I was stunned. "But—but how can you know?"

Lieutenant Nordbergh snorted. "I would have thought it would be obvious. But then, of course, perhaps you had not noticed his peculiar gait. I did, counting his paces that morning outside the Recollets' Gate at Montreal. He walks like a novice the first time on snowshoes."

The picture began to form in my mind. I knew that John Nordbergh was right. "But what is his game—think you?" I asked.

Nordbergh shrugged his shoulders. "That is the big question. This much we know, he is helping and encouraging the Dakotas to drive the Ojibway off Lake Superior."

My mind turned over pieces from the past. The mysterious intercepted letters from Captain Joseph Hopkins, now with the French in New Orleans, and his offer to a man not yet named. Was it Colonel Rogers at 'Mackinac? Were we in truth at war with the French and not at peace? The puzzle did not quite fit, perhaps because I did not want it so. "You think the French at New Orleans are behind this?" I blurted out at last.

He shook his head. "At first I thought so, until I had a talk on it with M. Cadotte." He paused for a time. "Abbé Guibault, Vicar General of Louisiana was at 'Mackinac last year; baptized Cadotte's baby and married him to his present wife. The Vicar General told Cadotte that the French commander at New Orleans was embarrassed by the ambitions of Hopkins and his crew of renegades in the Northwest and wanted no part of them. He assured Jean-Baptiste that this story of regiments ready to move was so much swill."

I grinned then at Nordbergh's serious, downcast face. "Come then," said I brightly. "If the French are not behind this, then why worry?"

The engineer-officer looked at me as he might a first-year cadet, bracing himself to explain the obvious with as much clarity as his patience would permit.

"Now look you," he started, wagging a long, lean finger under my nose. "Supposing the Sioux nation, led by the Dakotas, annihilate the Ojibway and take possession of this territory, with the help of the renegades and provided by them with arms. . . . And then, and then, my friend, Hopkins and his cohorts offer it to the French under conditions favorable to them, perhaps even with a readymade Governor. What would the French do?"

It was a question not requiring an answer, so I remained silent.

"And look you, Bayard," he went on. "Do you think that Whitehall would risk another war with France to regain it? Or perhaps you think the Canadians would take the field against France, eh? Is that it?"

I shook my head and Nordbergh, perhaps a little ashamed at his outburst, put his hand on my shoulder.

"The truth of the matter is," he said, "I know now how rich this country is—rich far beyond the dreams of man. And others know, men like Robert Rogers, and Hopkins, and Carver, and Tute, and Zeke Hutt."

Alexander Henry walked toward us. "What are you old soldiers so serious about?" he asked with a smile. "Whatever it is, I suggest you put it aside, and let's get moving. We have about eighty miles coastwise before we strike the river where the Ojibway copper lies."

John Nordbergh agreed heartily. "The sooner I get back to Fort Michilimackinac the better," he added under his breath.

But when we entered the wide mouth of the Ontonagon River thoughts of war and perfidy, of treason and strife, retreated from our minds.

It was a hot day, with the sun so strong that one could not bear the touch of a gun barrel. Our canoemen, all but naked, splashed one another with river water for a moment's relief. But neither the heat nor the power of the sun served to parch our excitement.

Now that we were at the water gate of the promised storehouse of copper riches, our excitement knew no bounds. I suppose our disappointment at the Isle of the Golden Sands should have tempered our enthusiasm but it did not, for I am told such tempering has no part in the makeup of a mine adventurer. The fever had hold of us.

Nine miles upstream we came to a waterfall, and the pool at its base was a frothing caldron of churning water. "Nahma! Nahma!" shouted our Ojibway hunters, pointing at the frantic water. Then I saw the cause of it—schools of spiny, steel-backed fish, some as large as a man, leaping and fighting as if each creature was seeking space of his own in the turbulent, cascading stream.

"Sturgeon," said Alexander Henry. "Enough to feed a regiment for a month on an hour's catch. I have heard the Ojibway come here each year at this time for the sturgeon. I suppose the Dakota raids have driven them off."

Less than a mile from the waterfall the river forked westward and our Indian guides indicated it was time to put ashore. At last we had arrived.

The bank of the river was, in fact, a limestone shelf

covered with the residue of spring high water. The two Ojibway walked ahead in the manner of men who knew where they were going, while the remainder of the party followed, looking this way and that. I spotted a strange stone half under a piece of driftwood. I picked it up and, although it was less than a foot in length, it was surprisingly heavy and obviously rounded by water. "Look!" I shouted. "Isn't this copper?"

Mr. Baxter was close by and examined it carefully. "By Jove! It is! Pure virgin copper!"

By this time others were making similar finds from lumps as big as a hen's egg to others of twenty or thirty pounds. "Shoad-stones, that's what they are," exclaimed John Nordbergh, not even trying to keep the excitement out of his voice.

"But they are copper?" I butted in.

Lieutenant Nordbergh made a face. "Of course they are. ... A shoad-stone, lad, is a piece that has been broken off a vein. So if you follow the shoad-stones, 'shoading' they call it in Cornwall, you find the vein." I decided to keep my mouth shut until I knew more about mining.

The Indians stood waiting, watching our excitement with the detached, half-amused air that one assumes when watching children in a game of blindman's buff. They spoke to M. Cadotte in their own tongue and moved on along the river bank. We followed, picking up rocks, casting some aside and talking wildly about others.

The Ojibway had stopped before a giant rock that stood out on the shore like some strange sentinel. Lieutenant Nordbergh, in the lead, stopped and stared. Then, as if he feared it was a mirage, he reached out and ran his hand over its face.

"Great Heavens! It is . . . it is!" He walked all around it and back to where he started. "It's all pure, solid copper."

By this time we were all staring or feeling the cold, burnished face of the rock.

"By Jove!" exclaimed Mr. Baxter. "It is in fact. In fact, it's the eighth wonder of the world."

Alexander Henry, being a practical man, tried to estimate its weight. "What would it be, ten tons?"

"Possibly seven tons at least," Baxter guessed after pacing around it. M. Cadotte brought us to our senses with a touch of Gallic wit. "Whatever it is, it will be a devil of a job to get it to Montreal. How about that, André, do you think you could get it over forty portages?"

We laughed uproariously, a strange laugh, as men would laugh if they had been led into the vaults of the Bank of England and told that all they could carry away was theirs.

"No," said Mr. Baxter when we had quieted down, "I don't think we will be moving this beauty. But the vein he came from—ah, that is a different matter."

A craggy hill rose clifflike not a hundred feet behind the copper rock. Both Lieutenant Nordbergh and Alexander Baxter, thinking alike, scanned it with their eyes. "It must have come from up there," said Nordbergh.

"Aye, but not the day before yesterday," agreed Baxter. "The waters of the river have rounded it."

The engineer-officer half-ran over to the base of the hill where an almost dried up mountain stream ran its course. What water there was was discolored, almost greenish. John Nordbergh thrust the head of his hammer into a shallow pool in a rock crevice—in time the iron head turned copper color.

"It's a leader all right . . . probably comes from the main vein," was his opinion. Mr. Baxter agreed.

The following day our explorations on higher ground resulted in the finding of a number of trenches, some as deep as five feet, with unmistakable signs that native copper had been taken from them. By then none of us doubted that we had indeed found the source of the sacred copper of the Ojibway nation.

Even so, the man from London insisted on a sample from the big rock. A roaring fire against one side, following by dousing river water on it, sending steam clouding into the air, helped achieve his wish—as did the untiring efforts of the Canadians, who also managed to dull every axe in the party. When it did split, a good hundredweight of copper gave way, much to the delight of Alexander Baxter, who must have known full well the stir it would cause in London.

We started the return journey to the Falls of St. Marys with a song in our hearts and a lusty joining in with the voyageurs' canoe songs. Even Alexander Baxter seemed to have cast aside his phlegmatic airs. As we passed the waterfall with its threshing sturgeon he called to our canoe. "John! That will help me recruit Cornish miners. Caviar by the ton right under their noses."

But even though we had found our mountain of copper it still had to be moved onto the high seas and so the planning was started. At each camp on that long journey, and it took us eight days despite favorable winds, details and duties were discussed.

"We must have proper shipping—can't move that much ore so far in canoes," was Baxter's first edict. "That means a shipyard as close as possible to the Falls of St. Marys. Any ideas, M. Cadotte?"

Jean-Baptiste considered the matter, relighting his pipe from a firebrand before answering. "I don't suppose there is a better location than Pointe aux Pins—sheltered, deep water within a few yards of shore. But I hope it wouldn't be a bad omen."

"What do you mean a bad omen?"

"La Ronde built his schooner there."

"Very interesting," said the Londoner drily, "but who was M. la Ronde and why should his building a schooner be considered bad luck for us?"

"I suppose because of his failure in his copper venture, and his death," spoke up Alexander Henry.

Baxter shook his head. "Will someone please explain, particularly now that the fellow is in the copper business as well as shipbuilding."

M. Cadotte took on the task, using the French language by force of habit. "Louis Denis, Sieur de la Ronde, was Commandant at Fort Chequamegan," he began. "That would be about 1735, thirty-two years ago. He had heard about the copper from the Jesuit Fathers and from the Indians and located a strike on the south shore in mountains the Indians call Kaug, which means Porcupine. He had a great dream; I remember all the talk when I was a boy. He wanted to mine the copper and sent it to France. He planned to ship his ore over the Toronto portage and needed a schooner on Lake Huron and one on Superior. And when this came about he was going to ship cattle and horses from Detroit and build a settlement on the St. Anne River. Well, God rest his soul, he did build his schooner for Lake Superior and at Pointe aux Pins."

Mr. Baxter listened intently. "And why did not his dream come true?" he asked, after a time.

M. Cadotte shurgged his shoulders. "He had no miners and not enough money. He begged the governor for both. Even petitioned the King of France. The best he could do was to hire twelve voyageurs but they couldn't handle the ore, and then his sloop was wrecked in a storm and he lost the most of his men. We thought he died of a broken heart."

Alexander Baxter nodded gravely. "Then I would say for us to use Pointe aux Pins is a good omen, not a bad one.

We are in a position to make la Ronde's dream come true. I will get miners, the best in the world—Cornishmen—and money? . . . When London hears of this there will be so much thrust at us we won't know what to do with it." He paused for a moment. "Tell me," he asked. "Did he have any difficulties with this place as a shipyard?"

"Non, M'sieur. Ah, yes, I remember. When he started his sloop the Sioux were on the warpath and a war party did raid it and burned the ribs and keel with fire arrows. But he began again and finished it."

The Englishman nodded. "We must take steps to see that doesn't happen to us. A man's a fool not to learn from the past."

If Pointe aux Pins was a legacy from the courage and farsightedness of Sieur de la Ronde then it was a rich one. Nature never contrived a better harbor for our purpose. It lay some six miles above the Falls of St. Mary's and the same distance from the open water of Lake Superior. The channel itself was three miles across to the west shore. Pointe aux Pins was almost crescent shaped, forming a natural protected harbor where the water lay some twenty feet in depth a few feet from the sand of the point.

The moon-shaped point itself was sandy soil covered with sand cherry and bilberry shrubs with the occasional outcropping of pitch pine. But at the base of it, and beyond, there was good soil. A fine stand of white pine stood within reach, like a forest of lance-straight masts, broken here and there by oak and elm.

Mr. Henry, Mr. Baxter, Lieutenant Nordbergh, and myself camped on the point for two days, measuring, pacing, taking soundings in the basin, cruising timber, and preparing interminable lists of supplies to be brought in before ice closed the waterways to the east.

Two buildings were to be erected. The first to serve as

quarters for staff, the second as a storehouse to which was to be added a forge and air furnace, suitable to assay metals.

A flat-bottomed barge of not less than 12 tons burden was to be ready when the ice went out, to be used to take supplies and equipment to the mine until the schooner was built, and for loading ore in shallow water.

Mr. Henry was confident he could hire men from amongst the winterers. "The Canadians are good timber men, excellent with the broadaxe," he said.

"Good," replied Baxter. "But you will still require a carpenter, two would be better, and a blacksmith. I will see what I can do at Detroit and Niagara on my way through."

I began to take stock of what had to be accomplished in the months ahead. And in winter! Heaven help us, I thought, is there no end to it. But this was not the end by any means.

"Now we come to the matter of defense," said the man from London. "Seems to me some sort of a stockade, strong enough to withstand light attack would suffice. What do you think, Nordbergh?"

"It wouldn't be too difficult, say a twelve-foot palisade around the perimeter with an adequate fire-step. There is plenty of timber available."

"Excellent! Now about the weapons—are they available?"

Alexander Henry said he had four cases of guns with rifled barrels in storage at 'Mackinac. "I got them from Albany for the trade, but since the Pontiac trouble it has been against the law to give an Indian a rifled gun."

"How about cannon? If we could get one it would serve to deter those with warlike ideas."

Lieutenant Nordbergh thought he had seen two brass swivel guns stored in the magazine at Fort 'Mackinac.

"Good. I presume you're an artilleryman, Master Bayard?"

I admitted weakly having once taken a gunner's course

in Holland. Le Bel Anglais favored me with a sly smile, obviously aware that I already had an attack of indigestion from the amount on my winter plate. "Yes, Ensign Bayard, and in your spare time you could unpack, clean, and grease the rifles—they need attending to."

But it was a shot fired over Baxter's head. "Those two swivel guns would be very useful. We could mount one on the schooner, when she's floated."

I stayed on at Pointe aux Pins with John Nordbergh for a day of measuring and staking but before the other two left for Cadotte's Fort, Mr. Henry managed a word in private.

"You must admit," he said. "Our Englishman doesn't let the grass grow under his feet."

I shook my head. "We haven't a charter yet to mine, nor have we raised any money. Seems to me he's taking a lot for granted."

He smiled. "I wouldn't worry about that. He was given a two-thousand-pound credit, now at Montreal, so that, if he was satisfied, he could get the work under way. If they have that much confidence in him, then he shouldn't have much trouble with the Royal Charter, or in raising money. Meanwhile, Vere, it looks like a busy winter."

And, indeed, it was. Mr. Henry and M. Cadotte were able to secure the services of six hearty Canadians, as able with the broadaxe and saw as their good humor was inexhaustible. Mr. Baxter, too, must have worked miracles, for his two carpenters did arrive, a New Englander from Niagara and a German from Detroit. Fortunately the New Englander had been engaged in building bateau so he was invaluable on the scow. And, too, Baxter had wangled the loan of a forge and blacksmith from the Indian Agent at Detroit. Even so, looking back on that winter, probably our greatest strength came from Pierre and Annette,

M. Cadotte's team of horses that we brought over as soon as the ice would hold them. How else would we have snaked the big timbers from the high ground?

But with the first snow came alarming news from Fort 'Mackinac—the Commandant had been arrested and charged with treason! Hostile Indians, mostly Ottawas and Potawatomies, enraged at the arrest, camped in such numbers about the fort that Captain-Lieutenant Spiesmacher dared not attempt to send his prisoner overland to Detroit, but was holding him for the arrival of an armed ship in the spring. There were rumors that Robert Rogers had attempted to bribe a Canadian to get help from New Orleans.

We doubled our efforts on the stockade and I did find time, after dark and by the light of our newly built fire, to unpack the long rifles and to clean them.

15

It was already the Moon of Flowers, but one would scarce have guessed it. The May sun, growing stronger day by day, had softened the ice and the snow ran rapidly before it, but it was a late spring hounding the heels of a hard winter of cold and deep snow.

Even so we, my Canadians and two carpenters, had accomplished much. The house was finished, of logs well chinked, with an ample hearth and fire that ate wood with the gluttony of a wolverine. The warehouse was finished, save about half the roof to be slabbed, and we had our forge up and working before the first heavy snow came. The barge had most of her planking hewn, some of it set, and would be ready for the water by the time the ice was out. The palisade, with an adequate fire-step, plenty of loopholes, and strong gates, had been completed around the whole perimeter of our shipyard headquarters. Even the little brass swivel gun stood, a well-polished sentinel, mounted high to give it a good field of fire. I was well pleased with our winter of building and labor and in the warming sun satisfaction grew in me, driving out memories of frostbite and the exhausting fight against drifting snow.

During the winter, snowshoe express had brought discouraging news from Fort 'Mackinac. Robert Rogers was in irons and in a solitary cell. Indians outside the fort had continued to increase in numbers and rumors ran like fox fire in Indian encampments that four battalions stood to arms at New Orleans ready to march northward to rescue the Ranger chief. By Strawberry Moon, perhaps before, he would be free.

What a hellhole of intrigue, this 'Mackinac, I thought, basking in my own satisfaction, yet sorry for my comrades of the Royal Americans. Poor Captain-Lieutenant Spiesmacher and Lieutenant John Christie with a winter of double watches seemingly without end, with the great bear of a Commandant growling in irons and the only hope the early arrival of an armed schooner and reinforcements. And then Alexander Henry and Jean-Baptiste Cadotte left for 'Mackinac, anxious lest the situation there might interfere with the movement of their fur and lest it would effect the London support for our venture.

Thus I was left in command and at once the burden of responsibility sharpened my thinking, leaving me alert and apprehensive. Retreating ice, moving backward in shifting, grumbling floes, now meant to me the opening of water routes to an enemy.

I put a day and night watch on the palisade, even though it reduced our labor force, and trained our little company on action to take in the event of an emergency. The long rifles stood always ready, with ample powder and shot.

I had all but come to think that my precautions were born of a fit of nerves until one sunny afternoon, when I was helping fit a plank in the scow, a shout came from the man on watch.

"M'sieur! ... Indians! Coming in from the lake!"

My legs all but outran me until I was standing by his side.

"There, see!" he said, pointing.

I did indeed and my glass picked up five canoes. After a time they became clearer. No fur brigade this. They were painted warriors. Before I shouted for a stand-to, I recognized the passenger in the lead conoe. It was White Fisher. And the speed of the craft as they turned in toward our shoreline told of the urgency of their mission.

I welcomed them at the shore and invited them to the house. White Fisher was grave and serious. Before he and Bright Forehead followed me he picked up a gun from the bottom of his canoe. We walked in silence and the Canadians stood in little groups, watching as if a foreboding cloud followed us.

"M'sieur," said White Fisher, "I bring bad news. The Dakotas are five days' journey from here."

"How many?" I asked, as calmly as I could, with a sickness coming suddenly to my stomach.

"About a thousand warriors. He-Who-Walks-with-His-Feet-Apart is with them. They have already destroyed three of our villages."

There was little doubt in my mind that they were headed for 'Mackinac, perhaps racing against the arrival of the armed schooner. They would most certainly come by way of the Falls of St. Marys.

"You intend to meet them?"

The tall young chief nodded.

"With how many warriors?"

He shrugged his shoulders. "Perhaps four hundred—the north rivers and lakes are still frozen so that the Men-of-the-Thick-Fir-Woods cannot join us."

Bright Forehead's eyes had been roving the common room of the house and were held by the stack of oiled rifles ready in racks near the door. He spoke in Ojibway to the White Fisher. I could not understand but twice caught the word "paushkesegone"—so I knew it concerned guns.

White Fisher held out the gun he carried and I took it. "The Sioux are armed with these—our scouts picked it up."

I turned it in my hands. It was not British; it might have been either French or Spanish. He pointed to the muzzle. It was rifled!

"The gun that shoots far," said White Fisher. "Twice as far as our guns. So I come to my friend because he has what we must have."

I opened my mouth, and closed it again. I looked for an opening, a way out, but could find none. The two Ojibway war chiefs stood wrapped in silence, waiting. They knew as I did that it was forbidden to give an Indian a gun with a rifled barrel.

"I will think about it, my friend," I heard myself saying. "Give me time to consider it."

White Fisher nodded. "My warriors wait at Pointe aux Iroquois—and time runs like a stream in the Flower Moon."

I left them there and went to my quarters, a boxlike room with a window facing the water. I stared out, scarcely seeing the Ojibway warriors squatting on their haunches by their beached canoes. I listed the facts in my troubled mind.

If I gave them the rifles I would commit a serious offense, probably it would mean arrest and trial. Worse still, Alexander Henry would lose his position as a preferred trader at Lake Superior and his license to boot; on the other hand if I refused, Mr. Henry would for all time lose his friendship with the Ojibway. The one seemed to cancel out the other and I was back where I started.

Suppose, I thought, I did give them the rifles and they were defeated by the Sioux, a not impossible conclusion considering the relative strength of the two forces and the reputation of the Sioux as fighters. Then the long rifles would fall into the hands of the enemy and would be used against us. Probably against my own regiment at 'Mackinac and Detroit. It was a grim thought. Still, if I refused and the Ojibway were defeated it would likely mean the Sioux would move through here and take them anyway. Again, the one argument seemed to cancel the other and I was left where I was.

There was one more fact involved ... our friendship and alliance with the Ojibway nation. If we denied them help we had available when their backs were to the wall, when they were fighting for life itself, how could we call ourselves friends? There was no cancelling out that one, it was the difference between black and white, between right and wrong. My mind was made up.

The two chiefs were still standing waiting, their faces showing no trace of the anxiety which must have been in their minds. Only painted masks of courage.

"Very well ... I have no choice as a friend; you may have the long rifles."

There was the suggestion of relief or pleasure in White Fisher's face. Before he could speak I went on, "On one condition ... that I go with them. And when we win the day I shall return with them."

Bright Forehead grunted approval. White Fisher reached out and took my right hand in both of his and shook it warmly and strongly. Neither spoke. Words were not needed.

While the guns and shot and powder were being loaded in the war canoes I gathered together my little company of workmen and told them the grim news. The two youngest and strongest Canadian canoemen I ordered to leave at once for Fort 'Mackinac to inform the commanding officer of events and to deliver a note to Mr. Henry. Two others were to leave as soon as possible for Cadotte's Fort and warn the people there, they were to take Madam Cadotte and the children on to 'Mackinac. At this place, I left my dour New Englander, Hiram Tuttle, in charge; the remainder to stay or not to stay as they thought fit.

Hiram looked at the others who were nodding. "Aye," he said. "We stay . . . there's a mite to be done. Got to get them shakes on the roof."

"Ja," agreed the little German. "Ve stay."

I penned a hurried note to Mr. Henry, the importance of which lay in my closing paragraph:

"The loaning of the guns with rifled barrels was my decision and I am fearful lest it would be contrary to your wishes, which it may well have been. I am aware of the orders and regulations in regard thereto; but under the circumstances and not having your direction available, I was forced to resort to my own reasoning and act upon my own conclusion.

I have the honor to be, Sir,
Your otherwise Obedient Servant . . ."

This, I hoped, would help Alexander Henry in his case to the commander-in-chief in the event that our purpose ended in failure.

Walking toward the canoes, I turned to look at our winter's handiwork. As I did so, the slanting sun flashed off the polished brass swivel gun that frowned out over the water. An idea struck me. I called to Hiram Tuttle, who a moment before had awkwardly shaken my hand.

"Get the other swivel gun, it's in the warehouse. And some swan shot and powder!"

While they brought out the little brass cannon and put it carefully in one of the canoes, I began to wonder how on earth I could put it to use. But never mind, I consoled myself, it certainly wasn't helping the cause, lying in the rubble of the warehouse.

The canoes seemed to have wings over the water and

naked copper shoulders and arms not once flagged or rested until we had reached Pointe aux Iroquois. During the journey I gave much thought to our circumstances. Certainly the forty-eight rifles would not of themselves assure victory. More than likely, the Dakotas had ten times that number. But the forty-eight rifles used with an element of surprise and shock might turn the tide.

I could not avoid the lesson of Bushy Run, not only because it was my first time under fire but because the odds were similar and Colonel Bouquet had turned disaster into victory—and that, by surprise, and the shock of unexpected fire from the flank, at the moment when the enemy thought himself grasping the scalp-lock of victory. The more I thought on it, the more I was convinced it was the answer. If it was the answer for the Delawares, Shawnees, and Wyandots, why not for the Dakota-Sioux?

We made landfall at dusk and, at our first fire, I made known my ideas to the war chiefs. I could see they were impressed.

"This way," I explained, "we can get the full effect of the rifled guns, and even our cannon. Our flanks would be well hidden so that at the first shock they wouldn't know where the fire came from."

White Fisher nodded gravely. "This is well spoken."

I was concerned about one thing only—these Ojibway might be brave enough but they were not trained soldiers like the Royal Highlanders or the 60th Foot at Bushy Run. To withdraw steadily in the face of overwhelming fire and losses required the discipline of the Black Watch or Royal Americans. I made my fears known to the chiefs.

"My warriors will do what they are told," said White Fisher.

"Then let every warrior, every man-jack of them, be told what the plan is and he'll know what is happening when it happens," said I.

On the sand of Pointe aux Iroquois, in the flickering light of the fire, was drawn the plan of our attack. The main body of Ojibway warriors would attack—or better still, be attacked by—the invading Dakotas. After the first shock, the Ojibway would slowly fall back, drawing the enemy forces into a prepared position dominated by the riflemen well hidden on each flank. At the right moment, the Ojibways would simulate a rout and, as the Dakotas rushed forward for the kill, the hidden rifles would open up, first from one flank, then the other. The main body of Ojibway warriors would then attack a confused enemy with all the fury they could muster—a role carried so well at Bushy Run by the bayonets of the Watch.

A simple enough plan; but executing it was another matter. Each sub-chief was brought to the fire and the plan explained in detail. There must have been nearly fifty of them who, in turn, explained it to the warriors for whom they were responsible.

The riflemen was another matter. Forty-eight of the best hunters, men used to the handling and use of guns, were picked for this duty as were two sub-chiefs, Me-gizz-ee, Gray Eagle, a calm, confident old hunter, and Nundu-wahqua, Bear Hunter, a lithe young man who walked with a limp. None had yet used a gun with a rifled barrel, so they must be taught the importance and difficulty of loading. Ramming a tight ball down so that it spreads and takes the groove, takes more than a strong arm, it takes skill. But the Ojibway hunter, like all Indians, is far quicker and surer in the use of his hands than the white soldier and before the next sundown I was confident they had mastered it. I shall never forget the look of grim satisfaction on the face of the warrior-marksmen as they got the feel of the long-rifle and experienced its range and accuracy in comparison with their own old, short, smooth-bore muskets, nor my satisfaction in their skill.

Two days later, our scouts brought in news of the Dakotas' advance. They were moving fast in a northeasterly direction. There was no time to lose. White Fisher and Bright Forehead had council with hunters who knew the territory through which the invaders were headed. There were no maps, but their knowledge was better than any charted course.

It was agreed that the Dakotas must be met at the fork of two rivers. One of these, running almost east and west, was a tributary of the Mississippi along which the canoes of our enemy now travelled. The other ran north and south and emptied into Lake Superior. Either the Dakotas would turn north here, to Superior, or continue eastward on their present course. Either way, here they must be stopped.

By good fortune, the fork of the two rivers was flat and open, gradually closing up into a valley that ran back to its head in high hills. Here, indeed, was the place to bait our trap.

We travelled with all speed now, more than a hundred canoes like living creatures moving arrow fast under the strength of brave, determined men. The rifles, and even my little brass cannon, were well covered under rush mats, for sooner or later Dakota scouts would be watching. Indeed, White Fisher gave orders that they were not to be interfered with, that they might report back our size and strength.

We arrived at our chosen ground at high noon the following day and it was as the hunters described it—an ideal place for our plan. Now the Dakotas were pressing closer as if anxious to have it over. The morrow might well be the day of testing.

Dawn light showed our warriors under White Fisher and Bright Forehead in position on flat ground near the river—they had lighted fires to give the impression of confidence. But they were silent men, fingering their weapons and making peace with their God in their hearts for they knew full well that, before another day, many would be travelling the "Ke-wa-kun-ah"—the Homeward Road across the sky, meeting the sun as it came up.

A thousand yards up the valley to the rear of our main force twenty-four riflemen were concealed on each wooded slope. But no one could know. Not a leaf out of place, not a bent or broken twig, no sound save that of birds and squirrels rustling in the leaves. I had my brass cannon in the center of the line on the right flank, lashed to two short logs to take the recoil and loaded with a heavy charge of black powder and swan shot, with a few balls thrown in for good measure. Even Little Meg, as I now called her affectionately, had been transformed into a stand of innocent ferns.

I lay beside Little Meg and waited, a loaded pistol close to my right hand. On my left, so close I could touch him, was the prone form of Gray Eagle. He had two sons who were to be blooded this day, young warriors down on the calm flats of the valley. The waiting seemed without end and I wondered what Gray Eagle's thoughts must be.

The sound of irregular firing from down by the river brought an end to the agony of waiting. I could not see and dared not look for fear of giving away our position, but the shouts and the increasing strength of the volleys told what was happening.

The blood-chilling cries of warriors and the sound of musket fire grew louder each minute. I hardly dared hope that they would commit all their forces in a frontal attack. Then I remembered Zeke Hutt! Of course it would be his idea. A bully at heart and knowing they out numbered us almost three to one, he would demand that caution be thrown to the winds. What bully wouldn't, particularly when someone else was doing the fighting?

But now I could see a part of the ragged battle line

without raising my head. White Fisher had withdrawn a good way, leaving room for more Dakotas to press in from the river. His great, tall figure seemed to be everywhere at once, dodging, dropping, raising, running. Twice I saw a warrior dropped either by musket ball or arrow close to his side—he must have a charmed life, I thought.

The noise that came out of the valley sounded as if the demons of hell had been let loose. Occasionally, over the gunfire and shouts, I heard the chilling shriek "JEEN-GO-DUN!"—the cry of an Ojibway warrior on the killing of an enemy. Fighting every inch of the way, White Fisher's warriors drew back. Now they were directly below us and I could see, sickingly close, the terrible losses the Ojibway were suffering. The Dakotas were so confident now that their warriors were actually stopping to scalp as others pressed forward. My brain burned with apprehension. This can't go on! It must not! The Ojibway will be annihilated....

I looked at the prone figure beside me. Gray Eagle's hard eyes were fixed on the carnage below—only his right hand moved, stroking the shaft of his war axe. With superb discipline he awaited the appointed moment.

Suddenly the Ojibway line seemed to wither away and, smelling the hour of kill, the Dakotas with an ear-splitting shout pressed in, their warriors behind crowding up as if fearful they would be denied their share of bloody trophies.

Gray Eagle was on his knees now, head thrown back. The cry of the timber wolf ran along the hillside—it was the signal! The agonizing wait was over! A ragged but terribly effective volley burst from our position. I doubt not but what every ball found its mark.

An amazing hush spread in its wake. From the valley, only the noise of those engaged in hand-to-hand combat. The great mass of Sioux stood in numb disbelief.

I struck my match—must give them time to reload. Now

a dozen or so Dakotas, seeing the smoke of our rifles whisping from the green cover started to move toward us. I counted, "One ... two ... three ... four ... five"; then I touched the match.

Little Meg leaped back with a roar that shook the leaves off the trees, the wooden cradle slammed against my legs. But if Little Meg never spoke again in anger she had her say that afternoon. The roar and the smoke were likely worth more than all the lead and iron crammed down her throat. I stood and peered through the pall of smoke. As it cleared in the breeze I caught sight of a white man, way back among the Dakotas. Like a puppet, his arms and legs began to go. A wounded Indian, half on one knee, tried to pass him going toward the river. He kicked the wounded man in the face to stop his progress. It was Zeke Hutt, raging, trying to stop the inevitable.

Then the volley from the other flank. I heard a war cry from below to my right. It was Bright Forehead, standing on a fallen log. It was a cry taken up by more than two hundred throats. The Ojibways, released from the necessity of retreat, hurled themselves on the confused Dakotas like avenging wildcats.

The Sioux were in complete disorder now—another volley from my flank—disorder was turning into a mad rout, a race for the river and survival.

I saw another white man join Zeke Hutt and the pair, fighting to get clear of the panic-ridden Indians, struck out for our flank. I picked up my pistol and ran the ridge hoping to cut them off before they reached water and safety. Over fallen logs, through brush, sliding and slipping, I could not seem to make my boots go fast enough. Then, as I slid and slipped down the far slope I saw them getting into a canoe. My legs shortened the distance with longer strides as I hit level ground. "Hold!" I shouted. "Hold!"

They pushed out. I stopped, took aim, and fired.

Between my breathlessness and overanxiousness the ball went over their heads. I threw the pistol away and dived in. As I reached the canoe the man at the stern dropped his paddle and picked up a gun. I upset them and Zeke Hutt came out on my side. Shaking the water out of his eyes he grabbed me in a rib-cracking bear hug. I hit him in the face with all the force I could muster; his arms loosened, but as I half-turned I caught sight of a gun butt raised over my head. There was a stunning crash. I felt as if my head had parted from my body. I was under water; I tried to struggle free but viselike arms held me; my body felt weightless. . . .

Then, I was on the shore being shaken, head down, with strong arms around my waist and, reaching for breath, I retched and vomited. My head cleared for a moment. It was White Fisher who held me.

After a time he sat me on a rock and I managed to look up.

"Kez-heche-gahda! Kez-heche-gahda!" he repeated, pointing toward the water. "It is finished! It is finished!"

With a supreme effort I focussed my eyes. Floating, face down, was a great bulk of a body that had once been Zeke Hutt—an increasing red tide ebbed about it in a widening circle. White Fisher's bloody knife lay on the sand where he had dropped it to pick me up.

"Thank . . . ," I started but I couldn't stop myself pitching forward, face down, and the world left me.

When I opened my eyes I seemed to be in the shadows —except a great glare of daylight over my feet. After a long time I figured it out. I was lying in some sort of a lean-to made of spruce boughs and the glare over my feet was, in fact, the open side. I stirred, but the pain in my head told me it was better not to. A figure that had been by my side, left.

After a time another came. As I rolled my eyes upward, it seemed ten feet tall. "You have been asleep a long time . . . this is the second day." It was White Fisher. I tried to raise myself on my elbows but the pain in my head caused me to fall back. I lay there trying to think things out, to bring them back, in order.

"It is better that you lie still for a time. Try and eat; they have venison broth for you."

"The Dakotas?" I asked weakly.

"Agh! It is over. They will not come back."

I ran my tongue over my lips "The guns . . . I must get them back."

White Fisher lowered his tall figure, squatting on his haunches beside me. "Do not trouble your heart, my friend. They are all here outside your lodge, well covered. When you are stronger we will take them back with you."

A warrior came in carrying things. "Turn over," advised White Fisher. "We will change your dressing now . . . it is good medicine."

They took off the fir-balsam dressing and washed the wound with a sweet smelling brew made from fern fronds. I bit my fist.

"It is doing well," said White Fisher. "In a few days you will be able to travel. The gun butt split your scalp wide at the back." He ran his long fingers over my head. "But the skull is not cracked. You English have hard heads."

"English?" I protested; but it was too much effort. Anyway, the White Fisher had already left to tend to his wounded and to finish burying his dead.

When we arrived at Pointe aux Pins, the two Indian canoes low in the water from the weight of guns, the whole company was at the water's edge to greet me. Mr. Henry helped me out of the canoe. "Welcome home, the conquering hero!" he said with a broad smile. I could not help but notice that it was no means all banter.

"I'm sorry about the guns . . . I . . ."

"What guns?" he asked, looking at me oddly.

"The guns with the rifled barrels . . . and Little Meg."

Mr. Henry shook his head sagely. "Dear me, I am afraid that was a nasty crack on your head, you're still imagining things." He paused and searched the clear blue sky with his eyes. "I see no guns, none at all." With that he put an arm about my shoulder, helping me to my quarters. "I have the best medicine for you in the world," he said. "Good news, the best ever! The King has granted us a Royal Charter . . . and Baxter is on his way with seven good Cornish miners."

Once I was made comfortable, Alexander Henry produced a copy of the Royal Charter from which besealed and red-splashed document he read me pertinent facts, pausing, now and then, to look over his spectacles at me, savoring the meaning of it all.

"To the Society of Adventurers for Working Mines in and about Lake Superior . . . the Grant of All Mines of Gold and Silver, of Copper, Tin, and Quicksilver, of Pearls and Any Other Precious Gems . . . to a distance inland of sixty miles from any shore of that Lake."

He paused in his reading, "And do you know who is our patron?" I shook my head. "No less a personage than his Royal Highness the Duke of Gloucester, brother of the King. And just listen to the other members of our company: The Hon. Sir Edward Walpole, that's Sir Hugh's brother; the Hon. Charles James Fox, a man who really believes in America; John Campbell, Doctor of Laws; Sir Thomas Bunbury; Baker John Littlehales; John Spottiswoode; Sir Samuel Touchet; Thomas Chabot, the refiner; John Townson; Martin van Mierop; Alexander Baxter, Consul for the Empress of Russia. . . . Ah, and listen to this, "Also the following gentlemen in America: Captain George McDougall of Detroit and the following, all of St. Marys near Lake Superior, Alexander Henry, Alexander Baxter, Jr., Jean-Baptiste Cadotte, Henry Bostwick, and Vere Bayard, Esquire, Ensign in His Majesty's 60th Foot, Royal American Regiment."

"Good Heavens!" said I, sitting bolt upright despite my head. "I never expected to be a member of the Society."

"Seems you are," replied Mr. Henry with an impish grin. "But you'll earn it." He thumbed through the document, "There is something here will keep you busy. . . . Ah, here it is. The Society of Adventurers is to annually lay before His Majesty in Council a complete account of the state of their works, including cost, the number of persons employed, the quantity of ore dug and to whom exported. So, when you're not running the mine, you'll be hard at it with the quill."

I had never seen a man so full of hope and excitement as Alexander Henry was that day. It put me in good heart and anxious to be up and doing. After disasters and suffering, his years were at last turning to fulfilment. He could scarce contain himself; he left the room and was back in a flash. "You know, Vere, it has just occurred to me, we haven't named this place. We must do that. How does Fort Gloucester strike you, a nice honor for our patron, eh?"

"Sounds well," I agreed. "Fort Gloucester on the River St. Marys."

"Aye, so be it. When you're on your feet again, we'll raise the flag, eh? And have a bit of celebration. . . . Fort Gloucester on the River St. Marys . . . sounds fine?"

He left me then, to read my packet of mail that had been brought down from 'Mackinac. A letter from an aunt, one from my uncle, and another from a cousin in military school brought news and family gossip from Switzerland. The fourth surprised me, it was from Captain Daniel Clause, and not from Montreal or Chaugnawaga but from London where he had been sent on Indian department matters.

"Your Superior adventure," he wrote, "is the talk of the City. A big piece of copper taken off the rock on the Ontonagon is on view in one of the best coffee houses and gentlemen and ladies, because I come from America, are constantly pressing me for information.

"Even Lord Hillsborough, chairman of the Lords of Trade, dined me and pressed me for information on it. Sir Sam Touchet is talking of grants of land and the building of towns where the mines are to be and a number of gentlemen of standing are soliciting to have Michilimackinac and Detroit made into Governments that these matters may be better advanced. I would be much happier about it all were it not for the fact that the expenses they are laying out for these mines of yours will arise to as much as all our department. Yesterday saw the King review Burgoyne's and Elliott's regiments, a most noble sight. . . ."

I folded the letter. Sitting on the edge of my cot, I could see out my window. The carpenters were all but finished with the barge; she was about ready for the water. Beyond, the warm sun sparkled on the water of St. Marys River.

It is all coming true, I kept telling myself. And I am a part of it. It was a good, warm feeling and already my bandaged head felt better.

16

Fort Gloucester, with the crossed flag of St. George and St. Andrew flying confidently now, was not long for me. My wound healed quickly, a tribute to the Indian herbs, and there was much to be done far afield.

The scow took to the water like a great, clumsy goose and I was much relieved that among our voyageur crew were men experienced in handling Lake Ontario bateau. We loaded her to the gunwales so there was scarce room for my two carpenters and the four Canadians going in with me, although they were useful enough on the sweeps. Our heaviest piece was the forge, although the iron that went with it was heavy enough, and we had some sawn lumber for sash and doors, tools, provisions, blankets, powder, and shot.

It was a long voyage up the south shore, for we dared not attempt to ride out a storm, she would ship too much water. Besides, I doubt that our little anchor would have held. Even with the fifteen-foot lug sail up and a fair breeze in our favor, I doubt that we made more than three miles an hour. In any event, two weeks had passed from the time we left the St. Marys River until we entered the mouth of the Ontonagon.

I decided to erect our buildings where the river forked and, although I had intended putting up three cabins, two for quarters and one for storage and workshop, the levelness of the ground and the availability of good timber made us change our plans in favor of a bunk-house for ten men. There was limestone in abundance and no difficulty in building a fine large fireplace at each end of the bunk-house for extra warmth and cooking. I held the scow for a few days so that the crew might help getting the larger timbers in place.

The days were long now and we labored from sun-up till dark anxious to be as far ahead as possible before the miners arrived. We need not have labored so hard. It was nine weeks before we heard the shot signal from the mouth of the river. We were down to the landing to a man, to welcome and for the first look at the Cornishmen that had come so far to wrest a fortune from the rocks.

As the scow was poled in, I looked for Mr. Henry or Mr. Baxter among the passengers, but in vain; obviously it was to be my responsibility to introduce the miners to our find and to get them established.

They clambered overside and onto the rock-shelf in great, heavy boots. My first impression was surprise that they were not larger men. I suppose I expected giants to which the splitting and carrying of rocks would be mere childs' play, but they were average-size follows. At least insofar as height, but strength was another matter—thick chested with a strength of arms that showed even through the heavy shirts they wore.

An older man of the group with graying black hair stepped toward me. "Good mornin', zur . . . 'ee be Maister Bayard?"

I nodded and stuck out my right hand. "Welcome to the mine."

"Thank 'ee, zur. . . . I be Will Tragear o' Redruth. Booys!" he called to the others, "Come an' meet the Purser an' Cap'n!"

They stepped forward one at a time, I assumed in order of seniority, and Will Tragear introduced them. For each a hand-shake, and I could soon vouch for the strength of a Cornishman's grip. "Dungie Crowgie o' Redruth; Petherick Kernick and Degary Tregarthen o' St. Just; George Tangye o' Camborne; Tom Triponey o' St. Agnes. . . ."

Will Tragear looked around for the seventh, but he could not be found. "Where thet booy gone to d' now?" he asked Dungie Crowgie.

Crowgie shook his head in a gesture of hopelessness. "David!" he bellowed.

There was a clatter of boots on limestone as a young man responded. "Iss, zur," he said, short of breath and with a sheepish grin. "Ded 'ee call?"

"Iss did I," shot back Crowgie. "I'll scat 'ees ears ef 'ee goes awf like 'at." And thus was I introduced to David Tonkin of St. Ives, who had the body of a made man and the face of a village choir boy. His age was a mystery, and I don't like mysteries.

"How old are you, David?" I asked out of curiosity and interest, both genuine.

"Sexteen, zur," replied Tonkin with an open and frank grin that bunched up freckles.

"But he's a good man in t' bal," spoke up Will Tragear.

"And a good wan before d' mast," added Dungie Crowgie.

"I work in the bottoms o' Wheal St. Aubyn for six years," added David quickly, "worked wid my faither . . . afore. . . ."

I slapped him on the shoulder and smiled, hoping I indicated we were not sending him home. "Good boy; now get your gear out of the boat and we will go to the barracks for a meal. That should tickle your fancy."

Poor Aaron Hill, our blacksmith who doubled as camp cook when he wasn't running the forge, had as much trouble with the Cornish dialect as I did, but being a Mohawk he quickly mastered the immediate problem by grinning and replying "Yes" to everything that was said to him. While Aaron busied himself with his pots on the hearth the miners stowed their slim possessions under the bunks they chose. Then someone spotted an untouched little pile of blankets and sea bags on the floor.

"Whose is dat?" asked one. It was quickly identified as the worldly possessions of one David Tonkin.

"He's gone again!" exclaimed Dungie Crowgie, making a quick move for the door.

"Now look 'ee here," spoke up another. "Don't 'ee be forever bally-wraggin' the booy . . . 'ee will make him chuff."

Despite the defense of his comrades, David rated a ticking off for leaving his gear in the middle of the floor and he got both verbal barrels from Will Tragear and Dungie Crowgie. There was nothing surly about the boy and he took discipline well.

"David," I said, when he had finished his task, "Tell me, is there something you're looking for outside?"

He grinned from ear to ear. "Iss, zur."

"Well . . . speak up, booy," said Crowgie. "Don't 'ee stand there like a buffle-head all of a grizzle. Tell the Cap'n what yer lookin' for t' see."

David Tonkin looked at me out of the corner of his eye. " 'Tis the rock, zur . . . es it fur?"

"The big rock o' copper," Will Tragear elaborated for my benefit. I realized that all the Cornishmen were looking at me, waiting, and that appetites or no, all thought of food had left their heads.

"There be not a village or bal in all Cornwall as not heard about it," said Tom Triponey from St. Agnes. "Two miners from Wheal Towan saw the piece off'n it in London town."

"Well, come on then . . . it's not far. It will give Aaron a chance to do his cooking without us under his feet." But before I had finished, most of the miners were already out of the door.

The effect of the giant bronze-colored rock on the Cornishmen had to be seen to be believed. For minutes they just stood with their mouths open. Finally two or three touched it, rubbing their strong fingers over it as if with affection. Another knelt, peering at its base, another tried to stretch his arms around it.

"Aye— 'tis the pride o' the country!" said one at last, low voiced like he was speaking in church. " 'Tis the pride o' the country."

"Nay," said another. " 'Tis the pride o' the world . . . the pride o' the world, I tell 'ee."

"Aye, 'tis a great bunch o' copper."

Will Tragear looked up at the cliff behind the stone. "We figure it must have come from up there, Will," I said. "And the main vein is in there somewhere."

The Cornishman nodded. "Aye, most likely. And those look like shoad-stones t' me . . . shouldn't take us long to find it." He smiled and added, shaking his head, "You know, zur, it will be the first time a Cornish miner ever went UP to bottoms and DOWN t' grass. . . . How about thet, booys?"

His remark brought a volley of guffaws, although I must admit at that time the point of his humor escaped me.

Young Tonkin did aught but stare at the big stone as if afraid it would disappear if he took his eyes off it. "Pride o' the world. . . . Pride o' the world," he said over, rolling it on his tongue. "Cap'n, zur, would it be fitten to call the bal, Wheal Pride?"

"Sounds like a good name for a mine," I agreed. "What do the others think?"

"Semmen to me 'tis a good name," said Petherick Kernick, whose left eyelid was permanently closed on an obviously empty socket and whose facial complexion was almost blue, as if it had been painted and the paint worn off.

"Aye, good. It's a right pride load, 'tis," chorused others. So Wheal Pride it was and I gathered all thought it well named. At any rate young David Tonkin, having thought of it, looked like the proverbial cat that swallowed the canary.

On the way back one of the men, who I had noticed coughing ever since he had arrived, had so severe a spell that he dropped behind. "That fellow has a bad cold," I said to Will. "There is a very good Indian medicine for colds—we'll get Aaron to mix him up some."

Tragear looked at me quickly, "You've never been down t' Cornwall, zur?"

I shook my head. "That is not a cold, that's a miner's cough. Most miners get it sooner or later ... semmen to me it's from the wet and water fathoms down. Fret 'ee not, George Tangye is as good a tut-man as you'll find anywhere, he no spits blood. Don't slow him down in t' bal any more 'an Petherick Kernick's blue face does him."

I could see I had raised a jumpy hare so I tried to change the subject. "By the way, what make's Kernick's face so blue?" I asked.

"Powder," said Will and, as I probably looked startled, he quickly added, "Gunpowder ... usin' a tam fuz. He wuz a lucky booy only losing wan o' his eyes—the doctors say it's unburned powder blown in the skin that turns it blue." He shook his head dolefully, "We have plenty o' miners about with no eyes. I guess the daid ones are not abaout, but I'd sooner be daid than to be led around and live on charity. . . . I be careful wid a fuz, I'm afeard o' dat."

Understanding the Cornish dialect was sometimes difficult and I did have trouble when it came to mining tools and mining. A mattock was not a mattock, it was a "visgy," a shovel was a "shouell," a log was a "mock," a chisel for rocks was a "gad," a short fuse was a "tam fuz" and a "needle" was not something to sew with at all, it was an iron drill for rocks. I soon learned that a place of mining was a "bal" but it took time to learn that a "branch" was a string of ore in a lode, that "teasible ground" was where you didn't require timber supports, or that "jigging" was dressing ore.

One morning Aaron Hill came from the forge to fetch me. Degary Tregarthen and Tom Triponey were there and he could not understand what they wanted. They knew what they wanted, they wanted a "graver-roz." Moreover, they explained, Hiram Tuttle, the carpenter, could make the "graver" if Aaron would make the "roz." Well, we all tried our best. The two miners tried to show us how it worked. They flexed the muscles of their big arms, bent their knees, straightened up and marched around the shop, arms out rigid in front of their bodies. Then stop, bend knees, drop arms to side. We scratched out heads.

"I know . . . I know," shouted Hiram Tuttle. "It's a . . . you know . . . the wooden thing across the shoulders you carry buckets on . . . a . . . yoke."

But no, it wasn't a yoke. As a boy in Switzerland I fancied myself at charades but this had me beaten and it wasn't until Will Tragear appeared that we had the answer. A "graver-roz" was a wheelbarrow! Even so, I had the last word. A "graver-roz" would not work in three feet of snow, so we settled for Indian-made toboggans.

Already, by night there was the tang of frost in the air and the Cornishmen lost no time in getting to work. They stoped the face of the rock cliff into steps and cut in to follow leaders, strings of ore that may lead to the lode or vein. We had finished the buildings and all was snug for winter and, while I was loathe to leave, I knew I must. The schooner must be built by spring if we were to move the promised ore from Wheal Pride. Before leaving, I promised myself a half-day's hunt. They could use fresh meat and Aaron Hill had not had time to leave his forge. "Would you like to go on a deer hunt?" I asked David Tonkin as the lad cleared the breakfast plates.

"Iss, zur, I would that."

"Good, I'll get you off work at the bal this morning. . . . I expect you could be of use to Aaron this winter and you best learn how to get meat." I looked at his heavy boots and gave him a pair of my moccasins. "Those boots of yours may be fine for rock mining but they are not much use in the woods. Now get a knife from Aaron, and a short length of rope."

He was off like a shot and back before I had scarce time to speak to Will Tragear. "Thank 'ee, zur," said Will, "for to takin' interest in the booy, you do us a service."

But they jibed good naturedly at David Tonkin as we left.

"Don't 'ee shut yer selve, booy," said one.

"An', David! . . . Mind 'ee don't go tumblin' down an owld whynshaft," said another.

"Aye . . . 'ee will scat 'ee skull."

David made a face at them. "Semmen to me it's a long way to a knacked bal—most likely t' Cornwall."

He strode alongside me carrying his knife and rope length as proud as a gladiator. "Tell me," I asked, "And what is a knacked bal?"

" 'Tis an owld mine, zur, mostly full o' water. There are scads o' them in Cornwall. Did 'ee ever hear o' wan here, Cap'n?"

I shook my head, "It isn't likely, seeing you and your friends are the first miners."

"Iss, zur."

"And David," I went on, seizing an opportunity. "Why do you miners address me as 'captain'? I'm not, you know, I'm only an Ensign, and a half-pay one at that."

David looked hurt. "But 'ee are a Cap'n, zur. Grass Captain o' Wheal Pride. Every bal has two cap'ns, a bottoms cap'n that looks after the bal warkin's like Will Tragear an' a grass cap'n that looks after everything up t' day, like tools, an' food, an' hirin' men an' bal maidens, an' the likes o' that. Besides, zur . . . 'ee iz Purser as well, does all the payin', looks a'ter time and books, like that there."

I nodded in what might well have been a gesture of surrender. "All right, David. Now let's get down to hunting, eh? Which means we go quietly."

It was a good morning for hunting. Heavy dew and what might have been a cousin to hoar-frost clung to the ground in low spots where the sun had not yet struck. Above, the morning sun picked out the occasional color showing on the maple tops and here and there sumac leaves pointed scarlet fingers at ground level. We had not gone far before I caught a glimpse of two does moving out ahead of us up a little valley.

I felt reasonably certain there was a buck in there somewhere. I explained the situation to David and sent him in a wide sweep to the other end of the valley with instructions to walk slowly toward me. Then I took up my position and waited. In front of me was a small clearing knee deep in meadow grass. Near the opposite side stood a gnarled old oak and a giant pine, side by side like old friends. Spreading out beneath them, like a skirt, a thicket of brambles and sumac and probably the inevitable stone pile.

I did not have to wait long. The boy could scarce have started up the little valley toward me when I heard twigs snap twice, then a fine buck came trotting out. At the clearing he slowed to a walk and stopped, head high, close by the thicket. He must have smelled me, for he raised his head suddenly and whistled alarm. It was just as I got my shot away, a good clean shot at short range, and the ball took him just back of the near shoulder. He went down as if he had been pole-axed and I knew a second shot would not be necessary. When he fell, he went sideways over into the brambles. I walked across the meadow, there was no movement, so I did not even wait to reload.

I had scarce reached the edge of the thicket when Tonkin came abounding. "Did 'ee shut wan, zur?" he bellowed. "Did 'ee shut wan?"

I looked along the edge of the brambles but no buck. I even parted them with my legs, still no buck. David looked disappointed.

"Is 'ee sarten 'ee shut wan, zur?"

"Of course I am," I shot back, a little piqued at the lad's lack of confidence in my marksmanship. "Here, hold this, I'll go in and find him."

I gave him my gun and tramped through the briars while he stooped over and peered through the low branches of the sumac. "There be a bit o' carn there, zur . . . maybe he's behind it."

By this time I was on the shale-rock pile and started to go down the other side when my feet slid away under the moving shale. In a sitting position I kept expecting my feet to hit something solid, but they didn't. Right through the tangle of briars I went, my feet kept going down. I grabbed frantically for the slim stump of a sumac and it held!

"What be 'ee doin', zur?"

"I'm down a hole; give me a hand David." I remember feeling foolish hanging on to the bush, my feet dangling below earth.

Digging his feet into the shale he pulled me out. "Do 'ee think he went down there?"

"I expect so . . . and after he had gone down the briars closed over it again. That's how I didn't see it."

"Fastenen rope on me, I'll go down and get him," volunteered Tonkin. With some misgivings but at his insistence, I tied the rope's end under his arms and lowered him down the hole.

"I can't see him yet." I lowered him some more, in fact as far as I thought safe.

"Can you see him?" I called, snubbing the end of the rope around the pine.

"No, it be too dark. Iss I do! He's down a ways yet, caught in the roots of a tree."

He came up then, bracing his feet on the side walls of the hole, and working his way up the rope like a monkey.

"Could you see bottom?" I asked.

He shook his head. "It's . . . it's like a whynshaft 'tis."

We dropped pebbles down the hole, but no sound came back. I thought to try a larger stone and started to pick over the shale. I found one, half embedded. It was twice the size of a man's fist and green in color. It was grooved around the middle. Then I saw another; and another, shaped like a chisel. Something of the truth began to dawn on me. I tore the rank brambles and branches away from the hole. Lying on my stomach I could see crude steps carved in the side, by man not by God, and lower down the hanging remnants of what looked like a ladder. I got to my knees. "David . . . I think we've found a knacked bal . . . and it was me who nearly scat my skull by falling down it."

"But how could that be, zur? . . . We be the verst miners here."

I shook my head. "Could you find your way back?"

David Tonkin nodded. "Then off with you. . . . Bring Will Tragear and the rest of the miners, and candles and lanterns, and rope, and anything else they need to go down a deserted mine."

He got to the edge of the meadow, stopped and called back, "But, zur . . . what about the deer 'ee shut?"

"Off with you, lad. . . . We will get him in good time."

While he was gone I amused myself by kicking in the shale-rubble. I unearthed more green-stone hammer heads and also a copper instrument that I would call a chisel but miners would call a gad. The head, or dull end, was splayed out as if struck a thousand times with a hammer. Another was like a bodkin with a socket for a wooden handle, long since rotted away by weather and time. I wiped them off and left them in the sun, in a row, evidence in my favor in case I brought them on a wild-goose chase.

One thing for certain, I underestimated young David Tonkin as a town crier. He not only arrived with the miners but every man-jack from the camp, with rope and lanterns and candles and axes sufficient to scale Mont Blanc.

They had the shaft cleared in no time at all and the first miner to reach bottom shouted up after a brief look, "It be a knacked bal all right. I'm down t' bottom at ten fathoms." A stirrup was soon rigged and, with two men winding the rope, we were lowered one at a time.

My feet on bottom, I could scarce believe the eerie scene before me. Blinking before me were miner's hempen candles, lit and placed on ledges along the rock passageway into blackness. The smoke stench from them caused me to cough. As the miners moved about, shadowy figures growing enormous against the walls, their voices echoed away like speaking from another world.

The bottoms captain spotted me. "The level runs dauon, zur. . . . But mind where 'ee steps, there iz plenty o' addle."

I looked down at my feet, my eyes not yet attune to the flickering light. He was right, in the middle of the long cavern were piles of refuse, mostly green-stone mauls and worn copper gads obviously discarded by the ancient miners.

"Must be ten cartloads," said Will Tragear.

He cast the light of his tin lantern up on the wall to my left, above the flickering candles. "Look, zur, they've been working big up there. . . . Looks as if they had a wooden scaffold o' some kind so they could get at the face high up."

I picked my way along the passage through the addle.

"Look 'ee sharp, zur!" he warned just in time. Right in front of me was a rock pillar left to hold the roof up. I felt the sides of it; it was polished smooth, perhaps by the contact of passing bodies.

There was the sound of trickling water, magnified a hundred times. It ran down the rock wall forming a pool at its base, then passing on through a crevice. "Need no adit here t' take off the water," said Tragear. There were objects in the water. I stooped and picked one up. It had been a wooden bowl but that section of it above the water had disappeared with the ages.

Two or three of the miners were standing nearby. "Look 'ee, Cap'n Will. . . . There be piles o' ashes and charcoal along the face here. What would that be?"

Tragear looked at it in silence for a time. "Well, booys, I never thought I'd seed it . . . thet's fire-setting. I heard my father tell about old workings in the Mendip mines with ash pits. They heat the rock real hot with fire then throw water on it t' split it. On'y thing 'ee could do wid out gunpowder."

"I'll say this for 'em . . . for sartin sure they didn't leave much. Not a smiggin o' copper have a seen below grass," said another, a little further in, holding his smoking candle high and looking up.

"Think 'ee not, Petherick? Then cawm an' look at dis!"

It was a huge boulder of pure native copper resting in the center of the cavern! They gathered around it, the candlelight glancing off its surface.

"Must weigh nigh on five tons . . . and pure copper! 'Tis a rare good bunch o' copper."

"Look," exclaimed another, "dey moved it on a sled." Under the mass, where the floor was wet, still stood the remains of oak runners. Somehow the ancient miners had dragged it this far. I wondered how many men it had taken —fifty, a hundred? And the struggling, sweating toil that had brought it this far!

"Semmens t' me," said a miner, "would ha' been better t' break it up." There was a pause.

"I wonder . . . I just wonder," said Will Tragear with a note of anxiety in his voice. "Semmens t' me we daunt know yet much abaut handlin' this pure copper."

Others had found an adit running down steeply from our level through a small hole in the face that we had to stoop to get through. I would as leave not of gone, for a strange feeling had taken hold of me. Somehow I felt we were intruders in another person's world, as if we had come, uninvited, through a trap door into the past.

But a shout from below brought us down quickly enough, with Will Tragear holding his lantern so that I could half see my way down the incline.

"We've found wan, Will!" an excited voice said. "We've found a miner at the end o' the adit."

"I think 'ee's daft," was Tragear's rejoinder, but we followed the voice. "We must be thirty fathoms down now."

At the end of the tunnel, water had come through from above and, level with the floor, a mass of ice remained.

Four or five of the Cornishmen peered at it, holding their candles close.

It was a body, encased in ice and half-preserved. The skin was still visible on the skull, and long, bony fingers were half closed as it waiting to grasp a maul. He didn't look Indian to me, but it was hard to tell.

More crowded around, incredulous, exclaiming. "Ah, the poor booy. ... He was a miner. ... I wish he could spaik."

"Maybe he was a Cornishman."

" 'Cause he was. ... 'Tis a miner he is."

"Let's take he t' grass an' give 'im a Christian burial." There were murmurs of agreement.

"No! ... No! ... Let 'im slaip in t' bal. ... 'Tis the right place for a miner!" It was David Tonkin. By the light of the candles and lanterns his face was white, working.

"You musn't say that, David Tonkin," said one of the miners seriously, standing. "It be bad luck on 'ee."

"I don't care if it's bad luck or no ... laive 'im slaip. ... My faither is in t' bal, eighty fathoms down in Wheal St. Aubyn. Leave 'im slaip."

There was a long silence in which I know more than one man had wished his tongue bitten off. For some time only the steady drip of water and the spluttering of candles broke the silence.

Dungie Crowgie stepped up to David and put a kindly hand on his arm. "Come, booy," he said. "We had best go up t' grass now."

One by one, and without speaking, we all left after that, each carrying with him his own thought to daylight. I, thinking and pondering what race of man had worked this mine. Was it five hundred years ago, a thousand, two thousand? I knew not nor could any man tell me. Was it men who strove for the precious metal before the Romans, before the Phoencians? How came they here . . . and where have they gone?

A hundred unanswerable questions crowded into my mind until I was pulled up into the stark, blinding reality of day. I saw David Tonkin sitting desolate on a log a little way off.

He raised his head as I approached. "I be a buffle-head, zur . . . the men will all think me a suckle-baaby."

I put my hand on his shoulder. "Now look you, my young friend, if we don't get busy and dress that buck deer we will both be buffle-heads."

So off he went to find his knife and rope length, wiping his face with his fists and pulling his shoulders back.

Back at camp, an express from Fort Gloucester was waiting, bearing an urgent request from Alexander Henry. The shipbuilder who was to come from the lower lakes could not be spared due to the decision to construct three new vessels for service on Lakes Ontario, Erie, and Huron.

"Captain Loring is very apologetic at not being able to provide a good man as he had promised," wrote Mr. Henry. "However, as we will be using the new shipping to carry ore on these lakes we cannot be too hasty to anger. Mr. Baxter informs me that one of the miners, named Dungie Crowgie, is master of a fishing vessel out of St. Ives and has had experience in building such craft. If such be the case, and if Master Crowgie is prepared to undertake the building of our vessel, I suggest you bring him back with you. I realize that by thus cutting the mining staff it will reduce ore output; however, without adequate shipping, production in any great amount would be to little avail."

I met with Will Tragear and Dungie Crowgie at once and they were both in complete agreement. Indeed, I rather thought Crowgie welcomed the offer and that the sea and not underground was his first love.

A disappointed young man was David Tonkin, ambling around donkey-faced and glum, so that at last Crowgie took note of it. "Pick your face up, booy. . . . I'll speak a word for 'ee to the owners and it may be they'll sign 'ee t' crew."

But it was Will Tragear who took me aside before we pushed off. "Semmen to me," he said, serious voice, "This copper be different t' any we have worked afore. 'Tis so tough we can scarce get a needle in it. You'd best send me another fifty kegs o' powder."

17

I suppose one has to be a sailorman to get the true feel of ships and of the sea. I shall never be that. A Swiss boy is not born with the salt in his blood.

But I came close to it that long winter when our lugger took shape and became a living thing ready for the waters of Superior. She was built by the eye, as the saying goes, by Dungie Crowgie's eye to be exact, and her shapely form knew no precise restrictions of the drawing board—it matured gracefully under the Cornish seaman's strong and magic hands.

Before the first heavy ground frost came we had her cradle set. Heavy blocks of timber, more than a foot square, were driven into the ground in a straight line and notched deep on top to receive the edge of the keel. When we first labored on these, I admit to thinking that Dungie was being overcautious as to their size and strength but later, much later, when I saw the strain and pull used to force the oak planking in place I knew the reason for it.

Then came the choosing and selecting of timber. Elm for the keel, the stempost, and sternpost, oak for the frames and beams. For a time, Dungie Crowgie was of two minds about the hull planking and as a result we cut and brought in enough clear white pine for the hull and deck—but in the end, he forewent the temptation of a quicker, easier task and planked the hull with good sound oak, two inches thick.

She was carvel-built, that is to say, the planking was fitted snug and tight by hand instead of clinched, a fact that brought much snorting and grumbling from Hiram Tuttle, the carpenter, who had served his time in New England shipyards. The stempost and sternpost were hooded to give greater strength when the keel struck bottom.

Indeed, old Hiram was at first so exercised over the extra work of fitting the tough oak planks, one by one, that I questioned Crowgie on it. I might as well have held my tongue.

"No ship is worth sailing less she be carvel-built," was his reply with definite finality.

"Is it peculiar to Cornwall?" I asked, trying to lead him on.

"Sailormen tell me it comes from the Mediterranean—and they do say we learned it from the Phoenicians when they came to us for tin. But, I'm telling 'ee, zur, 'tis the only way to build a trim ship." And then, having stood his ground well, he rounded it off with a touch of droll humor. "Besides, zur . . . it makes for a faster ship—how else could we outrun His Majesty's revenue cutters and make the coast o' France in less than eight hours?"

And in the end, long before the trim lady took to the water, Hiram Tuttle was taking as much pride in the fitting as anyone.

They did have one serious disagreement and didn't speak to each other for days on end. It was all over the stern of the ship. Dungie Crowgie had it in mind to give her a pointed stern instead of a squared transom.

This was too much for Hiram. "And what sort of a craft would that be," he snorted. "You couldn't tell whether she be going or coming."

"West o' the Lizard we wouldn't sail a craft less she was two-bowed," shot back Dungie.

Hiram snorted. "I suppose that is how you smugglers fool the customs officers . . . they don't know which way you're going."

That did it. But it was the Cornishman that gave way. "Well, they do build ships on the east coast o' Cornwall with square sterns, and there may be no harm in it."

But to me he confided. "Semmen t' me, zur . . . it wouldna be right for the little lady to look like a foreign woman in these waters." And so she got a square transom.

Her keel length was thirty-four feet, but she had a fine curved stem and straight sternpost, both well raked, that gave her an overall length of more than forty feet. A thirteen-foot beam and a hold depth of six feet gave room enough for many tons of copper ore besides room for a neat cabin for crew and passengers, three bunks on each side and a bunk for the ship's boy aft of the mizzenmast.

Dungie Crowgie was a practical man and gave consideration to the fact that the closer we could run inshore for loading so much the better. So he allowed for a draft for'ard of four feet and six feet aft. He would have wished her three good masts but, realizing the difficulty of getting crew, he reduced it to two, though I suspect he tried to make up the difference by adding canvas to the big lug foresail and mizzen.

And the two masts—there was an undertaking. Crowgie had us tramp miles on snowshoes before he found the two lance-straight fir trees he wanted; and then came the task of bringing them in, not to mention the endless hours and days of shaping with the drawknife.

The foremast, ten inches in diameter at the deck, was to rise a clear fifty feet above deck and the mizzenmast but eight feet less.

Winter let go its white-iron hold that year with startling

suddenness, at least it seemed so to us as we labored to finish the gleaming smooth hull and decks before open water came. Even so, the cry of the goose was strong in the air before the day of launching.

What a day that was! Petite Madam Cadotte came down to do the honors and the palisades of Fort Gloucester echoed with merriment. Two fur brigades were passing through the Falls of St. Marys and joined us for the occasion. Amongst them was Angus Macdonnell, the merchant-trader who brought his pipes, which, with the fiddles of two Canadians, left scarce a moment betwen reels and "la ronde." The entire two Indian villages were on hand with the inevitable swarm of laughing, happy children.

The choosing of a name was a matter resolved only by appealing to Alexander Henry.

"Well, now . . . all things being considered, I think the craft should bear an appropriate Cornish name and although my ancestors come from the west of England I'm not very good at Cornish. How about you, Ensign Bayard —have you any Cornish names locked up in your Swiss cupboard?"

I grinned and shook my head.

"Then it looks as if it's up to Master Crowgie. What do you suggest, Dungie?"

The Cornishman shifted his boots on the plank floor. "Thank 'ee, zur, thank 'ee. . . . I have a good name, a right name. But 'ee zee, zur, it be bad luck if the name is known before she is named on the ways."

We had raised a three-step platform, nicely decked in gay cotton, so that Madam Cadotte could grasp and swing the wine bottle against the bow as soon as she started to move. And so it was; blocks came out, and the fair ship started to move slowly and gently toward water. Madam grasped the bottle hanging by a ribbon and crashed it against the stemhead.

"Success to *Morning Song*," she proclaimed clearly. "Bon voyage et bonne chance!" The little brass cannon on the walls spoke her piece and it was the signal for a ragged "feu-de-joie" from Indian and Canadian guns.

Through it all, and occasionally over it, Dungie Crowgie's strong shouts directed willing hands. "Look 'ee sharp now, booys! ... Alaw boat haul,—haul, haul, haul!"

At this point, Angus Macdonell, carried away with enthusiasm, started a Jacobite air on his pipes and Crowgie thereafter, until she hit the water, competed with "Will ye nae come back again."

"Boat haulll!" he bellowed. "Haulll away!" Then, as she started to move faster, "Stump an' gooo! Look ee' sharp, booys. ... Stump an' go!"

The wave she gently pushed out ahead of her sent tinkling shell ice fanning out before her. At last she settled with great dignity on an even keel.

Dungie Crowgie stood for a time speechless as if struck dumb by the beauty of his own handiwork. "Aye ... look at her ... look at her, zur. She be a lovely thing!"

We worked for two more weeks, even with the help of the three Newfoundland seamen who had come up the lakes to help man her, before *Morning Song* was ready to sail. The masts had to be stepped, the two great sails fitted, blocks and running gear made fast, and a hundred and one other matters, enough to try the patience of any lubber like me.

I did find time to question Crowgie about the name. Said I, "I thought she was to have a Cornish name?"

"Iss, zur—and for a ship launched on May Day, what more Cornish than *Morning Song?* In my village the Morning Song is as much May Day as the hobby-horse and the wearin' o' flowers."

At last came the day when we were beating up the lake on her maiden voyage. There were white caps aplenty and a good wind. With a bone in her teeth *Morning Song* pitched gently in the icy waters, her great sails taut with strength and our Newfoundlanders, up for'ard, sending back to us snatches of a sea chanty.

"I reckon she's doin' close t' twelve knots," said Dungie Crowgie, with pride in his voice. "And 'tis a good blow. She'll stud out many a gale." He sucked on his fireless pipe and looked aloft to the head of the foremast. His huge hands inched over the giant tiller. "She's as gentle as a woman. . . . I be an impatient man, zur, . . . I can scarce wait t' see the look on the booy's face when he first sets eyes on her."

"David Tonkin?"

"Aye, an' he knows ships, mark ye. The booy was the best fisherman I had aboard the *Mary and Polly*. In any weather, clear or foul."

"You think a lot of David Tonkin," said I.

He put his barren pipe in his peajacket pocket and nodded. "As much as a son, zur. . . . Specially since his poor faither hold a house o' water in t' bal. His faither and I owned the *Mary and Polly* on shares."

"He was with his father when it happened?" I asked, recalling the incident in the deserted mine.

"Iss, zur. His faither shouted t' him t' run t' grass a second afore the water came athundering in. . . . They wuz down eighty fathoms."

Through my glass I spotted the scow working her way laboriously up the south coast. I wished them well and a fair wind for we needed the scow to carry the ore to *Morning Song*, for our draft would not let us too far up the Ontonagon River. The sooner the ore was loaded and the return journey started, the better. She would be a busy lady, this one, shuttling back and forth over three hundred miles of open water, carrying a king's ransom in copper gold on the first leg of its great water route to England.

It was a glorious day when we entered the mouth of the river, almost the first sun of summer touching all things with the matrix of warmth. I took it as a good omen; and the singing voice of the man with the lead for'ard called off the marks almost like a song of praise. As we dropped anchor Dungie Crowgie suggested a signal.

"They'd hear the cannon t' Wheal Pride," he said.

So Little Meg, shining bright in her lashings for'ard was loaded and fired. Her bark carried over to the hills and echoed back again before the puff of smoke had drifted lazily astern.

Crowgie stretched back his shoulders and rubbed his broad chest in satisfaction. "That'll bring 'em. . . . I can see 'em, scampering t' grass . . . and I'll lay 'ee the booy will outrun 'em."

We put the small boat overside and rowed up river against a current still swollen and murky from the spring run off.

When we passed the falls where the sturgeon ran in season the river current, churned by the falling tons of extra water, grew so strong that the man at the oars had to pull strongly to gain way. At last the landing took form and the figures on it.

"There be on'y four men there," said Crowgie in a disappointed voice. "An' I think one is the smithy fella."

As the boat pitched, I tried to size up the pile of ore. "It doesn't look like much copper, I must say. Not more than enough to ballast *Morning Song* for one trip. I thought they'd have ten times that much for loading."

"Look 'ee," said Crowgie, alarm taking the place of disappointment. "One of them is limpin' bad. . . . I tell 'ee there be something wrong. Here, give over one of the oars."

As we pulled in closer, the foreboding of Will Tragear's desolate figure came to meet us—no welcoming shout, just silence and dejected figures.

As they helped us out and made fast the boat, Will Tragear came to me, shaking his head sadly. "I be sorry, zur. . . . We be finished. We had a terrible accident. The copper is too tough an' the rock is agin' us."

Dungie Crowgie seized Will Tragear's right arm in his big fist. "David Tonkin? . . . Where is the booy, Will?"

The mine captain looked down. "It was more than a rock fall . . . the whole mountain seemed to slide in on us, like it moved sideways. We lost three men."

Crowgie shook Tragear, still grasping his arm. "An' the booy David, he was in it?"

Tragear nodded. "Iss, he was workin' big up t' face. The

other two, George Tangye an' Tom Triponey were closer t' day. Even so it took us near eight weeks to reach 'em; we buried them near t' Rock."

"An' David? . . . He's still in t' bal?"

"Aye . . . there must be thirty fathoms of rock t' move."

Like a man walking in his sleep, Dungie Crowgie turned away and started toward Wheal Pride.

"Dungie! Dungie Crowgie!" Will called after him. Dungie stopped and half turned. " 'Twas no my fault. It was well stulled. I was afeard o' the rock right from the start an' there were plenty o' stulls. We had lots o' timber for't. I dunno what it was, maybe the frost or thaw, I dunno; it just all shifted t' once wid out even a groan. Before God, Dungie, there was plenty o' timber, you must believe that, ask Petherick Kernick or Degary Tregarthen. . . ."

Crowgie held out his hand and took Will Tragear's. "I know, Will, I know it would be without asking t' others. . . . 'Twas an act of God, but why? Why?" Shaking his head as if to clear it, he continued his lonely walk to the mine, not pausing even at the two fresh graves as he passed.

But it was the end of Wheal Pride. Despite all the hopes, all the certainty, all the skill, it had come to a tragic, sudden end when it had scarce begun. Some awesome and fearful power greater than man had crushed us and pushed us aside. Truly, the sacred rocks of the Ojibway were indeed to be preserved.

The irony of it bit deep into the Cornish miners. " 'Twas the richness o' the copper beat us," said Will Tragear. " 'Tis too tough t' drill even enough for a good charge o' powder and when 'tis fired the blast goes round it. . . . Every bit o' that ore was chipped with gad and sledge, 'ee could na even spall it."

Only when I talked of the dull, gray copper on the north shore did their spirits rise. "Aye . . . sounds like some o' our best ore in Cornwall. 'Tis gray as lead."

Then, fearful that I might have raised their hopes too high, I made mention of the hard rock that went with it.

"An' praise be t' God," was his fervent reply. "We belong working hard rock."

I had a look at Degary Tregarthen's leg, but there was naught I could do. Falling rocks had broken it and they had set and splinted it. It had been foreshortened and the limp he would bear with him. He only grinned when I told him. "Iss, zur. It'll be right for t' work in t' bal with my long leg down t' stope and my short one high."

We started at once to dismantle, even before the scow arrived. The forge had to be taken down; iron, powder, and tools packed; and I thought it useful to take doors and sash. So, in a short time, the works and home of Wheal Pride became but a skeleton in the wilderness marking the determination and failure of man.

Once the ore was down the hold of *Morning Song*, I was determined to set sail at once with the four miners and sufficient tools to start afresh on the north shore, leaving the forge and other salvaged material to be loaded and brought down in the scow. The night before our scheduled departure the four miners came to me with a strange request.

"We wish a sarvice of 'ee, zur," started Petherick Kernick.

"It be for the poor booy . . ." broke in Dungie Crowgie, who then looked to Will Tragear to explain.

" 'Ee zee, zur . . . we be all Wesleyans. David Tonkin's poor faither, well, he was a good man, but a stubborn man, and he would no leave the Church like the rest of us and the booy David said what was good enough for his faither was good enough for him. Mind 'ee, zur, we be God-fearin' men and we haven't nowt against the teachin' o' the Church but. . . ." He floundered for a moment and I held up my hand to stop. I had heard from Alexander Baxter of the work of the Reverend John Wesley in Cornwall and how the miners had followed him, as much in protest against the mine owners, whose otherwise unsuccessful sons had taken over many parishes as priests, as for any other reason. I recalled also that neither press gangs for the navy, troops, nor imprisonment had stopped the movement. I let him know I knew of these things.

"Thank 'ee, zur." He went on with more enthusiasm, "Now we wondered, zur . . . if 'ee had a Book o' Prayer, if 'ee'd do the Sarvice in t' bal . . . for David Tonkin like."

I hesitated, but only for a moment when I looked at the four serious, expectant faces before me. "There is a Prayer Book in the sea chest of *Morning Song*. I'll have it brought. Do you suggest the morning, before we sail?"

"Aye, zur . . . thank 'ee, zur. We be grateful to 'ee, Cap'n," they chorused.

On the morrow I was abroad early. I brushed off my coat, put on a clean stock, and enlisted the aid of Aaron Hill, the Mohawk blacksmith, who was also by way of being a devout Anglican.

We clambered up the steep hill to the opening of the shaft that thrust into the cliff side. The sun did not penetrate far, but the miners had preceded me and on each side right up to the wall of rock that blocked the end stood a row of candles, quiet and still and flickering in the deadness of the air.

The four miners were a shadowy group scarce out of the sunlight. I moved forward until my feet were all but on the first of the rock-fall and thrust my hat tight under my left elbow. Aaron Hill, close by my side, held a candle so that its light fell on the pages and I began "The Order for the Burial of the Dead."

"I am the resurrection and the life, saith the Lord; he that believeth in me, though he were dead, yet shall he live; and whosoever liveth and believeth in me shall never die. . . ."

The words I spoke, and even Aaron Hill's responses, had

so strange a quality as they echoed back from the rocky, deathly cavern that though I live a century I shall never forget. Not that they were unfamiliar, for I had heard them before, when the bodies of an officer and three seamen were committed to the deep after we beat off a French privateer on the way out, and many times on the hillside at Bushy Run as I lay waiting for the surgeon's knife while the chaplain buried my comrades and Royal Highlanders. Even so, the memory of that Cornish lad we left in Wheal Pride will never quite fade.

As I walked out, I passed the four miners as they were kneeling. The sun struck me with a moment's blindness and its warmth brought with it the promise of a strong ship waiting at anchor. This, I reminded myself, was but the first skirmish and there were other fields to be fought over and, with God's help, won.

The news we carried to Fort Gloucester spread like a pall over the entire company. The loss of the three miners was tragic enough but the mockery of the mountain of pure copper within our grasp yet, by its very pureness, made too tough to crush was a double blow that took strength to counter. But Alexander Henry was no man to quit; within hours, our new plans were in operation. It reminded me of the principal of remounting a horse as quickly as possible after a bad toss.

We did not even unload the copper from the hold, but retained it as a ballast for the short run of sixty miles or so up the rugged north shore to our first discovery. With some irony, I recalled my disappointment at the first sight of the gray copper ore. Now in the very truth I knew that all that glitters is not gold.

It had a magic effect on the Cornishmen. Gone was their bewilderment at their failure to handle the richest and purest copper the world had yet seen. Now they were on known ground, working with metal they knew. As if to prove themselves from the shame of failure they labored from daylight to dark, eating their way into the hard rock inch by inch, foot by foot. Nor did it take them long to find the lode, a rich vein that measured four feet in width.

With two men on the sledge hammers and one holding the iron "needle," giving it a half-turn after each smashing rhythmic blow, they drilled in for the powder. We ran out of goose quills for fuses and the lighter quills, even from the largest wild geese and lake gulls we could get, gave Will Tragear concern. "Semmen t' me," he'd say, shaking his head, "they make a tam fuz. . . . I'm afeard they're too almighty quick. Stand well back, booys."

But they seemed to do the job. First the sinew-straining task of sledge and drill, the tamping of the charge, then the warning, "Fire!" and feet of ore would come sliding free.

By day's end, they were too body sore and weary to wish anything save a good meal and bed, and the crude shelter we had rigged as temporary sleeping quarters bothered them not one wit. I had moved in an Indian family and engaged the women to prepare food and the men easily secured enough game for meat, an appreciated change from the inevitable dried peas and corn.

Before I left the new mine for Fort Gloucester, to arrange for the transfer of the forge and to unload our ore, Will Tragear took me aside to put a confidence in my ear. "Semmens t' me, zur . . . this be silver country. I've found nowt but I veels it in me bones."

I told him of Lieutenant Nordbergh's opinions in respect to silver and his find of a piece of rich quartze. The old miner nodded.

"Iss zur . . . it be hereabouts. Will 'ee take back some o' this ore, and some o' that lead ore, and try it for silver in t' furnace? If there be any silver in't, then there must be silver hereabouts . . . an' a good bunch, I'll wage there be."

I cast my eyes about over the rocky crags and dwarfed trees. "Even so," I said, "And how would one go about finding it?"

Tragear looked at me out of the corner of his eye and grinned. "Now, zur . . . we be Cornish miners, if it be here ve vill vind it. I've been thinking on't and lookin' for the right sprigs."

And press as I might, I could not then get Will Tragear to explain himself further. But he had two small bags of selected ore for me before I sailed eastward. By the time we reached the River of St. Marys my bones too had begun to feel silver!

18

With urgent routine matters in the saddle, my impatience to get at the assay furnace with the ore samples had to be curb-reined for a time.

But at last came a free evening and, with my notebook propped open on an empty powder-keg, I meticulously followed directions in the preparation of the black reducing flux, measuring the tartar, niter, and borax for both it and the refining flux as if my very life depended on a thimbleful, this way or that.

The melting of the ore and stirring of the molten mass, so that it would not lump, until sulphurous flames no longer flickered, took long enough, but it was the hour of waiting for it to stand in the vial that seemed like an age. I tried the copper first and my hands shook with excitement when I saw the white matter take form. I went over my notes again. It could be lead, I had not thought of that! More black flux and more evaporation in the cupel. At last I held it before me—silver, pure silver! So small an amount that it would be lost in a priming pan, but silver it was.

Carefully, checking and thrice checking, as if I were counting gold sovereigns, I worked out the proportion of my speck of silver to the copper ore. It came out at fifteen ounces to the ton. I did better with the lead ore; in it, the silver ran forty ounces to the ton.

What was it Will Tragear had said? "If there be any silver in it at all . . . there be a lode, a houseful, of silver hereabouts." Even so, I thought, how does he propose to find it? The answer to that question must await my return to the mine.

"Refining gold, Vere?" So wrapped up had I been in my excited thoughts that I had not seen Alexander Henry walking toward the furnace in the dusk.

"No, sir," I said, with a bit of boasting in my voice. "Silver."

He lifted my notes off the powder-keg and sat down. I thought he looked tired, and put it down to the journey from Cadotte's Fort. But I had good medicine for this and I poured out my story of the silver as fast as my tongue could wag.

"What we sorely need now is more miners, so that Will Tragear can be spared to lead the search for the silver lode," I pointed out, my enthusiasm at white pitch.

Alexander Henry looked at me for a time, as if pondering what he should say; and as if what he must say was distaseful, he sighed. I felt deflated by his lack of enthusiasm and a little irritated.

"I am afraid, Vere," he said at last, "that we may be lucky to keep the miners we have. And as for the silver, we may not be able to wait for its finding."

My face must have worn a look of disbelief and mighty disappointment. Mr. Henry pressed on quickly with his bad tidings.

"Baxter has just had word from London that the copper market is in a serious way. The price of ore has dropped to six pounds a ton, and is still dropping. Some of the deeper mines in Cornwall have been forced to shut down."

"But why?" I exploded. "I thought that good copper ore was in short supply."

He shook his head. "We don't know why, yet . . . but we know 'tis so."

"And how will it affect us?"

He shrugged. "If the price stays down or goes lower, it will mean that it will cost us more than we will get for it. Under these circumstances, we could expect no more financial interest on the part of London."

"You mean . . . you mean . . . we would have to close down?"

"Aye, I'm afraid so."

The whole thing seemed so unfair. Now at last we had a good rich mine and a good ship to move the ore. It had not been easy. It had cost men's lives.

Alexander Henry put his hand on my shoulder. "Come now, m'lad. Don't look so glum. Who knows, perhaps the price of copper will go up, perhaps it's already up. And then again, perhaps you'll find your lode of silver."

But I was not to be lifted and we walked to our quarters in silence. Mr. Henry took the kettle off the hod, filled it with water and hung it on the fire-crane before he spoke again.

"Think not that I don't know how you feel, Vere. I've stood where you are standing more than once."

He got the tea-canister off the shelf. "I will just say one more thing." He stood facing me, with the lid open. "No matter what happens, remember this, it is not defeat, only a setback. We have found for the world a great storehouse of mineral worth, and shown them how to get it. When they'll need it, they'll take it . . . and need it they will, sooner or later. This is a great country, so rich it beggars the imagination to describe it. That is why I have long since decided to devote my life to it."

He measured the tea carefully into the pot and poked the fire under the kettle. "Now, lad. How about a cup of good strong tea?"

Courage rubs off. I knew that his entire savings from years of business in the fur trade had gone into our Society of Adventurers, but not once did he make mention of it, then or ever. I began casting about in my mind as to how we might best go about finding silver. He chose to change the subject entirely.

"Oh, by the way, you'll be interested to know that your regiment has gone east."

"No! You mean they've left 'Mackinac and Detroit?"

"Aye, the 10th Foot has relieved them."

"And where are the Royal Americans posted to? Florida, I suppose, to relieve the other battalion?"

He shook his head. "They are headed for New York. Some say for a foreign posting."

I shot forward in my chair. "But that's ridiculous! We were raised for service in America. We did most of our recruiting here."

He grinned. "Come, come, Ensign Bayard, do you expect *me*, a civilian, to explain the actions of Whitehall? I did hear 'twas because trouble in the American colonies is hotting up and, if it came to armed rebellion, Whitehall would like to be quite sure which side their regiments were on." He made a face then, and it was not the bitterness of his tea.

I snorted, but before I could give full rein to my tongue, he raised his hand. "Don't fret, Vere. No affront to the Royal Americans intended, I assure you."

Perhaps this news served to increase my determination to find the silver lode and I was off for the mine as soon as the last bucket of ore had been slung overside. But I'll not gainsay the departure of my regiment left a strangely vacant place in my heart. Though they were a week's journey distant, I had grown accustomed to thinking my comrades were near by.

When we dropped anchor off Pointe aux Mines, as the men had named it, I could see what the miners had accomplished. A great mound of ore rose by the lakeside. The whole Indian family, with the exception of Master Jimmy, who sat on a rock contemplating the operation, was hard at work breaking the ore into small pieces with hammers.

Will Tragear, full of confidence and pride, explained how he had recruited the help at the mine head. As we watched the women and children handling the ore, he said, "As vine a bunch o' bal maidens as I ever zaw. Zaves us time t' bring more ore t' grass." I had heard about the "bal maidens" of Cornwall and how the children as well as women were employed for this work at the mines. The Ojibways seemed to enjoy their new-found employment as much as the miners enjoyed having them, for they laughed and chattered constantly as they broke the ore on other rock that Will referred to as "anvons."

But of our new found labor force, I would say Jimmy himself was the happiest. He lay back on a rock, getting the full warmth of the sun. He was watching, I take it with some pride, his wife and children participate in this latest fad of the white man, the making of little rocks out of big ones. "Jimmy" was, of course, not his real name. His name was Kewet-ah-uhm, difficult for the English tongue, and its English translation, "He Who Goes Around the Point in a Canoe," a trifle cumbersome. As his first effort at the English language was "By JEMMY KNEE!" Master Jimmy he was from that day on and, of course, his good wife, was Mistress Jimmy.

For these many years, ever since they had taken him in and nursed him back to health during that bad winter in the nor'west, Jimmy and his family had been close friends of Alexander Henry. Jimmy's left leg had been so badly crushed in a deadfall trap that he could no longer face a winter in his hunting grounds so they wintered at the Falls of St. Marys under Alexander Henry's patronage, in return for the provision of fresh meat and fish and the sewing and snowshoe making of the women.

We walked into the mine, and I was amazed at the progress. It was nearly ten fathoms to the face where Dungie Crowgie and Petherick Kernick wielded great sledges as Tregarthen held and turned the drill. The dust-filled air brought me to coughing. The miners stopped work to welcome me, rubbing their hands over their sweat- and dust-caked bodies, for they wore ought else but heavy trousers. The caked dust, that made their eyeballs gleam white, could not hide from their faces the pride of accomplishment. How, thought I, am I to tell such men that their labors may well be in vain. Cowardly or no, I decided to put off the matter until evening.

It was then I became aware of a shadow. A very small shadow that seemed draped with powder-flasks, quill-fuse boxes, and extra candles. Will Tragear noticed my attention.

"Iss zur. Booy! Come and meet d' grass Cap'n."

The little shadow detached itself from the rock stoping and came forward. It was Jimmy's youngest son. At first glance he looked about eight, but he could have added a couple of years to that. He seemed almost to hop forward and his head turned quickly this way and that. The three miners grinned broadly.

"Dis is Penashe, Cap'n," explained Will Tragear. "When he grows he's goin' t' be a Cornish miner."

Penashe! How well named! "Little Bird." It took me back to my own boyhood. I remembered watching a falcon's nest on a Swiss mountainside, and the young birds, hawk-eyed, alert. Penashe, his bright eyes wide over a hooked nose, moved so. But I could see his eyes were all for Will Tragear, not for me.

The miners went back to their bone-jarring drilling and the air, charged heavy with rock-dust, started me coughing again. "Let's get t' grass, zur," said Will. Once out in the sunlight, he lost no time in seeking information on the ore assay. I told him.

He nodded confidently. "Aye, I knew it. 'Ee can count on it, there be a houseful o' silver hereabouts."

"And how?" said I, "do you propose to find it? Time is not on our side, Will."

"How zo, zur?"

I told him of the falling copper prices, even to the closing of deep mines in Cornwall. He said not a word for some time but walked back toward his shelter and I with him. The boy Penashe followed at a respectful distance.

"This be terrible news, zur," he said at last. "For me?" he shrugged his big shoulders. "It be not zo bad, me wife is dead and the children grow'd. But the booys? That be another matter, zur. Degary Tregarthen has twelve children an' Petherick Kernick, ten."

"But we have no definite information yet, Will," said I. "We don't even know what mines are closed."

He shook his head. " 'Ee don't, zur, but we do, the booys and me. 'Ee zee, zur, we know the owners. Semmens t' me they don't care a tinker's damn if our children starve or no, let a good bal water down fathoms deep they will an' put good booys out o' work, if they can't make the money out o' it they expect to."

There was a deep bitterness here I had not suspected. "Well, Will," said I, faking a lightness of heart, "the answer is to find your lode of silver. How do we do that?"

"I'll show 'ee, zur," he replied. He went into the shelter and came out with a stick in his hand. The boy, Penashe, came closer and squatted, his black eyes bright and alert. "Dis be it, zur!" He held the stick up proudly. It was forked and about a yard long, thin, almost willowy.

"Mind 'ee, 'tis not as good as iv it were from a peach tree or 'n apple, but it'll work."

I took it in my hands. At first, I thought it was a naturally forked branch but then I saw it had been spliced at the fork with some fibrous material.

"Green oak shoots they be," explained Will. " 'Twas Penashe that helped me find 'em."

The Indian boy had moved in close with the appearance of the Magic Stick. He beamed at the mention of his name.

"Here, zur. I'll show you how it works. 'Tis fixed for gold, have 'ee a gold sovereign?"

I shook my head. Then I remembered the small Swiss goldpiece I carried for luck. I half feared only a coin of the realm would do. "I have a Swiss gold coin, if that'll work."

"Aye."

He took it and placed it under his right foot, which he advanced about a foot in front of the other. Under his left foot he put a copper penny. Then he took a fork of the branch in each hand, palm up, the single stem pointing directly in front of him. He closed his fists about the branch, strongly yet almost tenderly.

Suddenly the stem turned downward, pointing straight at his right foot! He opened his fists, holding the branch, or allowing it to rest, on his finger tips. It returned to its normal straightness. Then he reversed the coins, putting the gold coin under his left foot to the rear. Again he held the rod. Instead of pointing to his right foot as before, the stem turned backward to point to his left foot!

Penashe's eyes were so big they seemed to occupy his whole small face. I expect mine would have been too, had I not been so full of excitement and unspoken hope.

"But what about silver?" I asked. "Will it work on silver?"

"Aye, zur. But it works on gold the strongest; after that copper, then silver, then tin, then lead."

He showed me where the rod had been carefully bored

and a small plug fitted. "I put filings in there—iron, lead, a bit o' silver, bone, an' charcoal, thet helps the draw to gold an' copper. When we go lookin' for silver I'll take out the iron, lead, and silver and replace them wid copper and maybe," he looked at me slyly, "maybe a filin' or two o' gold."

My mind raced ahead like fox fire. We would make more rods. There were the miners, the crew of the *Morning Star* and Jimmy's family, how many children were there? Six? Seven? Why, I thought, we can make a skirmish line long enough to cover a hundred yards at one sweep.

"May I try it?" I asked, anxious to get the feeling of it.

"Iss, zur. . . . But don't 'ee be disappointed, not all men can get a divinin' rod to work for 'em."

Patiently he went through the procedure. Not to grasp too hard, nor yet too weakly. "Like 'ee was maister but not greedy." And the mind must be right, too—perhaps there was the rub. "Nothing on the mind, zur, nothing. Jist let your mind sort of drift away like a mist afore the sun." I tried, I tried again, and again.

" 'Tis no use, zur," nodding his head as if he had known all along. "There not be many that t' rod will work for."

"The others," I suggested, in the hope that it was a native Cornish art. "Crowgie, Kernick? . . ."

He shook his head. Then, I thought, we must relieve Will Tragear at the mine, put Crowgie in charge, so that he can spend all his time on the hunt for silver.

Tragear agreed, but with one reservation. "I'll do de firin' myself," he said firmly. "I would not ask t' booys t' use them tam fuzs—tricky as a fox on the run, dey are. Dey can get de powder holes drilled an' I can blow enough t' once t' keep 'em busy for a day avter."

On the morrow, work went well. The crew made a good start on the back-bending work of loading heavy ore into the *Morning Song*, and the ring of the sledges on steel hardly checked all morning as the miners drilled powder holes to be blown in the afternoon.

Tragear had blown all but one of the drilled holes when I entered the shaft and a great mass of rock and ore lay ready for the miners to move out. I watched while he measured the powder from the flask, the sleeve at the top of the flask serving to pour the black grains into the hole. He emptied one flask and gave it back to Penache in exchange for a full one. He only measured twice from the full one, then laid it on a rock brought down by a previous explosion. The boy gave him fuses, then the hole was carefully tamped in. He sent Penache back to daylight, then looked at me. I moved along the rock wall to a safe distance as Tragear reached for his candle.

"Fire!"

It seemed to me that the miner's loud warning had scarce reached my ears when the whole end of the shaft moved out of the darkness toward me. A terrible, devouring roar came with it, and flame and dense smoke and dust that seemed to take over the world. For a moment that seemed an age I was stunned, then I remembered the all-but-full powder flask on the rock; perhaps the sleeve top had not been replaced and it would go up in the flame. My lungs could not bear the acrid smoke and dust. I went to my hands and knees, working my way over the fallen rock until I touched Tragear's body. I inched it weakly back in the shaft, every effort shortened my breathing until it seemed my chest was in a vise. I can't make it, I thought. Then I realized there were other forms beside me, touching me, moving backward with me and the dead weight of Will Tragear's moaning form. The Cornishmen had come in for their bottoms captain.

They laid him gently in the full sun and, still retching from the fumes and smoke, we ministered to him as best we could. It was all too obvious he had taken the full charge in the face. Indeed, there did not appear to be much flesh left, certainly not whole flesh. He began to bleed profusely from a number of cuts on his naked, blackened torso. Flying, jagged rock had cut his body worse than grape-shot. After a time he became restless, even tried to raise himself to his elbows. "Lie still, Will. It's all right, but we want to stop the bleeding and you help if you lie still."

My words did not serve to quiet him. "Dungie Crowgie ... Dungie, I want'ee," he rasped hoarsely.

"I be here, Will ... right beside 'ee."

"Am I up t' grass?"

"Aye."

"Is the sun shinin'?"

"Iss, it do shine right in 'ee face, Will."

He began to struggle and throw himself from side to side. "Me eyes are gone! My God, my God, why did 'Ee take my eyes? Let me die ... let me die."

Gradually his voice grew weaker, and he lapsed into merciful unconsciousness. I was forced to a quick decision. Obviously the man was too seriously injured to risk moving, let alone a long journey. On the other hand, it would take two—yes, perhaps three—weeks to bring the surgeon in from Fort 'Mackinac. But the latter was the only decision I could make. Meanwhile we must do all in our power to hold fast to the thread of life.

I picked two strong young Canadian canoemen, who were half the crew of the *Morning Song*, and dispatched them for the surgeon in one of Jimmy's light bark canoes. I knew once they reached Cadotte's Fort, untired men would take their places and that between here and the River of St. Marys their paddles would be scarce out of the water.

It was Jimmy and his family who saved Will Tragear's life and not the surgeon, and I have the surgeon's own word for that. Before the sun set that day, they had a summer lodge up on the spot. A dome-shaped wigwam with a frame of lashed poles, a roofing of birchbark and walls of mats woven from bullrushes to keep out chill night air. The floor was quickly covered with cedar, held in place by rush mats with a deep, soft bed of moss for the torn body of the unconscious miner.

It was eighteen days before the surgeon got there and the *Morning Song* had long since sailed with her load of ore. During this whole time, day and night, some member of the Indian family was in the sick lodge. They dressed his wounds constantly with fir balsam and washed them with a sweet-fern tea. His eyes were treated with scrapings from the root of the maple tree which, as Jimmy explained to me, had to be taken from the sun-rise side.

On the seventh day, consciousness returned to the injured man and he was fed meat broth with special herbs. I don't think he would have taken of it had it not been for Penashe, who squatted hours on end beside him, for all the world like a young hawk perched disconsolate in the rain.

"Aye, yourrr a lucky mon . . . a verry lucky mon," was Surgeon-Captain John Macdonnell's opinion after his quick examination. "I dinna think I could 'a saved your life. But ye've had guid medicine and care, laddie, and they've pulled you through."

"My eyes, doctor. . . . Will I ever see again?"

The surgeon shook his head, but motioned for the candles to be held closer so he could examine the eyes more thoroughly.

"No, laddie . . . y' will nae see again. The orbs ha' been burned by flame and the powder blown into them."

Will Tragear turned his head away. "Let me die then. In God's name let me die. If 'ee don't I shall take my own braave way up t' Heaven."

"Och! That's no the way for a mon to talk. Ye're still a braw lad, and with plenty to live for."

"It no be livin'," replied Will Tragear, "Being a useless creature, a burden to 'ee's brothers, takin' charity all the days of 'ee's life."

The next day, before I returned to Fort Gloucester in the surgeon's canoe, I tried my best to cheer him with thoughts of home.

"In a few weeks you will be strong enough to travel, Will," I pointed out. "Then we will arrange for your passage home."

He turned his sightless eyes toward me. "Thank 'ee, zur. But I will not be goin' home. I've been thinkin' anyway I shall never see the gorse by the roadsides yellow in spring, or t' sea breaking heavy aginst the red rock."

As I left the lodge I saw the Magic Stick standing in the corner with Penashe watching over it as if fearful I might demand it.

Surgeon-Captain Macdonnell was troubled when he left his patient. "Och, laddie," he confided to me. "We can bleed a mon, or cut off his leg, or sew up his wounds, or set his airm, but when it comes to a mon's mind . . . we ha' t' leave that to th' Almighty. That mon doesn't need his sight, he needs a reason to live, the poor devil."

My heart was as heavy as the ore the Cornishmen were carrying out of the shaft and I felt grievously the injustice of fate. If, as the good surgeon said, a troubled mind could only be left to the Almighty then I thought my sore heart must be left there too.

19

The tall spars of *Morning Song*, resting quietly at anchor in the basin off Fort Gloucester, spelled trouble to me. I knew she should have been unloaded long since and cleared for the mine. Even when I set foot ashore a foreboding came to meet me, for all the warmth of the summer sun.

I found Alexander Henry and Baxter, coats off and hard at work in the hot and tiny office.

"Thank God you're back," said Mr. Henry, looking up from the paper-strewn table as I stepped across the sill. "Now perhaps we'll get some order to this paper work and accounting."

He inquired of me concerning Will Tragear's condition and when I told him of the surgeon's report regarding his eyes he shook his head sadly. "Poor fellow, he will need all the courage he can muster. We'll have to do something for him."

"The miners contributed to a blinded man from their pay. It amounts to about ten shillings a month, I think. I fear we have enough financial responsibility already," Mr. Baxter put in.

Alexander Henry straightened up and looked at his partner for a moment of silence, as if considering whether or not the matter should be disposed of now. Apparently he thought it should. "I quite agree; it's a question of responsibility," he said. "And I happen to think that responsibility to a blinded man, and to the widows of the men killed, is a responsibility taking precedent over others. As I shall myself be a main contributor, I shall have to insist that this be done."

Mr. Baxter did not even look up from his work, let alone reply, so I thought it well to fill the silence.

"I can't understand about the accounts," said I, addressing myself to Mr. Henry. "They were up-to-date and in order when I left."

"Aye, I know," he paused for a moment. "But you see, Vere, this is really a final accounting—we are going out of business. Perhaps I should more correctly say, we are out of business."

I looked at Mr. Baxter and my face must have shown disbelief. He nodded and added, "I'm afraid it's all too true. I have been instructed to dispose of the ship and equipment and to pay off our debts."

"But in Heaven's name why?" I exploded. "Why now, when we are in to rich ore and moving it well?"

Baxter shrugged his shoulders. "Two reasons. First the drop in copper prices to as low as five pounds sterling a ton. This is forcing even Cornish mines to close. The Anglesey mines in Wales are most to blame. Ever since the Parys Mountain find, they've been flooding the market with cheap, low-grade ore, and it's right next door to Welsh coal. That's reason enough, isn't it? We can't compete with copper at that price, no matter how good our ore is."

"But," said I, "you said there were *two* reasons."

"Ah, yes, so I did. Well, I suppose the second reason is America."

"What's wrong with that? They knew it was an American adventure in the first place."

"Of course, of course. But the Society is much concerned over the spread of trouble in the Colonies and if it should come to open revolt they would sooner not have their money invested here."

Now it had come, it all seemed like a bad dream from which I hoped to awake any moment. Through the window I could see the *Morning Song* riding at anchor.

"But, sir," I said, wheeling on Alexander Henry. "Surely you will keep the ship. So often you've said how she could be of use to you in the fur trade, the more so now that you are trading more in the Nor'west."

He smiled and shook his head. "Believe me, I would give my right arm to have her, Vere. But it cannot be. It will take every penny I have to meet our obligations and I know half a dozen of my rivals in the trade who would be delighted to pay good hard money for her."

Mr. Baxter made a sound as close to a snort as he could manage. "It's a lot of poppycock, Alex, just sheer nonsense. I've told you we can arrange it between us."

Alexander Henry looked at Baxter calmly as he picked up his hat. "I thank you, I know you mean me well. But there will be no 'arranging' as you call it. She will be sold for the very best price we can get—and that's final." At the door he turned to me. "After you've supped, Vere, perhaps you'd check those figures for me."

After he had gone there was a long silence. "That Master Henry of yours is a very stubborn man, pon my soul he is," said Mr. Baxter. "He's just standing like an oaf in his own light."

That was spark to my powder. "He may stand in his own light but at least he takes care not to stand in others' light. Nor," I added as my temper exploded, "would he steal even a single candle."

Food had no attraction for me that night and I was soon back at work although, in truth, I had little stomach for that either. The candles had not burned far before Alexander Henry came in. He fussed through the papers for a time but obviously his mind too was on other things.

"It will take us a few weeks to finish things off," he said, half talking to himself as he pushed aside a packet of accounts. "I am sending up a Montreal canoe to bring down the miners. Do you think Tragear will be strong enough to travel in a week's time?"

I agreed that he might be. "But he did seem firm in his mind that he would not return to Cornwall."

"Perhaps when he gets over the shock of losing his sight he will change his thinking. Particularly when he realizes that his friends are leaving and it would be so much better if he travelled with them." He pondered the matter for a time. "If he insists on staying in this country he could stay on with the Jimmy family. I would see that Jimmy was taken care of for the extra mouth to feed, and he would not find it too lonely in the winters at Cadotte's."

We dealt with a few items of pending business but he finally threw in his hand. "I can't put my mind to it tonight," he said, and began pacing the floor. "Tell me, Vere, have you given thought to your own future?" I shook my head in reply.

"I had hoped you might change your mind about the fur trade. I would like to have you with me. More than that, this country needs you, and men like you."

"Thank you, Sir. For a long time now I have felt *I* need this country, but the fur trade has little attraction for me."

"I'm sorry, but I appreciate your honesty. Now that the mining venture is finished I shall push harder north and westward. If I can get men and canoes I would like to winter on the Great Prairie with the Assiniboines; it's a rich country."

"I find it hard to believe—I mean, the mining being finished," I said, more than a little sorry for myself.

"Cheer up, lad. It's not really finished, it's scarce begun. Look at it as a postponement. But I know how you feel, it's really the ending of a long-cherished dream that hurts most. Take me, now—for years, my dream has been to visit England and I was certain the mining venture would make it possible." He shrugged his shoulders. "Well, the dream has not gone, I face the disappointment of delay."

I lay awake most of the night trying to chart my best course but I ended up without any course. An ensign would starve on half pay, that was the only fact I was sure of. I could go back to Switzerland, but a bank appealed even less to me now than it did six years ago; besides it was like accepting defeat, and I could not keep my mind off all that copper and, more especially, the promise of silver.

The days passed slowly, each one filled with the painful task contingent upon the burial of a dream so long striven for. My own plans would not form in my brain, strive as I might.

So it was, until the tin kettle crossed my path.

It was evening, and as I was walking back to my quarters I heard the sound of an argument and an Indian voice raised in anger. I recognized one of Mr. Henry's clerks. The poor man was trying to placate the Indian, obviously without success. I stopped, for the Indian had a tin kettle in his hand and it looked as if he might use it on the unfortunate clerk. But finally, with an expression of disgust, he threw the pot away and walked off.

"What was all that about?" I asked the clerk.

He grinned foolishly. "It's those tin kettles again. They like them fine in trade, or did. All bright and shiny and light to carry." He shrugged. "I suppose the truth of the matter is that they won't stand up to use on an open fire, they burn through and then they bring them back, demanding copper or brass like we used to have."

Copper, I thought. The irony of it took hold of me. I picked up the discarded kettle with it's burned-out, black bottom and carried it to my quarters. I sat it on the table beside my coat and stared at it. A blackened, burned-out object that set my thoughts on edge where there had been none for days.

In the end I took both it and my thoughts to Alexander Henry. He saw the old tin kettle before I opened my mouth.

"I know, I know," he said. "In no time at all they become useless. And can you imagine what that means in the bush or on the trail in the winter? I will order no more tin kettles. But, on the other hand, how can I go back to copper or brass kettles? You know we had to give them up because of cost, mostly freight charges. I figured it out the other day that freight charges from Montreal on one copper kettle is about the same as charges on fifteen of the tin ones. And they are, of course, one of the most useful and important trade items so far as the Indian is concerned."

I put the tin kettle on the table and sat down. "I think I have the answer. Why not make the kettles here? We're certainly not short of copper."

Mr. Henry looked at me and smiled. "And do you know how to make copper kettles in numbers?" he asked.

"No, but I could learn."

He nodded thoughtfully. "It would probably mean smelting the ore. And there is no coal."

"I've thought of that. But I remember one of the Cornishmen telling me there was a shortage of trees some place in Cornwall due to the making of charcoal for smelters. Well, there is no shortage of trees here and won't be for many a year."

He got up and paced the floor. Eventually his silence caused me concern. "And, sir," I added. "It's not only the Indian trade I had in mind. There must be nearly two thousand settlers in Illinois country and as many at Detroit and at Niagara, and their numbers are growing. They all need such things."

He nodded. He stopped and stared out of the window for a time. "Vere, I think you have an excellent idea but it will take time, and no little courage to work out. For one thing it may take a year or more of study and even apprenticeship to gain sufficient knowledge."

"I've thought of that too.... I will manage."

He came and sat down, looking at me thoughtfully. "You can't do it on an ensign's half pay. And for now I can't help. In a year yes, but not now. In a year or more I should be in a position to help you get started in your industry, at least in a small way."

I thanked him for his offer. "So far as the next year is concerned, or until I have finished my schooling, I will find something to keep me going. What does worry me is where to start, how to go about it."

Mr. Henry smiled. "I've been thinking of that," he said. "And I think I know just the man to turn to, but for the life of me I can't recall his name. He's a silversmith in Boston, and a good one, has a shop near the head of Dr. Clark's wharf."

"Well, sir," I said with a grin. "I hardly had anything so fancy as silversmithing in mind."

"Oh, the fellow is more than a silversmith, he's pewterer and a dentist, among other things. Struck me as sort of a man willing to try anything new if he thought it worth while. The last time I was there was with my uncle who was getting new teeth; fact of the matter his, his false teeth are as famous as his goldsmithing. It's irritating not to recall a name. Sign of age, Vere."

He jumped to his feet. "Jove! That's it! There is a Vere in it. LeVere, no . . . deVere, no . . . Revere, that's it. Revere, Paul Revere. He's just your man, most likely has the information himself, or books on the subject. If not, he'll know who has. I'll give you a letter of introduction."

As the busy days passed, it became obvious to me that Alexander Henry was as enthusiastic about my kettle-manufacturing plans as I was, a fact that gave me much comfort. I was not unduly worried about the problem of finding employment the meanwhile but it did harrass me some, for I am the sort of fellow who likes to know the morrow's march route with some certainty. Little did I know that the answer was already on the way by military courier through Niagara and Detroit.

I did not know the seal and tore open the cover with some apprehension, for the place of origin, "Fort George," was outside my ken. It was from John Nordbergh, a Captain now and Commandant of Fort George on the southern end of Lake George, which he described as "not a pretentious command, being not much larger than your Fort Gloucester, but a happy one and not too far distant from my place in Connecticut."

I scanned the letter quickly, separating the meat from the bones. "I have news of the collapse of the copper market," he wrote, "and fear as to its effect on the Adventurers into Superior. It has therefore occurred to me that you might find it opportune to take advantage of the situation the regiment now finds itself in.

"The 1st Battalion is on duty in Jamaica. The 2nd, now being brought up to strength, is to garrison the West Indies Islands of Barbados, Grenada, and Tobago. I have no doubt that this will be a surprise to you, knowing that the Royal Americans were raised for service on this continent. As you can imagine, the soldiers recruited here viewed the matter with some apprehension. Parliament, however, with

God-like omniscience, has settled the legal aspect by declaring the Isles of the Indies to be part of North America!

"Your patron, fellow Swiss and fellow Canadian, General Sir Frederick Haldimand, is now Colonel-Commandant of the 2nd Battalion and Lieutenant-Colonel George Etherington has been given command. John Christie has been made captain and given a Company in which there is a lieutenancy available. All three of these gentlemen would welcome your return to the regiment in this rank.

"I know not your present situation at Lake Superior, nor of your immediate plans, but it is not improbable that the lieutenancy might interest you at this time. Moreover, a year's service in the Caribbean might serve to drive the fever from your aching, aged bones.

"I expect the battalion will take sea transport from Boston. If you are so minded, I presume you will travel down from Montreal. This being the case, I shall with double pleasure look forward to a visit from you at this place."

Bless you, John Nordbergh! And all my good comrades! I could have leaped from joy. Now for certain I would see Master Revere in Boston, and with a year's pay assured, my worries on that score had fled like a hare before greyhounds.

But more. I would be serving under George Etherington and John Christie. Etherington had commanded at 'Mackinac when Pontiac's warriors had by treachery put most to bloody knife and Christie had seared his own flesh on roof shakes at Fort Presqu'ile set aflame by fire arrows. They were men of this country, of my country.

My country! How strange. I had never given such thought to it before. But it had become, in very truth, my country.

In good heart, I reread the letter in comfortable leisure. There was one item of news that I read with ill-assorted feelings. "I have word from London that the old Ranger, who had travelled thence after his acquittal by the court in Montreal, has lost none of his verve. He was released from the King's Bench prison on bail but refused to pay fees and, as a result, fought his way out doing assorted damage to a number of jailers and turnkeys. However, 'tis rumored that he has kiss'd the King's hand and managed meanwhile to obtain four thousand pounds to pay his debts in addition to his back pay as Governor of 'Mackinac. Poor Rogers, how he must long for a war to bring him peace!"

His postscript kindled anew dreams of the morrow. "I long to know how you have fared in the search for silver. I presume it has been made known to you that the piece of quartz I found was assayed in London at seventy-five percent silver. I would to God the years had not added so much lead to my saddle."

My rare good fortune so captured my heart that not even the misfortune of others could gain foothold. At least until the canot du maître returned with the three miners and without Will Tragear.

"I do veel s' bad, leavin' the poor booy," said Dungie Crowgie, shaking his head sorrowfully.

"There be nowt we could do," said Petherick Kernick. "We bally-wragged him all night long, called him a bufflehead until t' last he would no even spaik t' us."

"Semens t' me," put in Degary Tregarthen, "he's doin' nowt but lookin' for a brave way t' heaven. Scarce eats, just sets and says nowt."

Alexander Henry did his best to cheer them. "I'm sorry he didn't go with you. But you have my word, should he change his mind I will arrange passage for him."

"Thank 'ee, zur, thank 'ee."

"But you know," My Henry went on, "It just may be that he will be happy here. If we can find something for him to do so that he won't think he is on charity. That is the answer."

"Iss, zur. But what can a blinded booy do?"

"Oh, it's not impossible," said Mr. Henry. "I know a blind Indian in the village of the Bay of Chagouemig who makes the finest snowshoes and the best toboggans west of Detroit. Don't fret, we will find something."

"Thank 'ee, zur," the Cornishmen repeated, but I could see they were not impressed. From their own villages they had a vivid picture of the utter hopelessness of the blind.

"And before I leave I will go and visit with him," I put in quickly. A rash promise in a way, for I could ill afford a sixty-mile journey westward. Still, it was the least I could do.

That evening I stood on the fire-step of Fort Gloucester, my mind turning this way and that. I wondered what service in the Indies would be like and was it too much to hope that Master Revere would have books on the manufacturing of copper pots. Back to school to learn to be a tinker! I smiled to myself, imagining the comments of my brother officers at that one.

And the hidden silver. Now it must await my return. I must remember to take poor Will Tragear a goodly supply of tobacco. As my mind so wandered, my eyes watched a duck hawk high in the sky already washed with rose-gray by the setting sun. Suddenly he struck and before he rose again with his prey in his talons the remainder of the flock soft-winged like arrows from the bay. Jove, I thought, that fellow must have good eyes. I hadn't even seen the ducks on the bay. It was then my idea came to me. On second thought it seemed so fantastic that I almost left it there on the fire-step. But thinking on it again, I could only ask myself, "Why not?" But I would tell no man until it was launched.

The big canoe was sent back to Pointe aux Mines to pick up the remaining mining tools so I went with it bearing tobacco, three feet of Spencer's twist, and high hopes in my plan.

I found Will Tragear pretty much as I expected to, sitting on a stump in front of his shelter, a slumped figure of a once-strong man turning unseeing eyes on life. Squatting close by, like a young hawk with ruffled feathers, the boy Penashe watched me constantly, as if I might do harm to the man whose shadow he had become.

Will was pleased enough to get the tobacco. "Thank 'ee, zur, thank 'ee. There be enough here for Jimmy too," adding as he ran his fingers down the three-foot twist. " 'Tis a good thing to have somat to give him, all the trouble I be to him and Mistress Jimmy."

It was my opening and I went in at the gallop. "That is what I came to see you about, Will."

"Tobacco, zur?"

"No, paying Jimmy and Penashe for their services."

" 'Ee be bally-wragging me, too."

I snorted, trying to keep as much made-up irritation in my voice as I could. "Look, Tragear, I didn't come this way to play games. Nor to look after your needs, or Jimmy's, for that matter. I want a share in this too."

He had a strange, bewildered look on his mutilated face, so I pressed on quickly. "Will, I want you to spend the next year looking for the lode of silver with your rod."

"Wid out eyes, zur?"

"No, of course not. With a very fine pair, better eyes than you ever had, I'll warrant."

I looked at the boy. "Penashe, you've got good eyes in the bush, eh?"

He jumped up. "Iss, zur," he said proudly.

"You see, Will. . . . And you have eyes that talk Cornish."

My heart warmed, for I saw the faint suggestion of a smile at the corners of the old miner's mouth.

"Well, lad," I said. "Hop to it. Fetch the Magic Stick."
He had gone about three paces when he stopped and turned. "I look 'ee sharp, me," he said solemnly.

Will Tragear's mouth widened to a grin, then to an outright laugh. I had a feeling I had already won.

The Ojibway boy passed wide of me as if fearful I might snatch the Magic Stick. He put the rod in Will's hands. The Cornishman opened and closed his hands about the rod, gently as if with great affection.

"It won't be easy at first, Will," I warned. "You and Penashe are learning together, each to help the other. You must be patient."

He stood up, with the rod before him, started to walk. Penashe, by his side with a small guiding hand on his elbow, scarce took his eyes off the pointer. They completed a wide circle.

"An' what do I do, zur, if I feel summat? I won't know where 'tis."

"Ah, but Penashe will. He will have already spotted landmarks that you would never have seen. Besides, he can stake out your lines and, if the bush be thick or the going rocky he'll blaze mark the trees."

Will Tragear nodded. "Aye. We can manage they, if'n we each do our own part."

I told him then of my plans for the making of copper kettles and of my quest for knowledge. "Smelting copper will be a problem. I don't suppose you know anything about it?" It was a shot in the dark for I knew Cornish copper was carried to Wales for smelting.

"Iss, I do that, zur," he replied with enthusiasm. "As a booy I worked at Sampson Swaine's furnace on Rosewarne Downs. Thet was afore they built the big Copperhouse Works."

"Good, good!" I exclaimed. " 'Tis more than I expected.

Although I fear I shall be snatching you away from the silver hunt."

The canoe was ready for the return journey next morning and I left Will Tragear with a parting admonishment, "And don't forget, Will. When you and Penashe find that big bunch o' silver, I'll expect a share in it."

"Aye, zur . . . an' t'will be a keenly lode. Enough for us all, and Master Jimmy too."

I looked back as the bow of the deep-laden canoe swung eastward and thrust forward under the Canadian paddles. The blind Cornishman and Little Bird were moving slowly together between craggy rocks, the Magic Stick thrust out before them. I felt a warmth of well-being throughout my body. Will Tragear had already found his "keenly lode," not of silver yet, but of life itself.

I journeyed straight up the River St. Marys and over the portage to Cadotte's Fort, from whence I would take a freight canoe to 'Mackinac, from there the water route to Detroit, Niagara, and Montreal.

I had thought to press on without delay but I counted not on the good cheer and hospitality of my friends who had gathered to bid me Godspeed. Alexander Henry, Jean-Baptiste Cadotte, André Perrot, even White Fisher, who had journeyed from his summer camp, were all there. Oh, yes, and Pierre Dupuis who was engaged in running freight from 'Mackinac. The Old One, still full of swagger and the joy of life, as the evening mellowed on Madam Cadotte's excellent dinner, produced his fiddle. Madam and I had many a dance and before dawn even my clumsy feet were atune again.

Both Alexander Henry and M. Cadotte were at the landing to see me off. Mr. Henry shook me by the hand before I stepped into the waiting canoe. "We'll be glad to have you back, Vere," he said, and I do believe he meant it. "But a spell with your regiment will go well with you. You are a good soldier, Lieutenant Bayard, and perhaps because of it you belong here."

"How so?" said I, seeking any road to lose my embarrassment on.

"Because, like Colonel Bouquet at Bushy Run, you have learned how to turn defeat into victory." He meant that, too, and I was deeply moved.

As the canoe edged out to midstream, M. Cadotte called out to me, "M'sieur! Be sure and bring a good wife back with you, we have room for another house in the settlement."

I grinned and waved but could think of no reply.

When at last we were through Le Grand Détour and about to enter the blue water of Lake Huron, the Canadian voyageurs brought their paddles inboard and knelt forward in prayer, each making the sign of the Cross.

I prayed too—that God in His mercy would bring me safe back to my people and my country, the better fitted to serve.

There was much yet to be done.

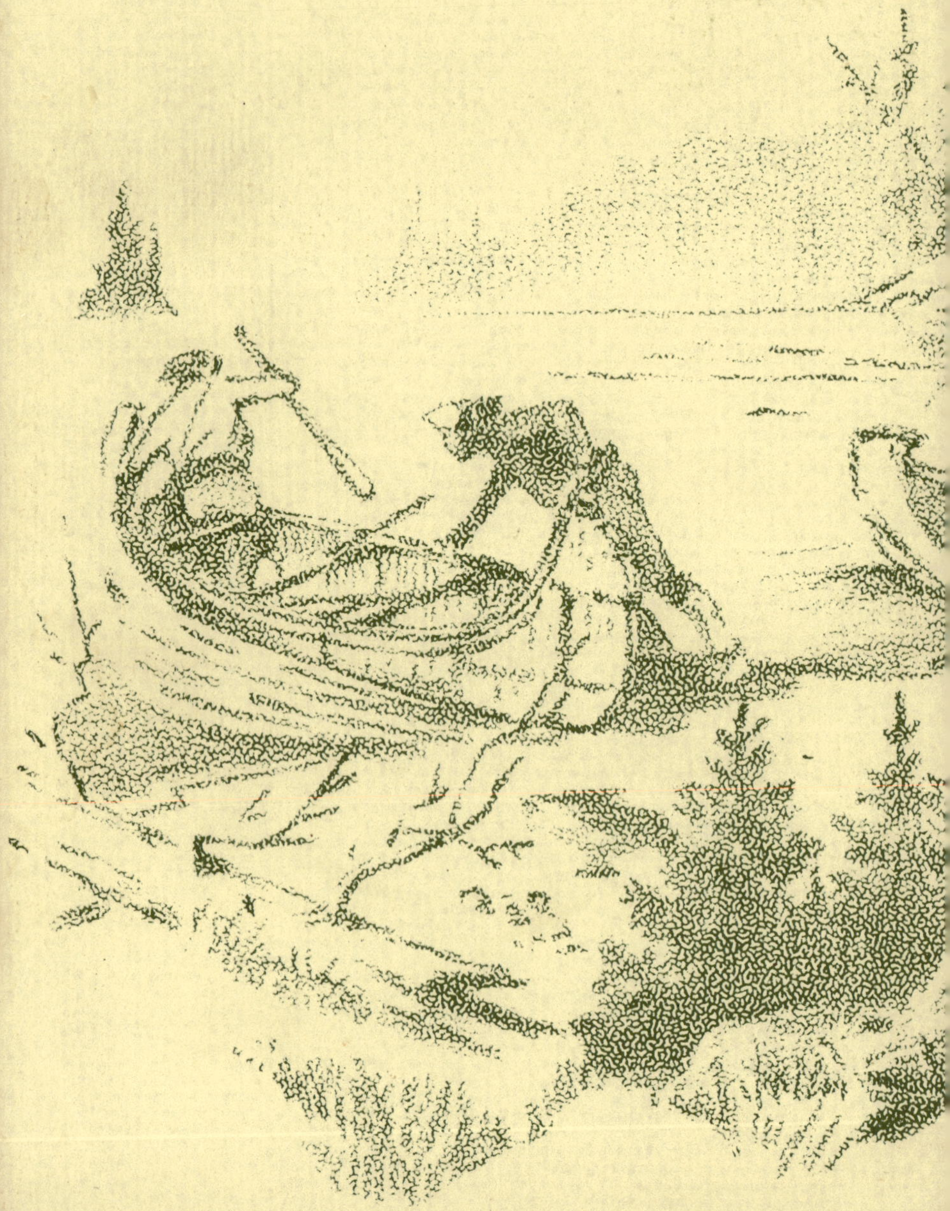